M000288062

Hawthorn Lake

REPRISAL

Paul G Buckner

This is a work of fiction. All names, characters, institutions, places, and events portrayed in this novel are either products of the author's imagination or are used fictitiously. Any resemblance to actual persons, living or dead, business establishments, or events is entirely coincidental. All rights reserved, including the right to reproduce this book, or portions thereof, in any form or by any means.

SPACEBAR
PUBLISHING, LLC

Copyright © 2019 Paul G Buckner

All rights reserved.
ISBN: 978-1-7323007-8-1

DEDICATION

For my wonderful wife, Jody and son, Chase

TABLE OF CONTENTS

ACKNOWLEDGMENTS

A very special thanks to the many fans of my first novel, *Siege, at Hawthorn Lake*. It has been more than two years for the long-awaited follow-up, Reprisal. I released *The Lost Gold Mine of Idaho Springs* as a short story to give you a little detail and background of an extraordinary character in the story-line. *The Lost Gold Mine of Idaho Springs* is the first ten chapters of *Reprisal*, which is included here as a refresher. If you have read Gold Mine, then Reprisal awaits you beginning in Chapter 11. I sincerely hope you enjoy this exciting series, and I thank you for being a fan.

1

...2005

"I gotta tell ya, you've had some crazy ideas before, but a lost gold mine?"

"I know what it sounds like, but it's the real deal," Steve said to his younger brother.

"So, let me get this straight, *Professor X*," Mark said, pausing long enough to recline in his chair and folding his arms behind his head. "Cause I'm a little fuzzy on the details. Like, what it is exactly that you're talking about? A second gold rush, huh?"

The three days of coarse, scruffy beard stubble did little to hide the smirk on Mark's face as he emphasized the word 'professor.' His brown eyes shined with a glint of smugness and more than a hint of sarcasm.

"Very funny. God forbid that I may know something that you don't," Steve replied. "But okay, pull up a chair and shut your trap, mutant. You might actually learn something."

1

The Turner brothers, both in their early twenties, were nearly direct opposites on most subjects. Steve, the oldest, was easy-going and relaxed while Mark could be impulsive and at times quite cynical. They were discussing the idea of a lost gold mine while sitting in the living room of the family farm.

"Yeah, yeah, whatever. Everyone knows about the Gold Rush, you're not telling me anything new, but it was in California in 1849, genius. Duh."

"Actually, forty-eight. January twenty-seventh, 1848, to be precise."

"What?" Mark scoffed, folding his arms across his chest now, defiantly.

"The California Gold Rush. It wasn't in 1849. It's called that because – oh never mind, that's not important. You get on my last damn nerve."

"Listen, Bub, Joe Montana did *not* play for the San Francisco Forty-*eighters* he didn't play for the San Francisco Fifty…fifty…neers, or whatever. The greatest quarterback in the history of the game played for the forty-niners!" Mark mocked. "And Mom always said you were the smart one. I call bull. Mic drop," Mark said, holding his hand out pretending he just dropped a microphone on the floor.

"You're an idiot. You know that, right? You have *got to be* adopted. Now, listen up, ape-ass ugly."

"I've been called worse by better," Mark said, needling his brother, again. He grabbed two pecans from a bowl on the nearby coffee table and cracked one open. He cocked his head to one side and stared up at his brother with a raised eyebrow.

Steve sighed and ran a hand through his blond hair in exasperation at his brother's nonsense and his own lack of restraint.

"Okay, whatever, but I'm not talking about the

California Gold Rush, you moron. I'm talking about the one right here in Colorado, a decade later. The one in California only lasted a few years because most of the gold found there was what is called placer gold or basically easy pickings. They could pan for it in the creeks and rivers. When it was discovered, the population boomed and when you have most of the gold on top of the ground, and an increase in population, it's not hard to figure why it didn't take long to mine it all. After that, it took specialized equipment to mine for what they call lode gold or veins in the rocks underground. Most people couldn't afford that, thus the ending of the California Gold Rush."

"Okay, great, but I still never heard of the Colorado Gold Rush, and I've lived here all my life," Mark said. "Sure, there are tons of mines all over, and everything is gold this or gold that, but the Colorado Gold Rush? Wasn't it just all one thing, California, Colorado, Utah, all the same thing, right?"

"And once again I must point out the fact that you're an idiot. Now do yourself a favor and shut up and listen."

"Okay, Einstein. Enlighten me," Mark said, popping a pecan in his mouth and crunching on it.

"In January of 1859, a guy by the name of Jackson discovered a large placer gold deposit near Idaho Springs. Remember placer gold deposits are ones that can be mined by panning? No big deal, but then shortly after, lode gold was found in a few different places not far away. Very big deal, which resulted in another gold rush. Thousands of people made their way up from Kansas and Missouri. Newspapers at the time reported that as many as 100 wagons a day would be seen passing by with emigrants on their way to try their luck at mining."

"Okay, so what does that have to do with that old box of books you found and this conversation?"

"Because in the bottom of that box was this," Steve said, waving his new prized possession in the air like a preacher would a bible on Sunday mornings. "It's a journal. Handwritten by one of those emigrants, Nathaniel Hackett. He and his brother William, along with a cousin named Bradford, made their way to the territory seeking their fortune in the gold mines. It's a log of their entire journey over a year long. The best part is, it tells about an incredible discovery, a natural cave filled with huge veins of gold. Easy pickings. So much so that they didn't know how they were going to get it all out and keep it a secret."

"I'm sure they figured it out and bled it dry of every last ounce."

"That's just it. I've searched every record that I could get my hands on, and I couldn't find much on these men or a mining claim registered in any of their names."

"So, it's all bogus?"

"No. Far from it. It's real, alright. As I said, I couldn't find much on 'em, but what I did find all match up, the names, the timeline all match up. It's the real deal. The journal's missing several pages, and some of it's faded and illegible, but something happened. It's not clear what, but from what I can gather, the men had mined enough gold by this time that they were going to load their mules and get out with what they could, but that's where the entries stopped." Steve held the journal up for his brother to see. "It picks up again with a final entry, a vow that none of the men would ever go back to the mine again and they would never speak of what they saw, which makes sense given that I couldn't find anything *officially* on the claim."

"Really? What the hell happened that would keep them away from a fortune?" Mark asked, completely taken in by his brother's story.

"That's the million-dollar question isn't it, but the thing

is, I think there's enough information in here that could lead us to that lost gold mine."

"Wait a minute," Mark said, putting his feet back on the floor and sitting up, suddenly more interested. "Seriously? You really believe that a hundred and fifty years later, nobody has already found it?"

Steve paced across the living room, giving thought to his brother's argument.

"Have you ever heard of a gold strike anywhere near here? Neither have I. The way the journal describes the discovery, I can see how hundreds or even thousands of people could've walked right by it and never seen it. Now, here's where it gets really interesting," Steve said, standing over his brother with a mischievous grin. "I found the journal in that box along with some other stuff. I'm sure that the estate sale folks running the sale had no idea what this was. They just come in and sell everything. Maggie Reese owned the house. Do you remember her?"

"Yeah, everyone knows old Lady-Bird Reese. She used to come to every baseball, basketball, or football game in town. She wore that old red and white truckers' hat with all the pins on it. So? She was a nut job."

"Eccentric," Steve said pointedly. "Not a nut."

"Potato, tomato, it's all the same."

"No, it really isn't. Nut implies crazy, eccentric implies wealth. She was loaded! Mark, you should've seen the place. It was huge. Who knows how many rooms were in it?"

"So, what? A rich nut job is still a nut job."

Steve rolled his eyes, but continued, "I did a little more digging, and as it turns out, Maggie Reese was married to John Reese, which is of no consequence. What's important here is her maiden name. You know, her family name before she was married," Steve said sarcastically.

"You're a regular comedian, aren't ya? I know what a

damn maiden name is, jackass."

"Good, then you'll be able to add two plus two. Her maiden name was Hackett!"

Mark stood and crossed the room.

Steve turned to meet his brother's eyes.

"You mean she was married to one of the gold miners?" Mark asked, incredulously.

"No, dumbass. She was only eighty-seven when she died last year. Do the math."

Mark punched Steve on the shoulder.

"Ow! You jackass."

"Serves you right!"

"It's not my fault that you're an idiot. Anyway, no, she wasn't the wife, not even a daughter. She is, however, the great-great-granddaughter of Nathaniel Hackett, and what's interesting is, she's never worked a day in her life. No telling how much her estate was worth. The house was huge, but apparently she also owned hundreds of acres of land and businesses around town."

Mark let out a long, soft whistle. "So, the old-bird was loaded, and they *did* find the gold!"

"I'm betting on it, but according to the journal, they left most of it behind and only got out of the mountains with a handful of pack mules."

"Why would they leave it behind?" Mark asked.

"I'm not sure, but what I do know is that I'm betting that with the information given in the journal that I know where to find it."

"Then, what are we waiting for big brother? Let's go find that gold mine!"

Steve smiled. "That's the first *smart* thing you've said all day."

2

With her soft, luminous blue eyes and long silky blond hair, Michelle Evers was considered pretty by most standards. This morning, however, she didn't feel pretty. Waking early on the hard surface of the small tent, she was sore and achy from the previous day's hike. She slipped on a fresh pair of socks before sliding into her shoes. Unzipping the tent, she ducked out and made her way to the fire. She stretched to wake her tired muscles then tied her hair up in a bun. She still wore the khaki shorts and the pink tank she had slept in.

Hot coals from the previous evening's fire glowed crimson as Michelle stirred through the ashes. She added a few sticks and built it back up and put on the small pot of coffee before turning back to the tent. Ducking inside, she quietly unzipped her friend's sleeping bag then with a quick motion jerked the sleeping bag away from her snoring friend.

"Rise and shine sleepyhead," Michelle laughed.

The early morning air was cold and brisk. The smell of pine mixed with campfire smoke and coffee was a welcome aroma to Jennifer as she stirred in her sleeping bag. She found the early morning cheerfulness of her best friend to be a bit annoying, but the smell of the coffee more than made up for it.

"I'm rising, but I'm not shining," Jenni grumbled. She slipped out of the tent and made a beeline for the fire. Grabbing a cup from the downed tree log they used for a seat, she poured it full of the black, steaming liquid and took a sip.

"How'd you sleep?" Michelle asked.

"Like a rock," she said in a gravelly morning voice. "I didn't wake up once all night."

Michelle scoffed. "I'll say. There was a squirrel or something messing around just outside the tent all night. I got up two or three times to shoo it away, and you never even stirred."

"No way? I guess I really must've been tired. It was a long hike yesterday, and that pack isn't light."

"It'll be another long hike today."

"But not before I get some breakfast," Jennifer said, raising a brow and glancing sideways at her friend. She brushed back a lock of brown hair out of her face and behind her ears.

Michelle scoffed, "It's not like you're going to get bacon and eggs out here. As much as you've complained about the weight of your pack now, I don't think a cast-iron skillet and a pound of bacon would've been a great idea."

"I'd trade the tent for a hot, buttery biscuit right now. These trail mix bars get old fast."

"It's just for a few days. Man-up and grow a pair, would ya?" Michelle teased. "Be right back."

"Where are you going?" Jennifer asked.

"I need to use the ladies' room if you must know. My morning continence must not be kept waiting any longer."

"Sorry, I asked!"

Jennifer finished her coffee, cleaned the cup, and put it away in her pack. Folding the tent flap back, she ducked inside and pulled on a fresh pair of socks and her hiking shoes before rolling up her sleeping bag.

The girls had left home only two days earlier for a three-day weekend hiking trip to the mountains. Both were sophomores in college and avid hikers, never missing a chance to be outdoors. Best friends since grade school, the pair shared many of the same hobbies and took advantage of any opportunity to escape to the mountains.

Jennifer suddenly tensed, the hairs on her arms standing straight up when she heard her friends' scream. She froze; the sound reverberated through the forest and echoed over the mountain.

***

"That's everything," Mark said, tossing the shovel in the bed of the truck.

"Where the hell is Chris?" Steve said. It was more of a statement than a question.

"Who knows. He said he'd be here by eight. It's almost nine, now. If he thought there was any work to be done, he's going to wait until the very last minute."

No sooner had Mark finished his statement when their attention shifted to the driveway. An old black Chevy 4X4 sped up the dirt road in a cloud of dust and slid to a stop just a few feet away from the brothers.

"Glad you ladies didn't leave without me," Chris said, jumping down from the raised off-road vehicle. He slammed the door closed as he jumped down, his small stature a stark contrast to the large truck. He hopped on the running boards on the back, grabbed his gear out and threw it in with the brothers'. Decked out in camo from head to toe, complete with boonie hat covering his military cut red hair and silver lensed aviators, he looked rather comical standing in front of the brothers with a big toothy grin. A longtime friend, he was never one to be left out of the action. He pulled the sunglasses off, "Hope you got plenty of food."

"Good God, man, are you ever on time? Never mind, I think we all know the answer to that, just get in and let's go," Steve said.

"Seriously? That's the thanks I get? You two clowns are always waiting 'til the very last minute to let me know anything. You call me up in the middle of the night, ask me to drop everything, pack up and be here ready to leave with less than a twenty-four-hour notice, and that's the thanks I get? Contemptible. Purely contemptible! You know, you're darn lucky I'm even here. I was supposed to be leaving for boot camp this weekend, but it got pushed back to next month. Paperwork got screwed up."

The brothers stared back in silence.

Mark shrugged; Steve rolled his eyes.

"Lucky," Mark said.

"Yeah! Lucky."

"Oh, dear lord," Steve said.

"You're here, aren't ya?" Mark said. "Let's go!"

"Geez, bust a guy's balls for waking up late why don't ya."

"If you had been any later, you'd be driving that piece of crap up the mountain by yourself, and I doubt that old jalopy would make it very far. By the way, nice fanny-pack there Peter Pan."

"Jealous much?" Chris snickered.

"Not really, no. It - completes you," Mark laughed.

"Whatever, dude. I'll have you know, within this handy

dandy little marsupial pouch is all the essential elements to make life in the wild a little more comfortable," Chris said, unzipping the pack strapped around his waist. "Why you got your toilet paper, wet wipes, pocket knife, fire kit, water purifying drinking straw, fishing line complete with hooks and a few assorted lures and, of course, one pistola."

"Enough!" The brothers shouted almost in unison.

"We get it. Can we go now, for Pete's sake," Mark said.

"Okay, okay. Don't get your panties all wadded up, my friend."

"Just move that jalopy of yours out of the driveway and get in, we need to get moving," Steve said.

"Right away, Captain. And take it easy on the ol' girl, she can hear you. The she-beast is old, but she's got a lot of miles left in 'er."

"Whatever," Steve said, sliding behind the wheel of his own truck. Mark jumped in the passenger side, leaving Chris to sit alone in the back seat.

"So, where exactly are we going?" Chris asked. "You were awful mysterious on the phone last night. Cryptic even."

"Steve here thinks he knows where a lost gold mine is near the campground, we all went to a couple of years ago."

"I think I have the area pinpointed, within a five-mile radius anyway. That's where we'll start our search. The journal is descriptive, and using Google Earth I think we should be able to find some of the terrain features. There weren't any mining claims in the entire area. None that I ever found a record of. Stands to reason that the mine has stayed hidden all this time," Steve said.

"So, old lady Reese is the great-granddaughter of this miner, huh?"

"Close enough," Steve said. "I've done some digging on

her too. For someone to be so crazy wealthy and never have worked a day, tells me that's old money. I'm sure that they found that mine, but unlike others, they didn't get gold fever. Basically, they hit the jackpot and cashed out. Pretty smart if you ask me."

"I wonder why? I mean, why not stake a claim and work the mine. If it were that rich, it would only make sense that they would be like everyone else and work it 'til it's dry."

"I wondered that too, but according to a few passages that I could make out in the journal, something happened. Whatever it was, scared them off. I can't imagine what *that* might have been. These were tough, rugged frontiersmen that battled more than the elements in their day."

Mark asked, "Do you think it could've been Indians? There had to be Native American tribes around, don't you think? Encroachment is more than enough cause to run 'em off, I'd think."

"I don't think so, but honestly, I've no idea," Steve said. "All I could gather is they were attacked several times when they were working the mine. Their supplies were running low, and they had lots of gold to get out, so they packed up what they could on the mules and hightailed it out of there. It could've been marauders, Indians, or even bears."

"So, what's the plan?" Chris asked.

"We find it," Mark said.

"Duh! I kinda figured that, smartass."

Steve laughed. "There's an old logging road we need to find near the campground and just off the highway. We'll take it as far as we can, and then we'll have to hoof it up. I think it'll take us a couple of days depending on how far that road goes back. Then, we do a grid search for signs of the cave. The good thing is, ol' Hackett was pretty descriptive of the terrain. I'm sure we can find it."

They drove for the better part of the day before Steve found the turnoff that led to the campground. Half an hour later they drove through the camping area and followed the dirt road leading past it in search of the old logging road. They bounced along for another ten or fifteen minutes. Just as he rounded a curve he slammed on the brakes.

Mark saw the obstruction too but had been riding along in silence, lost in his own thoughts, he was too slow to react. His seat-belt restrained him from the sudden stop, but not without its consequences. He slammed forward, but the nylon belt held firm.

Chris, who had been asleep in the back seat, was not as lucky. He wasn't wearing a seat-belt and was launched into the back of the front seats and swiftly deposited into the floorboard.

The Gaines brothers felt the impact and turned to look but couldn't see him.

"What the hell, man? That frikkin hurt," Mark said, rubbing his shoulder.

"Sorry," Steve said, trying not to laugh. "You okay back there?"

A long skinny arm shot up. Waving like a white flag of surrender, Chris gave a thumbs up. "I'm okay," he squeaked.

Steve shifted into park, turned the ignition key off, and got out to inspect the iron-post gate that stretched across the road.

"Now what?" Mark asked.

"I didn't come all this way to turn back because of a closed road," Steve said grinning. He walked over to the end of the gate and began moving some branches and rocks. "I think we can get around it. There's not a fence."

"Great, not only do I get body-slammed on this trip, probably have broken ribs and a fractured vertebra, but I also get to spend jail time for trespassing with brothers Grimm," Chris complained.

"Do you ever quit your whining, ya big baby?" Mark said.

"There's not a *'no trespassing'* sign hanging on the gate. Probably just an old logging road that the state didn't want to maintain. It's still public land."

"Right," Chris said. "A locked gate clearly means, *come the hell on in!*"

"Let's check it out," Steve said, ignoring his friend, and climbing back in the truck.

There was just enough room to get the gray 4X4 past the gate. They cleared the gate and bounced along the deserted road. Several areas had been all but washed out, but the four-wheel-drive had little issue navigating the rough, but dry terrain.

"How far do you think it goes?" Chris asked.

"Not sure exactly, but we'll go as far as we can and take a look at the GPS. No matter what, we're going to be doing a lot of hiking."

"Why didn't you go around on highway twelve and go up to Port Falls Campground?"

"Well, let's see numbnuts. If we go into a public campground with RV's and blue-hairs everywhere you turn, it might be a little suspicious to see three guys carrying a metal detector and shovels into the woods."

"I get your point."

Branches slapped at the truck as they pushed past. They were running out of road.

"I think we better find a good place to stop and make camp. It doesn't look like this old road's going much further," Mark said

"The GPS shows us only a few clicks from where I dropped the pin on the map. I was hoping to get a lot closer than that."

"I think the problem is the road's been pretty level and just curving around. It doesn't really go *up* the mountain," Mark emphasized. "Not nearly as much as it should. Are you sure it's the right one?"

"Yeah, it's the right one, but it's not been used in years."

"Then that means we'll be hiking a lot more *up* than anything," Mark groaned.

Chris leaned forward, pointing at the road ahead, "I hope you brought a chainsaw. That's one big ass dead tree across the road."

Steve stopped the truck just in front of a downed birch that covered the entire road. The forest growth was too thick in the area to go around, so he turned off the ignition and jumped out.

"Nothing else to do but start cutting branches, fellas. I have a limb saw in my pack."

"I've got a hatchet here somewhere," Mark said.

Chris threw open the door and stood on the side step, "How much further up the road is it? Maybe we can find a place to camp right here?"

"No telling, but looks like we can go quite a ways in," Steve said, scanning ahead.

"Hope so," Mark said as he came around to their side of the truck. "The GPS shows it at least four or five more miles back in there. I'm not packing all this crap any further than what I have to."

***

After the men had the tree cut up enough to get the truck through, Chris jumped in the back seat and lay down. He was asleep within minutes. A half-hour later, the slamming door woke him.

"What the hell?" Chris said. It took a moment for clarity to sink in. Once he had his bearings, he opened the door and jumped out.

"Glad you could join us sleeping beauty," Mark laughed. "We already found the gold and ready to head back now."

Chris yawned loudly and stepped around behind the truck. "*Right*. Cutting up that tree wore me out," he said as he stretched and yawned loudly. "Pardon me while I water the petunias."

"Let's get the tent set up and find some firewood before it gets dark on us. The sun sits fast up here in the mountains," Steve suggested.

Mark used his hatchet to cut up several dead tree branches and had a fire going in no time. Once the tent was set up, and sleeping bags unrolled, they settled near the fire to discuss their plans.

Chris poked at the flames with a long stick. "Man, this is the life fellas. I could live like this forever."

"You say that now, but we'll see if you still feel that way after a two-day hike up this mountain," Steve laughed.

"Not talking about climbing a mountain with Bert and Ernie," Chris sighed deeply, "I just meant this part, you know, sitting beside a warm fire deep in the woods with no cell phones, no boss yelling at me, no city traffic or idiot drivers honking their horns and cutting me off."

"Yeah, I know what you mean. It's peaceful up here, that's for sure," Steve said. "Speaking of no cell phone coverage, I picked up a map of the area. We have to go in pure analog. Sort of, I mean I doubt we will get any reception up here at all, but we have the Garmin."

"Good thinking, but did you happen to bring a compass, just in case?" Mark asked.

"Well, yeah. I'm not an idiot."

"That's open for debate."

Steve was too tired to bicker with his younger brother. He let the comment slide. "We need to get an early start in the morning and use all the daylight we can."

"So, what *is* the plan for tomorrow?" Chris asked while checking the magazine in the .45 he had brought with him for protection.

"Sweet. That new?" Mark asked, eyeing the firearm.

"Yeah, got it last week. Never can be too careful," Chris said. He dropped the mag and pulled the slide back to reveal an empty chamber before handing it to Mark to inspect.

Steve ignored their side conversation,

"We'll follow the ridge for about four or five miles before we leave it and make our way south. It shouldn't take long to reach that point, maybe four or five hours, but once we leave the trail, I suspect the terrain to get much tougher and slow us down considerably."

"That doesn't seem far away from where lots of people go camping all the time," Chris questioned.

"Yeah, really," Mark said. "I mean, this entire area has been logged, decades ago sure, but still that means that lots of people have been all over this mountain. Surely, someone's found the mine by now. How could it have stayed hidden all this time?"

Steve laughed, "Oh, no. Once we leave the trail, it'll take us the rest of the day, maybe longer, to get to the area where we start our search. Well away from any public hiking areas. I've checked the map several times. I'm hoping that the route will keep us near freshwater along the way. With all the snowmelt still coming down, that shouldn't be a problem."

The men talked quietly by the fire a bit more before the

brothers decided to turn in for the evening. Chris, having napped most of the drive up, decided to sit up awhile and enjoy the peace and quiet of the late evening.

"Goodnight fellas, I'll be in soon. I'll make sure to have enough wood on the fire to keep it going all night."

Chris tossed a few more pieces of wood on the fire then leaned back against a large log someone had dragged near to use as a seat. It was a quiet and peaceful evening as he watched the flames dance in the darkness. His eyelids finally grew heavy and soon, he was fast asleep.

He didn't know how long he had slept or what woke him up, but he was wide awake now. His senses were on high alert, and the hairs on the back of his neck tingled. The fire had died down to nothing more than a soft glow of embers. He kept still and quiet, listening for any noise out of the ordinary. There it was again. A soft rustling in the woods not far behind where he sat as if whatever it was, was trying to sneak up on the camp. More noticeably, whatever it was, was walking on two feet!

Chris had no idea who could know where their camp was located or what someone could be doing trying to sneak up on the boys. He hid behind the log, and with no fire behind him, he knew there would be no silhouette for him to be spotted. His hand slowly reached for the .45 he kept on his hip. The rustling stopped. Judging from the sound, whoever, or whatever was in the woods creeping up on him, wasn't more than twenty feet away. *Where is my flashlight*, he thought? He saw it lying just a few feet away. He grabbed it with his left hand while holding his pistol in his right. Rolling onto his knees, he aimed the gun and flashlight straight at the direction of the noise.

"Whoever you are, you better show yourself before I start spraying lead," he shouted.

He strained to hear any movements.

Nothing.

"I mean it. You better come on out," his voice breaking.

He heard a sudden crashing in the underbrush just to the left of his light. He adjusted his aim and waited. He was nervous, but not scared as long as he had his pistol with him. "I've got no problem busting a cap on your ass. They'll never find your body!" He continued shouting.

The tent flap suddenly zipped open, and someone stumbled out.

It was Mark.

"What's going on?" Mark asked.

"There's someone out there trying to sneak up on us."

"Seriously, dude, you need to chill with the Rambo crap. You're gonna get someone killed."

"Yeah, like me! You idiot!" Steve shouted from the woods. He stepped out from the trail and walked back toward the fire. "Get that damn light out of my eyes. You're blinding me. Dear lord, I had to go take a leak and couldn't find my flashlight."

"Sorry dude, my bad," Chris said, relaxing. "But how was I supposed to know that?"

"Because I walked right by you on my way out, you moron. Jeez, dude, you've been watching too much TV. 'Bust a cap on my ass?' Really?"

Chris turned the flashlight off, added a couple of sticks to the fire and shrugged it off. "If it had been a serial killer, you would be thanking me."

Mark groaned. "I'm going back to bed." He pulled the tent flap back and ducked inside "Chris, you're a complete asshat, I was sound asleep 'til you started yelling like an idiot," he shouted from the confines of his sleeping bag.

Steve was right behind him but said nothing more.

"Yeah, I guess I will too," Chris muttered and followed

the brothers.

***

Jennifer heard the scream and didn't hesitate. The girls never hiked without some sort of protection. She rifled through her pack until she found what she was looking for. Darting from the tent, she ran as fast as she could maneuver through the brush toward the sound of Michelle's voice.

"Chelle," Jennifer shouted. "I'm coming!" She saw a flash of movement and changed directions to meet her friend in a small clearing.

"There's something out there," she panted. "Not sure what it was, but I don't know, a bear maybe. A person, I don't know. Let's just get out of here."

"Where was it? How far away?"

"I don't know. Let's go."

"Okay, calm down and take a deep breath. In through your nose and out your mouth. Slow your heart rate down, or you're gonna keel over."

"You don't understand. Let's go."

When they got back to the camp, Michelle explained. "I was doing my business when I saw it. I just took off running. Maybe it was a bear, I don't know, but there shouldn't be anyone out here. I'm sure I scared it more than it scared me."

Jennifer laughed. "I'm sure you did. I'm going to have a quick look around."

"No, don't go out there. Let's get packed up and leave the area."

"It's okay, I have the Trail Guard with me," Jennifer said, holding a can of bear spray up. "I'm just going to have a quick look around to make sure it's not following us. I won't go far, start packing up. I'll be right back."

Jennifer made her way up the trail, stopping several times to look around and listen for anything out of the ordinary. When she reached the large pinion tree that Michelle had described to her, she studied the ground all around it but found nothing. She turned to start back when she heard something rustling in the bushes not far away. She looked around to make sure she had an escape route plan and holding the can up, she stood her ground and waited. A moment later, the brush parted revealing the source. She didn't bother with the spray. She ran as fast as she could back to the camp.

"Pack it up, let's get out of here."

"What was it? What did you see? Is it chasing you? Is it a bear?" Michelle asked.

Jennifer grabbed Michelle's shoulder and bent over to catch her breath before talking.

"No, not a bear. It was a huge, black and white skunk!"

"Seriously? Are you kidding? That's *not* what I saw, I swear!"

"I don't know and right now don't care. Let's get going."

"Sounds good to me," Michelle said.

It wasn't long before the girls were ready to leave the camp.

"We should probably go around, just in case your cute little friend is still out there," Jennifer said.

"Probably not a bad idea. We can skirt around through the woods and meet back up with the trail later. I don't want whoever, or *what*ever that was to follow us."

3

Steve was the first one up that morning. He lay awake most of the night reading through the journal, thinking about what it must have been like for those miners. One passage stood out.

> *Bears? We are not sure. But we are fearful with each passing night. If we are to make it home, we are in need of packing out as much of our fortune that the remaining mules can carry. We have made a pact. If we get out of this God-forbidden country, we shall never return – Nat. H*

"Tell me again why I have to be the one to carry all this stuff?" Chris asked.

Steve hefted the backpack to Chris's shoulders and helped him get it adjusted. "Because I have to carry the Garmin and navigate. I may need to scout ahead and stuff. Besides, you're a badass. Remember?"

"I'm also the smallest guy here!"

"Don't know why you're all pissed off," Mark said. "I'm the one carrying this stupid metal detector, and the tent, not to mention most of the food."

"If you two ladies are done bitching, think we can get started?" Steve said, "Chris put this topo map in your cute little fanny pack, so we have quick access."

Steve turned and led the way on a game trail that pointed in the general direction they were going.

Mark turned to follow his brother just as Chris stepped onto a large rock and jumped on the trail. Their backpacks collided mid-stride.

"Hey, watch where you're going, Magellan!" Mark said, giving Chris a playful shove that sent him stumbling to the side of the trail.

"Jackass! I was moving way before your pachyderm carcass lumbered out in front of me. It's a good thing my ninja reflexes kicked in."

Steve groaned and rolled his eyes but didn't stop to watch the two. They were following him now. The intrepid explorers had a long way to go over rough terrain, and he planned on taking advantage of all the daylight they could get.

The woods, though a misty gray in the early morning hours, were easily navigable. Steve kept to a game trail discovered as they began the first leg of their trek. He held the Garmin and gave the map to Chris to keep in his fanny pack for quick reference. Their goal for the first half of the day was to get to the top of the ridge cap. They hoped to do so by noon. There, they would take a short break then follow the ridge north. Steve had researched the area before their trip and used satellite images to pinpoint exact coordinates and distances between each one as he had them marked on the map.

Chris stepped on a dead tree branch snapping it under the weight of his boots with a resounding crack. The action caused a raven perched on a tree some distance away to caw loudly and flap off. Steve shot a glance over at him.

"Sorry," Chris shrugged before continuing. A few minutes later, he spoke up again. "Though I'm not sure why. I mean, we've been walking all quiet-like, like we're trying to sneak out of the church in the middle of the sermon to go have a cigarette or something."

"Yeah, I guess we have at that," Steve said. "Not sure why either." He chuckled a bit. "I guess it's just so quiet in here, tends to force that behavior through the power of suggestion. Really no reason for us to worry about disturbing anyone," Steve laughed.

Mark brushed past a long branch that caught on his pack. The limb snapped back slapping Chris on the face.

"Ow!" Chris shouted. "WTF dude?"

Mark laughed, "Sorry about that. What happened to your ninja-like reflexes?"

"You're gonna think ninja. That freakin' hurt ya mangy cur!"

"Sorry man, I'll try to be more careful," Mark smirked. He was never surprised by Chris's actions or words. They had known each other before they could even remember and were more like family than merely friends. It was just the way they carried on.

Steve had prodded along ahead of the two but had now stopped in a small clearing to look at the GPS and the map.

"What gives big brother?" Mark asked.

"Well," Steve began then suddenly paused a moment before continuing. The sky overhead was bright, but the forest had grown silent. Not even the birds chirped as he looked around. His eyes focused on an outcropping of rocks above them. The dark gray granite was shaped like jagged razor-sharp teeth of a vicious animal staring intimidatingly down at the small troupe. He shook the eerie feeling off and continued, "We've been following this game trail for a few hours but, unfortunately, it seems to turn here and head back down the mountain. We're gonna have to leave it and turn up," Steve sighed. "It'll probably get a little hairier from here on out through the brush." He turned and walked off quickly, not waiting for debate from the others.

Chris knew Steve's mannerisms and knew better than to argue. Something bothered him, but he wouldn't nag him. Not right now, anyway.

"I'm right behind you. Mark can ride drag," Chris quipped as he hurriedly jumped in behind Steve, cutting Mark off with a raised brow and a glib look.

"Whatever," Mark said, rolling his eyes.

***

Michelle stood on a rocky outcropping overlooking a small valley below. The wind, blowing from the south, tossed about several locks of her long blonde hair that had escaped the tight bun on her head, and dirt and sweat streaked across her face with from the countless hours fighting the elements of the mountain, a feeling she loved. Pine trees that once stood tall and proud now lay scattered in clumps at the bottom of the steep slope, uprooted from years of erosion and what appeared to be a recent washout. A small game trail wound down the steep hill just beneath her which may be safe enough for small animals but could prove to be too much of an obstacle for the hikers. From her position, she could also see the peaks and valleys of several other mountain tops far off in the distance. Though, a beautiful panorama, one far too dangerous for the moment.

"Precarious at best," Michelle mumbled.

"What was that?" Jennifer asked.

Michelle turned and smiled at her friend. "The slope. It looks too dangerous. I'd rather go around. It'll take a little longer, but it'll be safer."

"So much for a shortcut," Jennifer laughed. "Besides, we came for the scenery, right?"

Michelle laughed along with her friend. "Yeah, true. Besides, how were we to know the trail was washed out?"

"It wasn't recent, though."

"No, you're right, happened some time ago, but we've not been here in a few years now."

Jennifer thought about it as she watched a monarch butterfly flitting off among the weeds and wildflowers. "Yeah, at least two years since we hiked it last."

"I would like to get back to the main trail before it gets dark so that we can set up camp for the night. With any luck, it won't rain anymore today," Michelle said.

"I'm not so sure about that. I mean, look at the sky. Could break loose any minute and being that we have to go around this washout, it may take hours. It's already after two. I don't want to go back though; I think we just circle around and pick up the main trail on the other side?"

"I don't see why not. I don't want to back-track either."

"Well then, let's get moving.

The girls turned away from the rocky ledge, leaped over the scattered rocks left uprooted from the tree roots when the giant sentries lost their perch on the rim and landed with ease back on the dirt path. As Jennifer fell in step behind Michelle, an unkindness of ravens in the woods far below flocked away. Their wings beat hard against the wind, their shrill cries floating eerily on the breeze and echoing through the canyon.

***

"Shouldn't we have reached the top of the ridge by now?" Chris asked.

"It's not much further – maybe another hour," Steve answered. His face flush from physical exertion.

"I hope to God it is," Mark said. "I'm starving, not to mention tired as hell carrying all this crap."

"I gotta take a leak. You guys keep going. I'll catch up in a few," Chris said.

"Dude, you just did not more than half an hour ago. You have the bladder the size of an acorn, I swear."

Chris shot Mark a dirty look as he unzipped his camouflage pants. "That's because my body has to make room for *this* monster."

"Oh, dear lord," Mark said with disgust. He turned away to follow Steve. "Just catch up when you're done playing with yourself."

Chris watched the brothers leave then slid behind a large tree. He wasn't worried about getting too far behind, he was no stranger to the woods and having tracked plenty of deer during hunting season, following the trail of two men slogging their way through dense forests and vegetation would be simple.

He was small in stature, but Chris made up for it with blustery bravado. He was a good-natured and a fun guy to be around. He grew up near the Turner brothers and had been best friends with them since any of the boys could remember. Now in their early twenties, they couldn't spend as much time together doing the things they used to like hunting, fishing, and camping, so this trip was a welcome adventure. Steve had gone off to college right after high school. Mark went to a welding school, bought his rig, and traveled the country from job site to job site. Chris was the only one that stayed in Idaho Springs after graduating. He had worked in the local pizza restaurant through high school and now managed it. He never had the desire to continue to college. He was happy and content with staying home.

He dropped his backpack and laid it nearby. It felt good to be relieved of the heavy burden even if for only a short time. The pack weighed nearly sixty pounds, and for Chris, that meant over thirty-five percent of his body weight, which was more than most amateur hikers would dare to carry. He shook his arms and legs out to loosen up and rotated his shoulders several times while walking around the area. Satisfied the others were far enough away, he took off his fanny pack, unzipped it and removed the few items he needed. Finding a branch just above his head, he hung the pack over it before unstrapping his pistol and pitching it on the backpack. He was tired and sore even though the group hadn't traveled far yet.

***

"Finally," Steve said. "I thought we'd never get to this ridge."

"You're telling me, I'm exhausted," Mark said. "Looks like a good place to wait for Chris to catch up too. Lots of rocks along this ridge and as good a tracker as he is, even he may have trouble following our trail over this terrain."

"Yeah, good idea and it's a lot later in the day than I had anticipated, but look over there, freshwater to fill the water packs," Steve said indicating a runoff of crystal-clear snowmelt. He dropped his backpack and knelt beside the small stream. Cupping his hands, he drank deeply. "Ah, that's good stuff."

"I'll fill 'em in a minute. I gotta get this pack off and sit down before I collapse," Mark said.

Mark found a cool spot out of the wind on the shady side of a large boulder and dropped to the ground. He leaned against the rock and blew out a breath of air, relaxing for the moment. Even though the temperature wasn't necessarily hot, the physical exertion and arid climate were taking its toll on him. He hadn't hiked this much in over a year, and he was feeling it. His legs were aching, but the cool earth beneath him felt good enough to take his mind off it for the moment.

"I figured Chris would've caught up by now," Steve commented.

"Yeah, I know. I would guess that it was about a half a click back where we left him. Surely, he'll be along any minute."

Steve turned suddenly, "What was that?"

"What was what?" Mark asked, sitting up.

"I heard something. Sounded like a growl. Shhhh," Steve said, cocking his head and straining to hear.

Mark slowly rose to his feet as quietly as he could. He backed away from the rocks and stopped when he was next to his brother. A slow, scraping sound came from the other side of the boulders accompanied by a low-pitched growl. He whispered, "I heard it too, mountain lion?" he asked.

"Not sure," Steve said, looking around for a weapon.

Suddenly a shadow flashed accompanied by a loud piercing scream coming from the rocks above them. The brothers stood shoulder to shoulder to meet the attack head-on. The shadow leaped in front of them from the top of the boulder and landed with a heavy thud just in front of them rolling and then collapsing in a heap.

Chris lay on his back at the feet of the brothers, rolling back and forth, clutching his knee to his chest and moaning.

Mark took the opportunity to kick him.

"Ow! WTF dude?" Chris whimpered. "Have you no sympathy for a dying man?" He laughed.

"You're lucky I didn't kick you square in the junk, you jackass."

"Ha! Chris was laughing hysterically now, "You should've seen the looks on your faces. Oh wow, classic, epic even."

Steve turned away and walked back over to the water stream and began filling his water bladder.

"You're an imbecile."

"That may be true Stevie T, but I'm a damned funny one."

Mark scoffed. "Only in your head. I think you're just an idiot. Not the idiot savant type, but the idiot can't tie your own shoelaces type, can't walk and chew gum at the same time type, or even…"

"I get it, dude. Jeez. Go busting a guy's balls why don't ya," Chris said.

Mark joined his brother at the stream and filled his water bladders with the fresh and cold water of the Rockies after drinking deeply.

"Steve, it's getting kinda late, we should probably get moving now that the moron's back, don't ya think?"

Steve glanced over at Chris, who was limping around and mumbling about his knee.

"Yeah, grab your gear and let's get moving. Chris, get your stuff, let's go."

"Jeez fellas, can't a guy get a little break first? You've been sacked up right here under the shade for a good twenty minutes," Chris said, walking around the giant boulder to retrieve his backpack before he tried to scare his friends.

"Yeah, I suppose it'll give me a chance to look over the topography again, make sure we're on the right track. You got the map."

"Yeah, I got it right -" Chris began but stopped short when he realized he didn't have his fanny pack. His eyes widened when he remembered that he forgot to get off the tree he had hung it on in the woods when he had stopped earlier. "Uhm, I'd like to, but I don't have it."

"How could you have lost it?" Mark asked.

"It's not lost. I know exactly where it is."

"Oh, dear lord," Steve said. "Where is it?"

"Hanging in a tree where I just came from."

"Damn! I guess we don't necessarily need the map." Steve said.

"Yeah, but I have important stuff in that pack, not to mention a small derringer."

"Are you kidding me? How many guns do you need?" Mark said.

Steve threw his hands up in disgust, "You're killing me, Smalls! Are we ever going to look for the gold mine?"

"The good news is, I know exactly where I left it. The bad news is, we'll lose another hour of daylight. It's hanging from a tree where I stopped to use the bathroom."

"Then I suggest you hot-foot it back to that tree and retrieve it. We'll have to set up camp here tonight. Was hoping to make it a lot further than this before we stopped, but, nothing else to do."

"Sorry fellas, don't suppose either of you wants to tag along?"

They both stared at him as if they couldn't believe he would even ask such a ridiculous question.

"We'll get camp set up while you're gone," Steve said, turning away.

"Well, alrighty then. I see how I rate. I'll be back in a

bit," Chris said. He turned and trotted back down the trail.

***

Though some areas were dark and impenetrable by most sunlight due to the canopy of the massive old tree growth, Chris had no trouble finding his way back down the trail. In his haste to catch up to his buddies earlier, he had forgotten that he had hung his fanny pack containing the map among other things on a tree branch.

Half an hour later, he arrived. He knew he had the right place because his pack was now laying on the ground, open and all the contents lay scattered about.

"What the hell!"

His first reaction was disbelief. His second was worry.

4

"I'll get the tent set up if you want to gather up some wood for a fire tonight?" Steve suggested.

"Sure thing, I've got the water bottles filled," Mark replied.

Steve unrolled the tent and began setting it up on a level area he had brushed off with a tree branch. He leaned down to hammer in a stake when a drop of sweat formed on his temple. It would drop into his eye at any moment, but his hands were full with the hammer and the guy-line for the tent. He tossed his head back and tried his best to use his shoulder to wipe it away, but it was too late. The small droplet dribbled down into his right eye.

"Ah, man!" He exclaimed, dropping his hammer and the line.

"What's wrong with you?" Mark asked.

"Sweat and hair in my eye."

Mark shrugged his shoulders and continued gathering small dead limbs for a fire.

Steve stood and walked over to the stream. He kneeled next to the edge, reached in and splashed some on his face before dipping his head into the cold running water. It wasn't hot, but the physical exertion made it feel much warmer than it was. He also tended to sweat a lot.

Before he had gone to college, he was very active and spent a great deal of time outdoors. Steve loved to snowboard during the winter, but he preferred summer activities like swimming and hiking. In high school, he played sports, but he was more prone to academics.

"Remind me I need a haircut when we get home," Steve said. "This stuff is getting too long. I'm starting to feel like a sheepdog."

His brother laughed. "You're starting to look like one too."

Steve ran his hands over his wet hair and smoothed it back out of his face. The cold water felt refreshing.

"You say that, but you could definitely use one too ya know. That mess on your head looks like a rooster exploded," Steve said, laughing.

"Yeah, but I'm not complaining about mine."

"If you could see that mop now right now, you might change your tune," Steve said.

"Don't be a hater. You know how the ladies swoon over these locks. I have my choice. It's kinda like I'm Samson or something," Mark joked.

"Please, I saw the last one you dated. I thought you'd lost a bet!"

Mark stood and stared at his brother in silent indignation.

"What? No witty come-back little brother?" Steve taunted.

"There's no need to further the humiliation that I could bestow upon you. I've not seen your ugly ass date any *thing*, let alone any – *one*!" Mark said, haughtily.

"That's *only* because I'm a little pickier than you. I swear, your only caveat to dating is that they can walk and breathe unassisted. Critical thinking skills need not apply."

"Don't forget good looking. Besides, the only critical thinking skills they need to have is the ability to bait a hook, run a trot-line, or shoot a deer. Other than that, just look good."

Steve, tired of the banter, shrugged it off and went back to work on the tent. Once he had the tie-downs secure, he unrolled his sleeping bag and tossed it on the floor.

"Think I'll take a short nap."

***

Chris found the brothers exploring the campsite shortly after his return and explained how he had found his belongings.

"I'm telling you guys, no squirrel could've done that," he explained. "It was unzipped! That means opposable thumbs. I've never seen a squirrel with opposable thumbs."

"Could've been aliens. You should probably check to make sure they didn't probe you and then wipe your memory. You *are* walking a little bow-legged," Mark joked.

"Very funny ya jerk. Seriously, when I got back, everything was taken out of the pack and just dumped out on the ground. No way could an animal have unzipped it."

Steve, who was sitting on a rock near the tent, agreed with Chris.

"I think you're right about that."

"Thank you!" Chris said as he shot a glare at Mark. "I'm glad to see that one of you Turner brothers has a little common sense about 'em."

"I said I agreed with you that it couldn't have been an animal that unzipped it, but I do believe that an animal pilfered it because you left it unzipped when you hung it up in the tree. A bird could've seen it and took stuff like paper to build a nest with. That map is probably in some crow's nest as we speak. Way to go, Chris."

"There, that's a buyable explanation," Mark chimed in.

"I know for a fact that I zipped it back. I know I did. You can't convince me otherwise. I was there; I did it. It wasn't more than a few hours ago. I think I'd remember."

"Whatever dude," Mark said. "Just man up and fess up that you lost the map."

"I didn't just lose the map. I mean, yeah, I lost it, but not my fault. Besides, if it was a person, I don't think they would have left it behind, especially my derringer. They would've taken it with 'em. It had to be an animal that scattered it all out. As for a bird taking the map, yeah maybe, but why not all the toilet paper they had unraveled. That would've been easier for 'em to carry off."

"I think you answered your own question. It was all unraveled so, birds may have done that, but it was too long to carry off. The map being folded up was small and lightweight, easy pickings." Steve sighed. "At least we still have the Garmin; the map was just for backup."

"Yeah, well – anyway, what's for supper?" Chris asked.

"The same thing that we had for breakfast and the same thing we had for lunch, and the same thing that we had the day before," Steve laughed, pulling out an energy bar and tossing it to him.

"Oh, boy, can't wait."

"There's always twigs and berries," Steve said. "Being the outdoorsman that you are, why don't we have steaks on the fire?"

"Too heavy, I'd rather have some fresh trout," Mark said. "Why don't you catch us some fish?"

"Oh, and how do you expect me to do that? Stick my head in the water and bite one with my teeth? Besides, I doubt there's any fish in this stream. Probably just snowmelt."

"That doesn't mean there's not any fish in it. Besides, I just got a whiff of something from upwind that smells an awful lot like dead fish. Whew, nasty," Steve said, wrinkling his nose.

"OMG dude, are you sure that's fish? I just caught the smell of it too. That's one-hundred percent, grade-A stamped guaranteed frikkin' nasty. Putrid! Smells like rotting carcass," Mark said.

"Great place for a campsite. You two win the hiker of the year award for campsite location. Downwind of a stagnant pool of Dances with Wolves pond carcasses. I can't leave y'all alone for one minute."

"Oh please, that's not any worse than your feet. Which by the way, I'll need you to wash those things, or you are *NOT* sleeping in the tent tonight."

"I don't mind sleeping outside and away from your snoring. You sound like a cave full of hibernating bears for God's sake."

Steve stood and looked toward the sky, "The wind is changing directions again, so maybe we can stay downwind of whatever that smell is," he said as he turned back to the others. "It feels colder too, rain maybe."

Mark gave Chris a smug grin, "You're still sleeping outside."

***

Though the evening was blustery, it was not unpleasant. The wind drifted through the forest, carrying the sharp scent of junipers mixed with the sweet, pungent smell of firewood smoke. Michelle sat next to the campfire, reading her Kindle while Jenni, sitting across from her, fidgeted with a couple of fruit bars in her hands.

"This is nice, don't you think? Don't get me wrong or anything; I do miss my TV, my hair-dryer, curling iron, makeup, clean bathroom," Jennifer said, breaking the silence.

"You're bored, aren't you?"

"Yup, I sure am. Was thinking I was hungry, but neither one of these things look appealing to me. Dry leaves and mud almost seem better." Jenni laughed.

Her laughter was contagious, and soon Michelle found herself joining in.

"Buck up, you'll be back to your creature comforts of home in a few days. Right now, try enjoying the break away from all the other…" Michelle hesitated a moment before continuing, "Junk that goes along with it."

"Such as?"

"Such as getting up at 7 a.m. and going to class, cramming for finals, having Dr. Haiden stare at your boobs during his lectures. Shall I go on?"

"No, you had me at Dr. Haiden staring at my boobs. Eh! Just think I'll have to have one more class with him next semester. The guy makes my skin crawl. Does he think any girl would be dumb enough to sleep with him for a grade?"

"I know right," Michelle laughed.

"You're right, though, breaking away for a few days was a great idea. I can feel the stress drain away,"

Michelle closed her Kindle. "I think I'll turn in."

"Yeah, probably not a bad -"

Lightning suddenly splintered across the sky accompanied by booming thunder as if it were an orchestra solo of timpani drums rumbling over the mountain. Shards of pure white energy strobed against a black backdrop and crackled in a dozen directions illuminating the mountain in an eerie effect.

"Oh crap!" Michelle said. "That scared the heck out of me."

"Maybe we should stake the tent down extra tight tonight," Jenni said as she watched mother nature's fireworks show.

"Agreed. I didn't bring any rain gear. Didn't think I'd need it."

"Me either," Jenni said. Her amber eyes reflected the firelight and her brows wrinkled in worry as she looked at her friend.

"Probably just a little summer thing and it'll blow itself out long before any rain comes from it," Michelle said softly, unable to hide the worry in her voice.

***

The rain pelted the men's tent trying to penetrate the soft fabric with each wind-driven spike, but the men had taken caution to drive the stakes deep and pull the lines tight. Updrafts pushed and tugged against the tiny dome as if trying to uproot it and send it and all occupants flying off the mountain. The tent had seen more than a handful of thunderstorms, and the mesh had tightened through the use enough, so the men felt comfortable enough not to get drenched. The sleeping bags were lightweight and kept the cold night air at bay.

Chris laid on his mat with his hands cradling his head, staring up at the top of the tent, watching the bursts of lightning expose the rippling of the fabric.

"I think we'll be fine as long as it doesn't last all night," Steve said.

"Yeah, sometimes these things come in like a lion and leave like a lamb in minutes," Mark said in the cover of darkness.

"It must be forty degrees. I'm freezing," Steve said as he pulled on a fresh pair of socks and a long-sleeved t-shirt. "Sure wish we had a fire going in here."

Mark laughed, "We could build one, but Chris may not appreciate us using his sleeping bag and clothes for it."

Chris harrumphed, "And you thought I was nuts for packing my long johns. I'm quite toasty over here."

"Make no mistake there, probe-boy, we don't think you're nuts for that, we just think you're nuts in general."

"You're a real jerk, do you know that?"

"I've been told that on more than a few occasions."

"But, since you bring it up," Chris began. "I've been thinking about that. I know for a fact that I zipped that bag back up when I hung it on the limb. Otherwise, everything would've fallen out. I don't see who or what could've unzipped it and dumped everything out like that."

"Just too bad you lost the map," Mark replied.

"Just too bad you're a moron," Chris said, throwing one of his dirty socks in Mark's direction.

Steve rolled over and pulled his sleeping bag up over his head.

"If you two are going to talk all night, try to keep it down to a dull roar, maybe fewer decibels than the storm. I'm gonna try to get some sleep."

"I have no idea how you could possibly sleep through this storm, dude. It feels like it's going to blow this tent along with all three of us into the next county," Chris said.

"It's easy, just roll over and close my eyes."

5

Michelle hammered at the tent stake with a rock trying desperately to get it to hold. The wind raged against the small red and blue tent illuminated through the torrential downpour by constant streaks of bolt lightning. Jennifer did her best to keep the guy-line taught but struggled for a firm hand-hold.

"Almost got it!" Michelle shouted above the enraged roar of the storm.

The wind had pulled the stake loose during the night, which allowed the wind to push under the tent. The two women scrambled out of their bedrolls as quickly as they could to get it secured. The rain was cold in the mountains, and they were ill-equipped for it. They hadn't seen any rain predicted in the forecast.

Michelle hammered at the tent stake with a rock, desperately trying to get it to hold. The night was black and raging. In the torrential downpour, they could only catch brief glimpses of the landscape, the tent, and each other when the lightning streaked across the sky.

Jennifer did her best to keep the guy-line taught but

struggled for a firm hand-hold. Her hands were freezing.

The rock Michelle used as a hammer suddenly slipped from her grasp and came crashing down on her hand that held the stake. She screamed and fell back.

"What's wrong," Jennifer shouted

"Just busted my fingers, God it hurts."

Jennifer checked the line

"That should hold, let's get you back inside before we both freeze to death, or drown."

Michelle responded by diving inside and rolling over to her sleeping bag and using the outside of it to dry off before crawling between the zippered bedroll.

Jennifer helped her get back under the dry comfort of the sleeping bag, found a dry shirt, and dried Michelle's face and hair the best she could.

"How bad is it?"

"I don't think it's bad, but it hurts like hell right now because it's so cold."

Jennifer climbed in the bag, zipped it, and huddled close to her friend for warmth.

"Oh my God, this is miserable," Michelle said, shivering against her friend.

"You're telling me. We may be in this tent a lot longer than we wanted to be if this storm keeps up. I was hoping to make it to Mattie's Peak before heading back down the mountain."

"Me too. We'll just have to see what happens in the morning."

***

The storm finally passed. Lightning flashed in the distance, but its fury had burned out and moved on. Steve was sleeping comfortably when he suddenly awoke. He didn't know if it was a bad dream he was having or a noise outside. He rolled over to his side and closed his eyes to go back to sleep. That's when he heard it.

He heard a thick, throaty grunt and sniffing just outside the tent. *The bear had found them*, he thought. *Is this small pistol enough to stop a hungry bear?* He sat up slowly and quietly, trying not to attract attention.

"Shh," Chris whispered. He was already awake. "Bear. It's been sniffing around for a few minutes now."

Steve nudged his brother to see if he was awake.

"I heard," Mark whispered.

Chris pressed his small derringer into Mark's palm.

"Just in case it tries to get in. I have my 45," Chris said softly.

Steve pushed back the top cover of his sleeping bag, being slow and cautious. He didn't want to feel trapped in case it tried to get in. Chris had already done so.

They could hear the animal as it walked near the tent wall. The low, guttural huffing and sniffing were distinctive, but Chris was confused. Even though he was sitting up, he was still relatively close to the ground. The bear, if that's what it was, seemed to be very tall, well above their heads from where they sat. Whatever it was, it was huge.

The animal moved away from the tent. Chris changed positions and began the slow, calculated risk of unzipping the front. Steve reached out to stay his hand, but Chris insisted and pushed ahead. When he had the zipper up enough, he pulled back the tent flap to see if he could get a look.

The rain had stopped and moved on, but the erratic wind gusts blew the tree limbs above the tent. The occupants could hear the large droplets of rainwater fall against the tight weave of the fabric and bounce off. Though the sun wasn't over the horizon yet, the gray, misty morning light provided some visibility.

Chris poked his head out and let his eyes adjust. He could hear the footsteps of the bear and knew that it was walking away from the camp. He took a chance at not alerting the bear to their presence and pulled his boots on. He clambered out trying his best to be stealthy. He pulled the tent flap back and mouthed the words, "*Hold this*" to Steve.

Steve was reluctant and gave Chris a questioning look. "You can't shoot it unless it attacks us," he whispered.

"I'm not," Chris said. "Just want to see if it's gone."

Chris ducked under the opening and stepped into the clearing cautiously peering around. He wrinkled his nose when he caught the same putrid smell from the night before on the wind and motioned to Steve with a wave across his nose. He moved painfully slow, but he didn't want to alert the bear to his presence if he could help it. He held his .45 in an outstretched hand ready to use it if necessary. He had no intention of shooting the bear unless for some reason the bear decided to attack.

The small clearing where the men had made camp was protected on one side by huge boulders and several yards from the forest line on the slope above and below. Chris thought the bear had gone down the mountain, judging from the sounds he had heard. He moved over to the firepit they had made and saw that the creature had scattered it out. As he examined the camp, he heard a sound coming from the direction the bear had moved off. He ducked down, spun to face it and brought his sidearm up. He wasn't sure what he was looking at for a moment; all he could see were the trees. Then movement. Very slight, but still, movement from something that shouldn't be there. Chris knew not to look directly at the subject; he used his peripheral and let it adjust to it. The bear must be standing on its back legs. It was massive. Chris figured it to be eight or even nine feet tall. The creature had its back to him, so he felt somewhat safe that it hadn't noticed him. He watched the beast for a few seconds before it moved off into the forest.

"Did you see it?" Mark asked, now standing beside him. Steve joined them.

"Holy hell!" Chris said. He had been so focused on the animal that he never noticed Mark walk up. "Give a guy a frikkin warning, would ya! But, yeah, dude, that thing was huge!" Chris exclaimed. "I saw it walking off into the woods, but the funny thing is, I think it was walking on its back legs the whole time."

Chris explained what he saw when the creature was beside the tent.

"Is that typical of a bear? To walk on its hind legs that much?" Mark asked.

"No, it isn't," Steve said. "Bears only walk on their back legs for short periods and usually only raise up like that when they feel threatened and want to look big and impressive to another bear or something. Or possibly an injury to the front paw."

"Still, it was huge. We need to be careful and not leave any food out. I'm freezing, and I doubt we could get a fire started at all. We should've brought some wood inside to keep it dry overnight or something." Mark said, turning back to the tent and ducking inside.

"I'm right behind ya," Steve said.

After the men dressed, they had all their gear packed and were ready to leave by the time the sun was up over the horizon. They were grateful that the storm came in the night and that they wouldn't have to hike all day in the rain or lose valuable time waiting it out.

"Hey, fellas, check out these tracks," Chris said.

The tracks made by their midnight visitor were long and wide just outside the tent.

"These don't look like bear tracks. They look almost – human," Mark said, kneeling beside them.

"Nah, can't be. Bears do tend to step into their front tracks with their back paws giving the appearance of a single foot or bipedal. But this one was strange; I'm telling you that it was walking on its back legs the entire time."

"Okay then genius, explain how it could have stepped into its front tracks if it were walking on its back legs?" Mark said.

"Well, hell, I don't know. Maybe it stood up when it got to the tent."

"I don't know either, but what I do know is, we're losing daylight, and we lost enough of that yesterday," Steve said, casting a mindful glance at Chris.

"Okay, already. Let's get going," Chris said, ignoring the look.

***

Daybreak found the ladies sleeping peacefully in their bright orange and gray tent. Michelle was the first to wake. Her hand ached, but not bad. She examined it the best she could in the dim morning light. There didn't seem to be anything broken; all her fingers worked when she opened and closed her fist. Though she was a bit stiff, only a dull pain remained and that should work itself out once she was moving.

Jennifer rolled over onto her back. "How is it?" Sensing what her friend was doing.

"It's fine really, just hurts a little, but not bad," Michelle answered in a gravelly morning voice.

"I'd like to have some Starbucks right now."

"Me too, would you settle for some finely ground, dark, rich and bold Michelle pour-over special in a not-so-venti?"

Jennifer laughed. "Perhaps in a short?"

"Yes, a very short collapsible tin cup."

Michelle playfully pushed her friend out of the sleeping bag. After getting dressed, she crawled out of the tent and found the Sterno. She had the small fire going and the portable camp stove around it with water heating a few minutes later while Jennifer started packing the gear.

The long, flat sheets of altostratus clouds shielded the sun allowing only enough sunlight through to let them know it was daytime. Even though it was technically summer, the mountains were cold, especially during the nights with rainy, cloud-covered conditions. The two hikers were experienced and knew how to pack for their excursions properly.

Jennifer had everything packed by the time Michelle had the coffee made. The small camp stove worked perfectly to heat enough water for two small cups of the steaming liquid. The smell alone was comforting.

"Got the bacon and eggs ready yet?" Jennifer asked.

Michelle was vegan, but she knew how her best friend felt about it. Jennifer was one-hundred percent carnivore.

"Sure, come and get it," Michelle laughed.

"Mmm, the coffee certainly smells good. That makes up for having to eat these nasty bars for a week."

"Ah, don't be so glum. Think of it as a flash diet, a cleansing."

Jennifer scoffed. "A cleansing? Ha! My kind of cleansing involves lots of tequila, Cozumel and a tall, dark and handsome man named Manuel."

Michelle laughed out loud at her friend. Jenni wanted to go to Mexico for a summer vacation, but Michelle had talked her into a more secluded hiking trip to the mountains. The selling point was the cutting-away from the world, the complete stripping of technology and isolation from the city. They both agreed that it would be nice to live without constant texting and social media.

Jennifer sat on a small rock next to the little camp stove. Looking around, she noticed a short stack of stones, not more than twenty feet away.

"Why did you stack those up?"

Michelle followed Jennifer's gaze until she spotted what it was her friend was asking about.

"I didn't do that."

"Then who did? I didn't notice it when we set up camp, and I was walking all around. That's strange."

"I've no idea. I'm sure they've been there for a long time, and we didn't notice until now. Weird things happen naturally."

Jennifer considered her friend's suggestion, "Yeah, maybe. Just seems – odd really."

Jennifer stood and walked over to the rocks. There were five rocks stacked on top of one another. A large stone followed by four more each smaller going up. The ground was soaked from the rain, but Jennifer saw a few places where the rocks had been freshly pulled out of the dirt.

"Um, Chelle, these weren't naturally put here like this. Come take a look."

6

"Guys, we've been at this for days now," Chris complained. "There's absolutely nothing out here. We haven't found any of the signs where you say they should be and we're running short on food."

"Yeah, I'm starting to think he's right for once," Mark agreed.

Steve stood in a clearing overlooking a small pond. Sweat poured down his temple and threatened to sting his eye. He used the back of his hand to wipe it away.

"I know, but somehow I feel like we're close," Steve said, staring off into the distance. "I just know it. Tomorrow will be a better day. Let's find a place to make camp."

He lingered a moment longer before turning to face them. With a glance and a shrug of his shoulders, he walked between the two men to continue down the trail. He wasn't ready to give up. Not yet.

Chris traded looks with Mark who shrugged, imitating his older brother, then followed him.

The sun had just gone down as the three men finished

pitching their tent, the last of the daylight retiring over the mountain. It took a while to find enough dry wood to build a fire, but they soon had one going well enough to warm up. The heat felt good as they sat quietly waiting on the water to heat up for coffee. Chris took his shoes off and rubbed his feet.

"Look, I'm not saying it's not here. We need a better plan," Chris said, breaking the silence. "What do you say we plan another trip later in the fall? Maybe by then, Steve can dig a little deeper into that journal and figure out why the mine isn't where it's supposed to be."

"I'm not ready to call it quits yet. Let's give it at least another day," Steve said. "I know this is the right area though, I know it!"

Mark stood and looked around. "A hundred and fifty years of weather can change the landscape. At least we know this area a little better now. I mean, that creek you said, the one where the miners worked near the entrance to the cave, it could've dried up, changed course or even went underground. We have no way of knowing."

"I'm game to give it another day," Chris said.

"Me too. We can get an early start in the morning and make a grid search pattern for the creek. Even if it's dried up and changed course, we should still be able to find the old bed where it ran," Mark suggested.

"Okay, then we're all in agreement. We give it one more day. Then, if nothing turns up, we head home and make another plan to come back in a few weeks," Steve said.

"Now that that's settled, how about getting some sleep, I'm freakin' exhausted," Mark said.

The morning came quickly, along with a fierce wind. Steve was the first to wake. He lay in his sleeping bag and listened to the wind howling across the ravine less than a hundred yards from the camp. Each gust shook the small red and black tent violently, but the stakes held firm. The other two men were still sleeping; he could hear them snoring. He rolled onto his back and stared at the ceiling and watched the ripples as the structure danced in the wind. The dim light of daybreak filtered through the window.

The gold mine kept sleep at bay. He lay awake most of the night thinking about it. It wasn't necessarily the thought of gold that drove him; it was the thought of piecing together all the clues that were over a hundred and fifty years old and finding the mine. The find itself is what propelled him. *I know we're close to it, I just know it*, he thought. He sat up and stretched, accompanied by a huge, sleepy yawn. *Where did I go wrong? The clues are all right there in the journal. The creek could've changed course over the years as Mark suggested, but the dried-up creek bed would still be there, but it's not where I thought it would be.*

He couldn't lie idle any longer. He slipped on his clothes and boots and scrambled out of the tent, eager to get started. Poking at last night's firepit remains, he found a few coals and had a warm blaze going in no time.

A weird sensation suddenly came over him, causing the hair on his neck to stand as if he were being watched.

"Thinking about that gold mine, aren't ya?" Chris asked, startling his friend. He had woken and slipped out of the tent without Steve noticing.

"Yeah, dude, I know we're close. I can feel it."

"Damn, it's windy. You got the coffee going yet?"

"Working on it. Yeah, this wind kept me awake most of the night. I pretty much dozed off and on."

"Sure wish you two would clam up out there, I'm trying to get my beauty sleep up in here," Mark half-shouted from the tent.

"If anyone needs their beauty sleep, it's damn well going to be you, but honestly, if you slept for a hundred years it wouldn't help your ugly ass," Chris said.

"Very funny. What time is it?" Mark asked as he ducked out of the tent rubbing his eyes.

Steve looked at his watch. "Time to get up and get moving."

Three trail-bars, two cups of coffee and a half an hour later the three men were back on the trail in their search for signs of the gold mine.

***

"We never should've left the trail, and now we've been doing nothing, but walking around in circles all day. We're practically out of food, I'm exhausted, and I want to go home. Face it - we're lost," Chris complained.

Steve turned and looked over his shoulder at Chris. A heavy sigh escaped his lips.

"Yeah, I know. Trust me, I know. We lost the map," Steve said, looking at Chris before shifting his gaze to Mark, who was sitting on a rock rubbing a sprained ankle. "Now the Garmin is toast, so I think the best thing we can do is try to back-track our way out."

"We could be out here for days, weeks even, and no one would ever find us," Chris chimed. "We'll starve to death first."

The Turner brothers turned and glared at Chris.

"I thought you were a tracking expert," Mark said.

"I am, I can track just about anything, but after the storm this morning, any signs of our passing have all been washed away. Face it, fellas, we're gonna die."

"Seriously, Chris, shut up," Steve said. "Let's get

moving. We need to get Mark down and a warm fire going so he can rest until that ankle is better. Once we find a way down to the bottom of this ravine, then we can follow the mountain runoff to the bottom. Surely, we'll come across a road or a trail, something."

"I'm sorry I cut our trip short you guys, this totally blows," Mark apologized.

"We just have to remember to bring a backup GPS next time," Steve said.

"And a map," Chris chimed in.

"Hey, wait! Look over there. It's hikers," Steve said.

***

Michelle stopped suddenly and held her hand up for silence.

"What is it?"

"Shh," Michelle hushed, motioning for her friend to listen. She thought she heard something and concentrated on hearing it again.

A few minutes later, she turned and shrugged. "Eh, guess it was nothing."

"What'd you think it was?"

"I could've sworn I heard someone shouting. Sounded like a man."

Jennifer laughed. "I've been telling you if you don't find a man soon, people are going to start thinking you play for the other team."

"Ha-ha, aren't you funny?" Michelle deadpanned. "Just remember this, it would be years, *if ever*, that anyone finds your body out here."

"Shhhh."

This time it was Jennifer that heard it. The trail they traveled ran alongside a vast ravine that dropped down several hundred feet, and equally expansive across. The wind blew over the mountain and came across the chasm, picking up speed and whipping against the side where they stood in a constant gale. Sounds swirled on the wind, like autumn leaves of maple trees scattering across a lawn. There was no way of knowing which direction the sound came from.

"I heard it too," Michelle whispered, holding her hand up to remain quiet. "There it is again!"

"Yeah, no mistake about it. That's a man shouting. Where's it coming from?"

"There! Look, on the other side," Jennifer said, pointing across the ravine.

Two people stood waving to the women on the other side about halfway down. It was more than a few football fields across, so they were hard to see at first glance and with the wind blowing so hard, they could barely hear them yelling.

Michelle quickly dropped her pack and pulled out a bright colored t-shirt and waved it high overhead.

"Are you okay?" she shouted, but it was no use. He couldn't hear her, but she knew he was in trouble. It would take a few hours to get down the ravine and back up to where he was. She held her hands up to indicate they should stay put. "Stay there," she shouted when the wind died down for a brief second. "We're coming to you."

Nearly three hours later, the two girls reached the bottom of the ravine. There was no fast or safe way down and across, and the going was slow. A small creek lay at the bottom, but there were plenty of large boulders and downed trees that enabled them to cross. Once over, it didn't take them long to reach the area where they thought the stranded hikers were.

"I don't see them now," Michelle said, looking around.

"Hello!" Jennifer shouted.

"Up here," they heard a man's voice yell.

They hurried up the slope, climbing over dead trees and rocks. When the girls arrived, they saw there were three men, not two like they thought.

"Thank God you heard us. We got lost and were on the way back down the mountain when Mark here fell on the rocks, twisted his ankle pretty bad."

"It hurts, but I don't think it's broken," Mark said.

"What happened?" Jennifer asked warily.

Steve pointed at Mark, who leaned back on his elbows, his legs outstretched in front. "As embarrassing as it is," he began, but Chris cut him off.

"We were on our way back to the campgrounds at Mist Falls," he said, pointing in the direction they were traveling. "That's when Mark fell and twisted his ankle. That's all."

The girls both looked at Chris. They knew there was more to the story, but chose to say nothing now.

"Can you walk at all?" Jennifer asked, turning to Mark.

He sat up and gingerly rubbed his ankle. "With a little help, I can."

"It'll be dark in a couple of hours," Michelle said. "We should get him down to the bottom and make camp near the creek."

"Yeah, there's no way you're getting off this mountain in the dark," Jennifer said.

Steve glanced around at the evening skyline. He sighed, "Yeah, you're right about that. Let's get him on his feet and get moving."

Jennifer and Michelle asked a lot of questions of the men on the trip down. They were leery of meeting three strange men in the middle of the woods. It didn't feel like much of a coincidence, but stranger things have happened.

Were they just hikers with bad luck? Or, is there more to their story? Michelle thought. Either way, the girls had to be cautious.

By the time the group reached the bottom of the ravine, the women felt more at ease around the men. Enough so to share a campsite. They seemed genuine in their predicament.

The group quickly set about getting the camp set up for the night. Michelle helped Steve gather dead tree limbs and built a fire. There was a natural spring nearby to help make some coffee. The sun went down, leaving the night pitch black. The wind settled, blowing in storm clouds and blotting out the moon and the stars, making the night even darker. The rain held off, but lightning flashed off in the distance. There was a good chance they would be hiking off the mountain the next day in the shower. Mark sat near the fire, holding a small cup of coffee when Jennifer sat down. "How's the ankle?"

"It's better. I'm sure it'll be fairly stiff in the morning, but I should be able to put some weight on it."

"That's good. So, what are you guys doing out here?"

Mark turned back to the fire and used a stick to poke at the burning wood, sending tiny embers floating. "Just camping, you know, getting away for a few days."

"When we were up on the hill, your friend said you were heading back to the campgrounds at Mist Falls."

Mark said nothing, just nodded and continued poking at the fire.

"Trouble is," Michelle said, joining the conversation. "Your friends could've helped you down here. You didn't need us. Not to mention, the direction you were heading isn't anywhere near the direction of Mist Falls."

"It's okay, Mark," Steve said, walking over to sit beside his brother. "You can tell 'em."

Jennifer traded looks with Michelle. *What have they gotten themselves into*, she thought?

"Truth is, we're lost."

"We're not lost," Chris said, sulking.

"Don't listen to him; he's an idiot. Yes, we are lost. We've been out here running around looking for a lost gold mine for the last three days, and got turned around."

"A lost gold mine? Really?" Jennifer asked.

"Yeah," Mark said. "Steve here believes there's a lost gold mine somewhere out there. He found a book in a yard sale that he believes tells of its location."

"It's not a book; it's a handwritten journal," Steve said, proudly displaying the tome.

"Yeah, yeah, whatever. I'm beginning to think you're nuts."

"So, where are you guys from?" Michelle asked.

"Idaho Springs," Steve answered.

"Oh, okay, Clear Creek, I should've known," Michelle laughed. "We're from Golden."

Before Steve could ask *what* she meant by her comment, he was cut off by his brother.

"Seriously," Mark said. "If you two hadn't come along when you did, who knows if we would have found our way out. You *do* know the way out, right?"

Michelle hesitated a moment. Unable to hold back any longer, she laughed. "Yeah, we know our way down. We parked at Mist Falls too, and we hike here all the time. That's why when we saw you on the other side of the ravine, we knew something was up. It's only a day's hike out so, yeah, we can save you."

They all enjoyed a good laugh.

"Is there any coffee left, or did you drink it all?" Steve asked.

Mark's ankle would be stiff in the morning, but the slow

hike out would have him moving and flexible quick enough. He rubbed it gingerly with one hand and sipped down the remaining bit of coffee from the thermos. He slurped loudly while eyeing his brother over the top before handing him the empty cylinder.

"Nope."

"Gee, thanks a lot mutant," Steve said dryly.

"Hey, I'm an injured man here," Mark said.

Michelle and Jennifer chuckled at the brothers as they set their tent up on the other side of the fire opposite the boys. They overheard them talking about finding the gold mine, and what they would do with the money they could make. Chris talked most of the time about joining the military and would have to put all his share of the fortune in the bank until he got out. Mark had plans to buy a beach house and retire while Steve cautioned them that they hadn't found any gold yet.

Jennifer finished rolling out her sleeping bag and joined them around the fire.

"What makes you think that this journal you found is legit? I mean, it could just be a book, pure fiction? Couldn't it?"

"I've researched it thoroughly. The people, the places, everything matches up. I think this is legit," Steve said. "Besides, even if it's not, we still got to go camping."

"And got lost and saved by two girls," Chris chimed in laughing. He bristled at his own words. "Sorry, no offense. I mean, it's not that being saved by two girls is embarrassing because you're girls, but because we got lost in the first place and…"

"Just shut it, Chris," Mark said. "You're only digging yourself in deeper."

Michelle and Jennifer laughed.

"It's okay. I'm just glad we were here to rescue three lost

and wayward souls."

"So are we, and thank you. I don't think we've told you that yet, but we appreciate the assist," Steve said.

"No problem, code of the road, so to speak," Jennifer said. "You can't leave stranded hikers."

The more the group talked, the better the girls felt about being around the men. They seemed like average guys who put their minds at ease about being alone in the woods with perfect strangers. There was nothing creepy about any of them and everything they said panned out as far as the school and town and events. No one seemed suspicious about anything in case they were up to something.

7

Michelle was the first to wake the next morning. She unzipped the tent and slipped out, careful not to wake Jennifer. The fire went out sometime during the night, but she added more wood to the coals and soon had it blazing again. The heat felt good and knocked the chill off the early morning. The storm clouds remained, blocking the sunlight and leaving the woods in a misty gray hue.

"Good morning," Steve said, his voice low and ragged.

Michelle spun. "I didn't notice you get up. Scared me."

"Sorry."

"No worries, I was just about to make some coffee. Want some?"

"Sounds good. I'll give you a hand."

The smell of the coffee brewing was eye-opening, but Steve felt much better after the first sip. He sat across from Michelle and tossed another small dead limb on the fire.

"The others will smell it and be up soon I'm sure," she said.

"I'm sure you're right."

"Hey so, I'm curious, do you mind me asking about this

lost gold mine? Is that for real or was it just a joke to hide the fact that you guys got lost and two women had to save your bacon?"

"Ha, very funny," Steve laughed. "I suppose it won't hurt to tell you."

Michelle listened as Steve told her the story of the lost gold mine. Before he finished, the others had woken, poured coffee for themselves, and were listening quietly.

"I'm guessing you never found any sign of it though, or you wouldn't be leaving," Jennifer said.

"No, we didn't, but I know we're close," Steve said.

"I don't believe it exists," Chris said.

Steve shot him a nasty look.

"What? What I'd say?"

"Oh, ye of little faith," Steve chided. "It's out there; I know it is. I need to do a little more research. The weather here in the mountains can be drastic and can change the lay of the land over the course of a hundred and fifty years, you know."

"I understand that, but for all we know that cave or mine, or whatever has been caved in for years from rock slides or avalanche, we may never find it."

"Chris could be right," Jennifer added.

"Maybe, but I'm still going to try to find it," Steve said. "I'll come back alone if I have to."

"Would you mind if I looked at the journal?" Michelle offered. "Maybe I can help. I've been hiking this mountain ever since I was a little girl. My family comes here to camp and hike all the time."

"Sure, I don't mind at all." Steve hurried to get the journal and his notes out of his pack and returned a moment later.

"While you two look over that stuff, we'll get packed up," Chris said.

Michelle took the journal and read through it and referenced Steve's notes.

"Steve, let me ask you something. There's a reference to a creek they had to cross made from mountain runoff of two mountain peaks, one being half the size of the other. They crossed just below where they joined. From what I can gather, mind you the journal is faded in places, there was a pool where they stopped and made camp."

"Yeah, and there's another place later where he mentions the pool again," Steve said. "Something about standing under the waterfall. That part is hard to make out. Just too faded, but I think that the two mountain streams probably joined and cascaded over rocks that made the waterfall. I think they crossed below all of that because the fast-moving water of the falls was probably slowed down by the pool before running over and on down the mountain. Does that make sense?"

"Actually, it makes perfect sense. I think I know where that is."

"Seriously?"

"Yeah, but it doesn't look like that now, of course. Several years ago, loggers built a road back in that area. The road didn't last long because of all the rock and mudslides. It was abandoned after a few years, and the loggers made new roads on the other side of the mountain. I remember my dad telling me about it. I've only been through there once maybe, but I remember it. I'm more than certain that's where they crossed."

Mark limped over and sat down next to Michelle. "Okay, say that is the place they crossed, that still doesn't tell us where they went after that, does it?"

"It doesn't, but the journal talks about once they made it to the other side of the creek the going got much easier. They climbed the mountain following the runoff of the smaller peak. They neared the top and then moved westward along a ridge. That's when they found the valley — made camp in the meadow near a clear mountain pool. His writing is very poetic. People don't talk like that these days. That's when they discovered a hole in the ground that turned out to be a cave. *The* cave," Steve said.

"I read that part. Apparently, over the next few days is when they discovered the gold, but that's also when something started happening. The missing pages sure could help explain what happened, but I take it they were attacked. Whether it was by other prospectors, Indians or animals, it doesn't say. It's a mystery."

"He made mention that during the crossing, they lost a few of their supplies that weren't tied down good on one of their mules. They found the pack that fell off later, but there was nothing left as the animals must've made a feast of it. When they found it, it was torn to shreds, and all the goods were gone. It could've been bears or mountain lions."

Michelle stood suddenly. "Could be. Is anyone in a hurry to get back home?"

Everyone said no or shook their heads.

"Why?" Steve asked.

"Well, depending on how Mark's ankle feels in the morning, I'm sure that I can guide us to that spot!!"

***

The hike up the mountain to the area where Michelle thought could be the trail of the miners didn't take long. By early afternoon most of the clouds had moved out and the sun shined brightly, raising the temperature. The group stood on what looked to be the old logging road. Following the path, they came to an area that had been washed out and were forced to skirt around it. The underbrush was thick but manageable.

"We're pretty close now. Shouldn't be more than a half hour's walk from here to the place where the two mountain flows came together," Michelle said, stopping to wipe away the sweat from her forehead.

"I sure hope you can find your way back. It's like canopy jungle up in here," Chris said.

"Oh, quit worrying ya big baby," Mark quipped.

"I'm not worried. Besides, I'm part Cherokee; I can find my way out."

Steve scoffed, "Right, need I remind your dumbass that before these two ladies came along, we were *lost*?"

"No, we weren't. I had it under control."

Steve laughed, "What direction are we facing now?"

Chris stopped walking and looked around. "That way is west, so we are traveling due north."

"I rest my case. Chris – you're an idiot," Steve said, shoving Chris out of the way and moving forward.

"What was that for? What'd I say?"

Michelle and Jennifer laughed at the exchange and followed Steve over the rocks.

Mark shot Chris a look of feigned disgust and shook his head in disbelief, "If we depended on you to find our way out of these mountains, we would all die. Whoever told you the sun sets in the north? Dumbass!"

***

"Wow, look at that," Jennifer said.

The group came to the edge of a cliff to look down into a beautiful scene below. A small stream cascaded down step-stone rocks to splash into a crystal-clear pool surrounded by lush, green foliage. A meadow filled with tall, golden-brown grass waved in the breeze that flowed over the mountain, changing directions like a school of fish. Thick, green cattails grew around the edge of the other side of the pool.

"Incredible. It's beautiful. Look at the water falling over the rocks. I bet you could stand under it," Steve said. "Wow!"

"Wow, is right. That's awesome. Completely undisturbed by man, purely natural. I'd love to build a small cabin right there in the middle of that field," Chris said.

Steve didn't miss a beat, "Then it would be disturbed, and it would look like your old truck in no time. Beer cans laying all around, empty TV dinner trays mixed in for good measure and, of course, an engine hanging from a tree."

"What is this, pick on Chris day?"

"Well, you do ask for it sometimes."

"Do you guys go at each other like this all the time?" Jennifer said more rhetorically than questioning. "Let's get down there and check it out."

"Sorry," Steve offered, "I agree, besides, I bet that's the place that they talked about in the journal," Steve chimed in.

"That's what I'm thinking too," Michelle said. "I remember this place from years ago. My parents used to bring the family to the mountains to camp. Our dog ran off and got lost, and we searched for him for two days. My dad found this place then. I've not been back since but had always wanted to find it again. Hikers don't come here because it's too far from the trails and I don't think anyone knows about it."

The group backtracked the way they came for a short distance before cutting back through the woods until they arrived at the runoff. They crossed the fast-moving stream over large boulders in the middle of it and followed its path back up toward the pool in single file.

Michelle's yellow and orange backpack stuck up above her head and bobbed up and down with each step over the mountainous terrain. She wore khaki shorts, a blue t-shirt, and hiking shoes and carried a walking stick she fashioned out of a dead tree branch. Her arms and legs were naturally tanned from the summer sun. Steve couldn't help but notice as he followed closely behind. She was strong, smart and capable with confidence about her that he found attractive.

"You said you're from Golden, right?" Steve asked.

"Yup, born and raised."

"A Demon, huh? That's cool. We have family that lives there," Steve said, doing his best not to sound nervous. Idle chit-chat wasn't his specialty when it came to the opposite sex.

"Yeah, Jenni and I grew up together there. Been best friends since we could walk."

"You commented yesterday when I told you we're from Idaho Springs. What was that about?"

Michelle laughed, "You also said that you were looking for a lost gold mine. Isn't the Clear Creek High School mascot the *Gold Diggers*?"

"Damn, never thought about that," Steve laughed.

The trail beside the stream was skirted by the tall grass and was well worn. The hikers saw several tracks of different animals along the way but saw no indication that the animals were still there. Elk tracks mixed with lots of deer made up the bulk of what they saw. When they parted the grass and entered the clearing near the pool, they all stopped in their tracks. Standing on the far bank, a doe with two yearlings were drinking the cold mountain water. The hikers watched for a few minutes in silence so as not to spook them. The mother, ever diligent in her protective watch, however, knew something was off and quickly moved the two youngsters out of the area.

"It's even more beautiful down here," Jennifer said. She moved past the group and dropped her backpack down near the pool. Dropping to her knees, she leaned down and cupped her hands under the overflow and took a drink. "Amazing. Tastes better than Fuji."

The others quickly joined her. Mark slid his pack down off his shoulders and pulled the water bottle out. His ankle was a bit stiff, but he wasn't in pain. He knew he had slowed the others down, but there was nothing he could do about that now. They decided to search for the mine knowing all the variables. He issued a long sigh that seemed to come from far away. He was tired.

"It's already getting kinda late in the day; maybe we should get the camp set up?" Mark suggested.

"Yeah, I agree," Michelle replied. "We may have enough time to explore before it gets too dark."

"I hate to say this, but I have to be back at work on Tuesday," Jennifer said.

"I hear ya. I have to be back on Monday, so if we don't find anything by tomorrow, we may be out of luck," Steve said.

"Let's grab something to eat and get camp set up. After that we should have a little time to explore," Steve suggested.

"Good idea," Jennifer said. "I'm starving. Haven't had anything since the energy bar earlier today. What I wouldn't give for something different right now!"

Chris, who had moved off to explore the pool, overheard Jennifer. "How about a nice, fresh salad?" He asked.

"There he goes again," Mark said.

"That would be wonderful," Jennifer said. "But I don't

think we can get delivery out here in the middle of nowhere."

"I'll admit, I don't have any raspberry vinaigrette dressing, but I have the greens," Chris said, smiling.

The others walked over near him for an explanation.

"This cattail has everything we need. They're actually nutritious and don't taste half bad."

"What, pray tell, is cattail?" Michelle asked.

"This," Chris said as he pulled one of the tall green stalks out of the pool. "The lower parts of the leaves can be eaten raw. You can make a salad out of it. There's a lot of different ways to use it. This yellow pollen can be added to soups and stews or mix it with flour for bread. The roots can be dried and ground up to make flour too, lots of protein."

"I've never heard of cattail," Jennifer admitted.

"It's also called bulrush," Chris said, breaking a few leaves off and munching on it. He handed some to the girls.

"Now, *that*, I've heard of," Michelle said, taking a bite of the green leaf. "I have to say, it's not bad."

"Look at you, Mr. Survivalist," Jennifer laughed.

Chris smiled, "I'll take that as a compliment."

A short time later, after the two tents were up and a fire pit made in the center, the group split up to explore. Making their way along the banks of the pool, Steve and Michelle headed for the waterfall. The cold, crystal clear mountain water glimmered even in the fading light of the early summer evening. Huge boulders, broken and splintered by thousands of years of natural erosion, formed a long oval pool where snowmelt from the two mountain peaks crashed down a path of least resistance. The deep pool only gave pause, a slight hesitation in the incremental cascade as it joined with other runoff streams, forming a roaring river far below. The crashing of the break, however, seemed almost divinely inspired alongside the beautiful, peaceful valley filled with tall, graceful grasses and scattered gray-barked birch trees in a never-ending crescendo. The entire scene, majestic, wild and untamed, was a complete work of art, a masterpiece painted by the greatest master of them all.

The intrepid explorers climbed the layered rocks to the top of the falls. From there, they could see much of the valley below. A bowl-shaped arroyo formed below the two mountain peaks and stretched strategically from the rising sun of the east to the western horizon almost as if by design. They were aligned perfectly to catch all the day's radiance for a perfect balance of vegetation. Scattered across the valley floor grew mountain harebells and beautiful bright blue and purple alpine forget-me-nots. Standing on the rocks, they could feel the power of the water as it flowed over the twenty-foot fall and crashed with all the force of a locomotive into the pool below.

"Let's cross over on those rocks and look around on the other side," Steve suggested.

"I'll let you lead the way," Michelle laughed. "I like my water frozen."

"A skier, huh?"

"Snowboarding's my thing. Every chance I get. What about you?"

"I ski, sort of. Guess you can call it that," he laughed, leaping from one large, flat rock to another one. "I'm just not that athletically inclined, I suppose. Your turn."

She took a quick-step run and leaped across the four-foot span with ease. There were several large rocks scattered across the stream that allowed them to get across safely. Once on the other side, they clambered down the edge to the base of the falls. The misty spray of the falls was thick and soaked their clothes quickly.

"Well, we're wet now. Might as well keep going," Steve said, smiling at her. He smoothed back the dark brown hair out of his eyes.

Michelle laughed at him. Her hair, also wet, stuck to her forehead and covered her eyes. Dozens of tiny water droplets clung to her face until the moisture collected too much water and finally slid down her suntanned bronze skin. Her chest heaved from the sudden exertion of scurrying over and under the rocks and the frigid, rapid flow of melted ice and snow.

"Oh my God, it's cold in here," she said.

"You're telling me. I didn't think it would be this cold. You could store meat in here."

They stood at the edge of a fissure directly behind the sheets of falling water. The freshly melted snow from high on the peaks poured down the mountainside and emptied into lakes and rivers below. The power of the flows created pockets in the rocks like the one they stood in now. What little daylight was left allowed them to see only a few feet into the cave.

"I wish I had brought my flashlight with me."

"Yeah, me too," Michelle said, staying close to Steve as they inched their way further in. "Not much sunlight left. We'll have to come back tomorrow and check it out." Her voice echoed off the cave walls.

Steve held his arm out in front of him to feel his way around and shuffled his feet to inch further inside. "Hello!" His voice, bouncing off the solid rock walls replied with an eerie, rapid echo.

"That's cool, but I don't think we should go any further. I can't feel where I'm at, and I dang sure don't want to fall into a bottomless pit."

Michelle groaned, "Ugh, that would be bad. When we

come back, remind me to bring a can of Febreze, this place sure has a nasty funk to it."

"Agreed!" Steve laughed. "Probably a mixture of dead fish and decaying carcasses from beavers or something. It is a bit – rank."

As darkness began closing in on the hidden valley, the spelunkers meandered back to camp and joined Mark and Jennifer around the fire they had built earlier. They changed out of their wet clothes and lay the wet things near the heat to dry.

"What happened to you two? Go for a swim?" Mark asked.

Michelle sat down as close to the fire as she could. Her body still shaking from the cold. "Not a chance. That's ice water. We found a cave entrance beneath the falls. Not sure how far it goes back, but the echoes of our voices made it sound huge, didn't have a flashlight though, so we couldn't explore it."

Steve chimed in, "Yeah, dude, we've got to go check it out tomorrow."

"Cool, I'm game. Maybe that's where the gold mine is?" Chris said, plopping down near the fire and leaned on his elbow to one side. He immediately winced in pain.

"Rock?" Jennifer asked.

"Must be," he answered. He sat up and dug into the ground. A few minutes later, he held up an object that seemed to be made of iron.

"What is it?" Michelle asked.

"Not sure," Chris said, scrutinizing the object. "Looks like something that may go on a harness for horses maybe."

"Or pack mules," Steve said. "Can I see that?"

Chris handed him the metal object consisting of an iron ring attached to a dried out, brittle piece of leather.

"Yeah, I'm sure of it. This looks like a piece of a harness

for packhorses or mules or something. What else could it be? This must be the place. No doubt in my mind," Steve said.

"Okay, that's freaking awesome," Mark said. "That mine has to be close then. Too bad it's dark now, or I'd say let's get going!"

"Speaking of that, where's my flashlight? Jenni, do you mind coming with me to the little girls' tree?" Michelle said.

The girls took their flashlights and left the camp. The tall grass swayed gently in the evening breeze, making a swishing sound each time a gust picked up. Owls hooted in the night in search of meals and bullfrogs croaked nearby. No stars lit the way. The only light came from the small flashlights they each carried.

8

"I think I'm turning in as soon as they get back," Steve said. "I'm exhausted. Doubt I can sleep, though. Too pumped up about the gold mine. The journal talked about everything we've found so far – the crossing point, the valley, the waterfall, and the cave; its gotta be close!"

"I hear ya. I guess I may finally believe you now," Chris said.

***

Jenni followed her friend through the tall grass until they came to a small clearing near a large tree.

"I can't believe just how dark it can be out here," Michelle said.

"I know it's a little eerie," Jennifer answered.

"A little? This place, as beautiful as it is in the daylight, is equally as spooky at night."

"What was that?" Jennifer spun around with her flashlight.

"What is it? What'd you see?"

"Heard something. Hey, who's there? This isn't funny you guys?"

A grunting sound came from somewhere in the darkness, followed by a loud *whooping* noise.

"We are not amused, you guys. This isn't funny at all," Michelle shouted.

Suddenly, a large rock landed just a few feet away from the girls and rolled to a stop near their feet.

"Oh my God," Jenni said, grabbing Michelle's arm.

"Leave us alone," Michelle shouted.

The girls shined their flashlights, searching for any sign of the unwanted guests but the buffalo grass was four to five feet tall, and they couldn't see but a few feet around them. They huddled together closer, Jenni grasping at Michelle's hand. They jumped at every little sound from the wind tickling the grass to the flutter of unseen birds. Suddenly, a towering figure loomed up from the grass standing at least eight feet tall. They knew immediately; it wasn't the men. Jennifer dropped her flashlight as panic overtook her. A shout froze in her throat. Michelle screamed. A high-pitched, fear-filled scream. She grabbed Jenni's arm, spun her away from the hulking figure, and ran.

***

The fire had burned low. Steve added a few more sticks of dry wood to make sure there would be adequate coals for in the morning. He couldn't survive without his morning coffee. Hopefully, the rain would hold off, but the storm clouds from earlier weren't promising.

Mark stared silently into the flames as the fire danced in the darkness. Tiny embers floated on the gentle breeze and burned themselves out within seconds. Suddenly, the solitude of the quiet evening was shaken into chaos as screams from what had to be Jennifer and Michelle pierced the night. The men jumped to their feet in an instant and searched the darkness in the direction they thought their voices came from.

"Where are they?" Chris asked.

"There," Mark pointed. "I saw the flash of light."

Steve was already moving with his small flashlight in hand.

"Wait up," Mark said. "I'm right behind you."

Chris ran into the tent, grabbed his backpack, and located his pistol. He was only seconds behind the brothers.

"Where are you?" Steve shouted. He could hear the girls panicked screaming. They were on the move, running from something. Mark reached his side.

"Anything?"

"No, I lost 'em," Steve said. "Not sure which way they went."

Chris reached the brothers, flashlight in one hand and pistol in the other. "Anything?" he asked.

"Nothing," Steve said. "The last I heard, I think they were running in that direction. This grass is so damn tall!"

"Tell me about it, I could hear you hollering, but I couldn't even see your flashlights," Chris complained.

As suddenly as the shouting began, the evening fell into an eerie silence. The three men stood silent, looking in all directions for any sign of the girl's flashlights or voices.

"Let's head in that direction then."

"Mark, maybe you should head back to camp and wait there in case they come back. I can see that ankle is still bothering you," Steve suggested.

"I'm good; I can keep up."

"No, you really can't. You'll slow us down. Besides, what

if you step on it wrong out here in the dark? We'll have to carry your ass back. Not happening. Just wait for us at the camp."

Mark knew his brother was right. Any misstep out here and he could do worse damage to the ankle and be of no use to anyone.

"Okay, I'll build a fire up as high as I can. If you get turned around, head to the high ground and look for it."

"Sounds good," Steve said. "Let's get going, Chris."

***

A limb slapped back and hit Jennifer in the face as the girls raced through the darkness trying to allude whatever was chasing them. She didn't notice as fear-infused adrenaline coursed through her veins. They could hear the weight of the beast crashing through the trees and underbrush, each step shaking the earth beneath it from its enormous weight as it ran after them. Whatever it was chasing them, it was for sure not a person.

They raced through the tall grass as quickly as they could, but there was no way of knowing which direction the campsite was now. They were not tall enough to see the glow of the fire. They found a narrow path that led into the woods. Thinking it would be easier going, they took it and picked up the pace.

"Is it still following us," Michelle panted. "What was it? A bear?"

"Can't tell. I don't hear it anymore. Turn off the light," Jennifer said.

They heard nothing except their own breathing as they stood in silence in the darkness. Whatever had been chasing them seemed to have stopped, for the moment.

"What's that?" Jennifer whispered.

"Sounded like Steve."

They listened carefully, straining to hear which direction he may be.

"There, that's definitely Steve," Michelle said. "But I don't see where he is."

"Oh my God, look!" Jennifer said, pointing in the distance. It was the campfire.

9

Mark gathered more wood for the fire and built it as high as he could. When he finished, the bonfire was blazing at least ten feet into the night sky. When he was satisfied, he gathered as much wood as he could to keep it going. There wasn't much deadwood remaining in the area. He hoped the group would be able to see it and make their way back as soon as possible.

He leaned down to pick up a large branch when he heard a loud, *whoop, whoop* coming from nearby in the darkness.

"Who's there?" He shouted.

A huge, hulking figure suddenly raised above the tall grass just before him. Mark shined his light into the face of a fierce-looking beast of the likes he had never seen before. The face was like black leather with deep sunken eyes that glowed red. The nose was flat and spread out almost as large as its mouth with lips darker than its skin. It snarled, bringing the lips together on one corner and exposing sharp jagged teeth on the other side. The hideous beast was pure predator. Mark froze in fear as the creature glared at him. He turned and ran back to the fire, his heart racing much faster than his feet.

***

Chris shouted, "Michelle, Jennifer, where are you?"

"Hey, turn your light off a second," Steve said. "Look! Over there."

The glow of a flashlight lying on the ground could be seen just a few feet away.

"This has to be theirs," Chris said, as he picked it up.

"Which way did they go?" Steve mused. "Ground's too hard to pick out any tracks, especially in the dark."

"If I had to guess, I'd... Oof!" Something hit Chris from behind, knocking him to the ground.

"Chris!" Steve shouted. He saw the huge limb that struck his friend. Someone had thrown it from behind them. He reached down and helped his buddy to his feet. "Let's go!" He shouted.

The two were on their feet and running through the head-high grass. Another massive figure suddenly appeared in front of them. A blood-curdling scream from the creature stopped the two men in their tracks. Chris brought the pistol up instinctively and fired three shots at the beast. He heard it yelp in pain before Steve pulled him in the opposite direction.

"Run!" Steve yelled.

***

Michelle whispered into Jenni's ear, "Let's leave the flashlight off and head towards the fire."

"We can't walk around out here in the dark. We can't see anything," Jennifer whispered.

"We have to try," Michelle said. "I'm not standing out

here to be eaten by a freaking bear!"

***

Steve felt the ground disappear beneath his feet.

"Oomph!" He fell straight down and hit with a hard thud against the dirt-floor of an underground cave entrance. Chris, following closely behind him, was unable to stop in time and fell crashing down on him.

"Are you okay?" Chris asked.

"Yeah, yeah, I think so," Steve finally responded. "Nothing seems broken anyway."

"Do you still have your flashlight? I dropped mine, and it must've gone out," Chris asked. "I've gotta find my gun. I dropped it too when I hit. Thanks for breaking my fall by the way."

"Glad I could help. No, I dropped mine too. Let's feel around. Maybe we can find one of 'em and figure out where we are before that damn thing finds us. What the hell is it?"

"I don't know, but I know I hit it. At least once anyway. I heard it holler when I shot at it."

Steve scrambled to his hands and knees and felt his way around. "Found your gun," he reported.

"Hey, that's something," Chris whispered. "I feel a hell of a lot better now."

"I'd feel a lot better if we had at least one flashlight to see with. I don't want you shooting me!"

"Here it is," Chris said, turning on the flashlight. He put a finger over the end of it to keep the beam small as not to be seen by the animal chasing them.

"We need to get out of here and find those girls before that damn thing does!"

"What is that thing? A bear?"

"That wasn't a damn bear dude! I don't know what the hell it is, but that's not a freaking bear!"

"Then what the hell is it?"

"Whatever it is, it's flesh and blood, and that means it can die, especially filled with .45 slugs in its ass!"

"Where are we anyway?" Steve asked.

"Not sure, but it looks like it goes back ways, but we don't have time to explore it now. Not if we want to live!"

"Hey, shine that light over here again," Steve said.

Chris turned the light over to where Steve indicated. Shoots of gold surrounded by milky quartz gangue shined in the bright LED light on the cave wall.

"Holy Hell! We found it!"

"Yeah, but we also found why those miners got the hell out and never came back!" Steve said.

"Okay, what do we do now?" Chris asked.

"We get out of here, find the girls, and get them back to camp."

"How do we find them?"

"I'm hoping that when you shot the damn thing, it ran off. Let's get going."

The two men climbed out of the cave opening, which was only about five feet below the surface. They were careful to listen for any sign that the beast could still be lingering, but once they were satisfied it was gone, they backtracked the way they came.

"Damn, that's a hell of fire he's got going on," Chris said when he noticed the blaze a few hundred yards away.

"I'll say. Surely the girls will see it too and make for it!"

No sooner had he said that when they heard a rustling in the field coming from behind them.

"When it gets closer, turn the flashlight on and light it up! I'll blow his ass away," Chris whispered.

They hunkered down in the tall grass and waited. The

sounds of something making its way through the grass grew louder with each waiting second. Just as they were about to jump up and surprise the beast, a flashlight beam flashed on the ground in front of them.

"Don't shoot," Steve whispered. He stood and turned his light on. It was Michelle and Jennifer.

"Oh my God, are we glad to see you," Michelle said.

"Did you see what it was?" Chris asked.

"No, not exactly," Jennifer said, trembling.

"I saw it," Michelle said. "It wasn't a bear, but it was just as big if not bigger."

"I don't care what the son of a bitch is, let's get back to camp. Mark's alone there, and he's all gimped up," Steve said. "Chris, you have the gun, lead the way."

***

Mark grabbed the longest branch he could find in the fire. Whatever that thing was that was chasing him might be afraid of the flames. He could feel the beast moving right behind him. He turned and waved it menacingly at the massive creature. He was right; the animal was afraid of the fire and retreated into the darkness. It screamed furiously but ran away.

***

Chris led the way back to the camp in a single file with Steve bringing up the rear. He kept the flashlight beam as small as possible in his left hand and the pistol at the ready in the other. The group held one hand on the person in front of them and moved along steadily. Chris stopped the group several times to listen for any signs the beast could be close, but when hearing nothing, they continued. The camp was less than a hundred yards away.

Jennifer stumbled and fell forward into Michelle's legs, knocking them both to the ground in a tangled mess, almost taking Chris with them.

"Ow!" Michelle said, falling to the ground. Her elbow landed hard on a rock. Rolling onto her bottom, she sat up rubbing it gingerly

"Sorry, Chelle," Jennifer whispered. "I tripped over a rock or something."

"I'm alright. Let's get going."

"Shh, don't move," Chris whispered, clicking off the flashlight. "Something's following us."

Steve heard it too this time and felt around for anything to use as a weapon. A large rock was all he could find. Adrenaline pumped through his system, and his heart raced, threatening to burst out of his chest.

Chris eased around the girls as quietly as he could and waited with Steve. Whatever was following them stopped whenever they stopped.

"Let's force it out," Chris whispered. "When we do, the girls can run back to camp, and I'll shoot it. I have fourteen rounds of .45 left. I don't care what it is; it can't live filled with lead."

"I'm game," Steve said.

"Okay, as soon as we jump up and run at it, you two run as fast as you can, back to camp. We're gonna end this thing," Chris explained to the girls.

They understood and made ready to run.

Chris gave the signal. The girls bolted for the camp. He and Steve stood, screaming as loudly as they could, trying to be as intimidating as possible to their adversary. The beast stood and rushed at them. It was massive. Chris was ready and fired several shots. The creature fell within a few yards of the men.

"Let's go!" Chris shouted.

They bolted for the camp not far behind the girls. An enraged scream pierced the night from somewhere in the middle of the tall grass. Chris held onto the firearm as tightly as possible. If he fell, he couldn't afford to drop it again.

The two men arrived at the camp moments after the girls. Mark had the fire roaring with massive logs.

"What the hell are those things and how goddamn many are there?" Mark asked.

"I don't know, but they're not bears!" Steve shouted. "We need more fire. Spread it all around us. Maybe it will keep them away."

"One of 'em attacked me here at the camp, but when I shoved fire in its face it backed off," Mark said.

"We gotta get out of here," Jennifer cried.

"There's no way we can make it out of these mountains at night," Steve said.

Lightning flashed several times, and thunder shook the valley.

"Are you freaking kidding me?" Chris yelled, ducking into the tent to search for his pack.

The rain began slowly at first, but within seconds had picked up, falling hard and pelting the campers. They watched in silence as it sizzled in the fire and slowly began extinguishing the flames.

"What are we going to do now?" Mark asked.

"The cave!" Michelle shouted, looking at Steve. "The one behind the falls. If we can make it there, we can hold them off until morning and then get the hell out of here."

"Chris, how many rounds do you have left?"

"Eleven in this mag and another full mag in my backpack, 28 rounds."

"Make sure they count!" Steve said. "Chris, you lead the

way."

Just as Steve said that, a huge rock crashed into the middle of the fire scattering pyramid stacked logs and sending wet coal ash and sizzling embers into a plume. Chris turned the direction the rock seemed to have come from and let loose a three-round volley.

"Move!" Steve shouted.

Chris led the way to the falls as quickly as they could manage in the dark. With only a couple of flashlights, soft earth turning to mud, and scared out of their wits, the trek wasn't easy. Michelle followed Chris, Jennifer was in the middle, and Steve and Mark brought up the rear.

10

Lightning flashed across the valley followed closely by booming thunder shaking the very ground beneath their feet. Chris saw one of the beasts in a flash of lightning and chanced a couple of rounds. He heard the creature scream loud and piercing, possibly from pain, but it could have been rage and anger. He didn't know if he hit it or not. He kept running.

They made it to the base of the natural rock staircase that went up and crossed over the falls. The rain was pelting down so hard that they had trouble seeing even with their flashlights. They clambered up the twenty feet to the top to cross over to the other side. Another bolt of lightning crackled, and thunder boomed near them, causing Jennifer to stumble. Momentarily blinded, she fell into the water below. Mark made a grab for her and was able to catch hold of her shirt.

Steve was at his side in an instant. Together, they hauled the girl out of the water and onto her feet.

"We gotta keep moving," Steve shouted.

BOOM BOOM BOOM

Steve saw the muzzle blasts as his friend opened fire behind them, but he didn't want to look back. They managed to get to their feet and jump across the rock slabs to the other side. Once across, they climbed down the rocks and found the ledge that led behind the falls.

"Turn off the lights; maybe they won't see where we're going now," Steve said.

One by one they slid along the ledge, careful not to slip off the rocks into the crashing water below. Chris felt along the wall until he felt it give way to the interior of the cave.

They crowded together into the opening of the cave and stood huddled together. Jennifer was crying and near hysterics, but Mark was holding her in his arms, trying his best to comfort the girl. "We're going to be okay, we're safe now," he soothed.

They stood huddled for several minutes before anyone dared speak.

"Maybe they're gone now. Back to wherever they came from," Chris whispered.

"I don't know, but I'm not leaving this cave until daylight!" Steve replied.

Michelle, listening to the exchange reached a trembling hand out to feel for Steve, her voice shaking from the bitter cold, "If this st...storm doesn't le...let up, that may be th...the day after to...to...tomorrow."

"Let's move back from the falls; maybe it'll be drier and warmer," Steve suggested.

Chris shuffled back into the cave using Michelle's small flashlight. Keeping the beam small and low on the ground, he found some driftwood that may have floated in at some point. "Maybe we can build a fire and warm up?"

"With what?" Steve asked.

"There's a bit of driftwood here that seems dry, and I have my fire starter kit in my pocket."

"Okay, but let's move further back in so the light isn't seen from outside," Steve whispered.

Chris gathered up the few pieces he could find that lay near his feet. He didn't want to shine the light all around the cave from fear of being seen from outside. Kneeling, he pulled out his fire-starter kit and went to work.

After several minutes, Steve said "It's not gonna catch dude, might as well give up. Need some kindling."

"Yeah, you're probably right, but it's freezing in here. We need to huddle together and stay warm. We'll wait em out until morning."

Easing down to the hard-rock surface, Steve leaned against the cave wall. Michelle next to him, huddling together. The others joined them, no one speaking, just breathing and trembling.

"What was that?" Michelle whispered.

"What? I didn't hear nothing," Chris said.

"Yeah, me either," Steve said. "We're safe in here. Those things don't know where we are, and besides, Chris has the gun. We'll be okay."

Chris leaned back against the cave wall, keeping one hand on his pistol. "Hey, let me see that flashlight," he whispered.

He clicked it on, once again, careful with the beam keeping it small and near the ground. "There's a field mouse nest here. We're in business,"

"What's that mean?" Michelle asked.

"It means," Mark said. "He can use it as kindling and get a fire started. Maybe."

Chris pulled the nest apart and laid it in the center of the group. Grabbing the driftwood nearby, he stacked it on top and pulled out his Firestarter kit.

"Cross your fingers."

After a few strikes of the flint, the dry grass caught. It burned rapidly, but Chris and Steve added just a little to it at a time to keep it burning as long as possible.

"Damn, not sure if it'll be enough to get the driftwood going too."

"Oh my God, it's catching. It's going to burn," Michelle said.

The driftwood caught fire in one small area, just a tiny candle sized flame, but it was burning. Soon, the blaze grew larger until a large portion of the driftwood burned. The small band of hikers scrunched in a circle close to the fire. Michelle saw Steve looking at her. She tried a smile but felt that it came more of a grimace under the circumstances.

"I'm starving," Mark said.

"I can't believe how warm it is with such a small fire," Michelle whispered. "What is that smell? It's atrocious."

"It's all of our body heat," Steve replied.

"Can't be that it feels…stuffy," Chris said. He switched on the flashlight. He never had a chance to fire another shot.

Jennifer's scream was ripped from her throat.

11

...2012, seven years later

"Listen, Cameron. We just can't go barging in like this. I'm sure the hotel manager has a million other concerns at the moment. They're getting ready for a busy weekend coming up from what I understand," Judith tried appealing to her husband.

"That may very well be, but I think more could be done in regards to security. Before they can, though, they need to know what happened, don't you think?" Cameron asked. He knew his wife would never complain about anything to anyone if she could help it, but this was an issue that he wasn't about to let go.

"Yes, of course, but couldn't we call first and arrange a meeting in the morning? The manager may not even be in at this hour, and I'm exhausted." Judith rolled her eyes, huffed, and sat down to tie her boots.

"We could, but I'd rather not wait," Cameron said. His tone sarcastic, annoyed at his wife's tone. "What happens if this… this… prowler comes back? What then? Maybe it *was* kids messing around, or maybe it wasn't. We just don't know," he finished zipping his coat and turned to look at her. "It's certainly not my job to find out."

She finished tying her boots and stood to face him.

He softened his tone and placed his hands on her shoulders to look his wife in the eyes.

"Look, babe, we paid a lot of money for this trip, and we paid even more to have our privacy. I had hoped to avoid all of the drunken frat parties at the hotel, and spend time with you." He finished with a soft kiss on her forehead before pulling away.

Cameron tugged at the stocking cap covering his salt and pepper hair knocking his glasses off in his haste. He bent down, scooped them up, and settled them back on his face. His green eyes blinked a couple of times before readjusting to the lenses to peer over them at his wife, expecting a comment that never came.

The two had been enjoying the evening after dinner with a relaxing soak in the outdoor hot tub in the backyard when strange noises, grunts and what Cameron called chittering, disturbed their solitude. When he shouted for whoever or whatever it was to stop, a rock was thrown in their direction hitting the side of the tub, narrowly missing them.

Judith turned away from her husband, pretending she hadn't noticed his clumsiness with his glasses or his condescending smile. She wrapped a bulky wool scarf around her neck, pulled her long blond hair out, and grabbed her coat. She drew a stocking cap over her head and followed him out the door of their rented cabin, her boots crunching on the frozen snow.

"At least that atrocious smell is gone now," Cameron commented as he trudged through the compacted snow making his way to the car.

After the rock was thrown, they hurried inside the cabin, but not before the terrible smell came over the area. The smell was so intense that Judith heaved and wretched before ducking inside the cabin.

Cameron clicked the key fob, and the car chirped. The lights blinked when the power door locks released with an audible click.

"Seriously, what do you think it was? Could it have been the plumbing backing up?" She asked.

"No, I don't think so. Everything inside is working just fine. Whatever it was, it was putrid, almost like a dead animal carcass. It's gone now, so hopefully, it won't be back."

He opened the passenger door and helped his wife in, closed it, and jogged around to the driver's side.

The couple had traveled to Hawthorn to stay at the new resort that opened just a few months earlier. They frequently traveled together when he went on business trips, but this time was strictly a vacation. A much overdue vacation as she had pointed out on more than one occasion. They were in their late forties, loved to ski and had spent many getaways together in the snowy mountains.

Judith, two years younger than her husband, had an outgoing personality and made friends quickly with an enchanting smile behind sky blue eyes. An athletic build and the better skier of the pair, her husband would often quit earlier than she, leaving her alone to hit the more challenging runs he didn't feel comfortable on.

The hotel and ski lodge were the newest resort in Hawthorn. Owned by Cohen Group, Inc., the holdings consisted of the charming Hawthorn Valley Hotel and Ski Lodge located near the town square, and the Buckhorn Lodge higher up on the mountain. CGI has many other properties, but these were the newest and most prestigious ones in the portfolio. Though a bit on the trendier side, the hotel was still affordable for those coming to town for a ski vacation or to explore the picturesque countryside year-round. The Buckhorn Lodge was the more luxurious and extravagant option situated on the mountainside overlooking the town. It catered to a higher-end clientele and had every amenity those clients would expect. The hotel also rented several cabins on the mountain for a more remote and private setting, which is where Cameron and his wife were staying. These were located further up and scattered five to eight miles away from the lodge. Backcountry enthusiasts could enjoy the uncrowded trails made possible by the newly built roads.

It took nearly two years to complete the project. The area needed the uplift in new investments that catered to a wider range of clientele. The resort opened with a full house and a long waiting list for the season. The snow reports were better than expected, and all the lodges were operating at full capacity. It couldn't have been any better for the planned grand opening celebration.

The rented cabin was a fifteen-minute drive away from the Buckhorn lodge and at least half an hour from town.

"It just seems so unnecessary is all I'm saying," Judith commented as she watched her husband climb into the orange Subaru. "I'm sure a simple phone call would take care of it. Maybe we should call the police or the mountain patrol instead of being so…impetuous?"

Cameron started the vehicle, put it in drive, and pulled out of the driveway. He let out an exasperated sigh. "I thought we discussed this and made a decision? Besides, I thought about that, but I think the lodge would probably be best. They have their own security, and I'd rather give them the opportunity first before we go that far. If it *is* one of their guests being jerks, then they would probably prefer to deal with it themselves if possible."

Judith reached down and tugged at her coat that was pinned under the seat belt.

"Dammit!"

Cameron huffed and turned to his wife. Pushing his glasses back into place he said, "Listen, babe, I hear what you're saying, but I've found that a phone call is usually not treated as important as a face-to-face meeting with someone. You know how people are, body language is half of communication, and I want them to understand just how important this is to us. What if I hadn't been there? No telling what that jackass would've done," he said in an apologetic tone and a fake smile.

She took it as condescending. "Please don't patronize me. I'm not a child." She turned away but not before shooting him a nasty look. "I hate it when you do that," she said tersely.

Cameron scoffed and rolled his eyes. He knew he should keep his mouth shut, that he had pushed his wife too far, but he also knew no matter how hard he tried, he couldn't.

"I am not trying to be insensitive. I know you don't like to complain about things, and I understand how you are, but I wish for one second you would simply trust me to make the right decision…"

Her head snapped around. "Oh, just shut up, would you? I get tired of always doing things your way. You never listen to me. It has to be at your impulse, and it can be so embarrassing to me how heated you get over *nothing* sometimes."

"Whatever," Cameron snarled. He turned his attention back to the road, accelerating as it changed from gravel to blacktop.

Silence.

A few minutes later, Judith harrumphed and slapped her hand on the console between them. "You don't have to drive like an idiot just because you're upset with me. Slow down."

He knew he had pushed her as far as he could. He let his anger fade and turned to look at her, putting his hand on her leg. His voice softened. "I'm sorry dear, I promise not to embarrass you. I'll simply ask that they increase security in our area so that we can relax and maybe they can send someone out in the morning to check things out. How's that?"

She turned to give him a reassuring smile, but something in the road caught her eye. She went rigid; her eyes opened wide as fear overcame her. She sucked in a breath, then screamed, she braced herself for the impact.

Cameron looked up in time to see it too. They were going too fast to avoid it, and his reaction was too slow to stop in time. He cranked the wheel and slammed on the brakes. The vehicle careened into a slide, caught the shoulder, and spun wildly out of control. He turned the wheel back the other way and the tires caught dry pavement. The Subaru flipped over onto its side and slid down the embankment. The small car hurtled through the trees and underbrush rolling and sliding down the treacherous mountain.

For Cameron, it was as if the entire scene was playing out in slow motion, yet he was helpless to prevent it. He saw the windshield explode and mix with pieces of the red tail light lens, bursting from the impact of trees and granite. He heard his wife's screams with each violent jolt. The hood latch broke and the momentum flung the square piece of orange metal up, catching a large sapling and crinkling around it. The hot coolant from the radiator spewed and hissed into the snow. The car rocked back and forth on the embankment before sliding to a stop and coming to rest upside down.

The dark forest of Hawthorn Mountain swallowed the small vehicle and continued its silent and apathetic vigil. It was over in a matter of seconds.

***

"Com'on Tammy, let's get going. This is the last run of the day. Let's hurry before they shut the lifts down," Leon urged his wife along.

"I'm coming," she said, "*I'd rather take the Voodoo Trail though,*" she muttered under her breath as she picked up her snowboard and slogged behind to catch up to her husband.

Leon and Tammy Souter lived in Dallas, but often visited the mountains of Colorado and especially loved spending time in Hawthorn. Tammy enjoyed the shopping in town and considered it just as much physical activity as the skiing on the mountain.

Her husband was an outdoor enthusiast, and though he liked skiing and snowboarding, he was not as skilled as she or nearly as adventurous. He preferred his camera rather than skis. His wife only agreed to the easy slopes so that they could do it together – and, of course, to keep the peace. Leon was more into photography than he was the adrenaline rush of extreme sports as she was. The mountains provided the incredible scenery for his hobby no matter what time of year or season. He was never without a camera handy, even if it was only his smartphone.

Leon barely glanced over his shoulder at his wife as he hurried toward the lift. Most of the other skiers had already left the mountain for the warm confines of the lodge, but there were still a few people out for the evening runs. Night skiing was popular, though only portions of the mountain remained open. The operators would be shutting the lifts down in the other areas soon, including their favorite one, and the couple wanted to get in a final run before they did. There was no line now, so they didn't have to wait, which was not the case earlier when they stood in line for over an hour.

"Hold your horses. I'm coming," she yelled. "Nothing like a candy run to end the day," she muttered under her breath as she hurried to catch up with her husband.

The couple moved over to the lift-chair and sat back for the quick ride to the top of the run.

"Maybe we can split up tomorrow," he said. "I know you're only doing this for my sake."

"Oh, you heard that? I'm sorry," she replied. Her voice not implying an apology, but rather embarrassed that he heard her.

He put his arm around her shoulders and pulled her closer. Leaning in, he clumsily attempted a kiss on her cheek but jerked back when their goggles clinked together.

"Though I appreciate the gesture, that kinda hurt." She laughed as she readjusted her goggles to rest more comfortably on her forehead.

Leon laughed and readjusted his own.

"Sorry, it's hard to be graceful when you're wrapped up like a mummy and holding these poles while thirty feet in the air,"

"You know I love you, dear, but yes, I would like to hit the Voodoo trail tomorrow," she said.

"Why don't you do that in the morning, and I'll go take some photos. We can meet in town for lunch," he suggested.

The lift glided smoothly up the mountain at a brisk pace taking the pair to the slope called Kerrigan's Run. It was marked as a blue square trail and was Leon's favorite hill.

Tammy had taken her gloves off and worked diligently on fixing her jacket that seemed to have ridden up when she sat on the lift. Suddenly the chair jerked, and Leon quickly pulled his arm off her shoulder and frantically tore his gloves off to reach into his pocket, one of which dropped straight to the snowy ground below.

"Oh my God, do you see that? I can't believe it!" He said.

"For heaven's sake, what are you doing? You're going to knock us off here. Would you please -"

She cut her statement short when she saw the look on her husband's face. As he held his cell phone aloft, she followed his gaze but saw nothing.

"What is it?"

"Look at the ridgeline near the top, between the rock outcropping that looks like a doubled-up fist and an old rock slide. Do you see it?"

"I don't see anything - just rocks, trees, and snow."

"Are you serious?" He asked in a haughty tone. "Surely you saw it too? It's gone now, but I swear, there was someone or something on that ridge. I'm not kidding. I have it on video. I finally saw one with my own eyes!" He said. "I can't believe it. I can't believe that I actually have it on video. I have proof, video evidence. You can't refute video footage!"

"I can't believe it either," she laughed. "What in the hell are you babbling about? Okay, so you saw someone on the ridge — big deal. Look, there go some skiers. See how easy it is."

"I swear you're going to think I'm crazy, but I believe it was a Bigfoot!"

"Why would Bigfoot be at a ski resort? I doubt they make ski boots that would fit him," She mocked.

"I'm serious, check out the video for yourself."

"I'm sure it was just a backcountry skier wearing dark colors," she suggested. "That's too far away to know for sure."

Leon quickly pulled the video up to show his wife, but when she viewed it on the small screen, she concluded that she was right in her assessment that it was just a person wearing dark colors.

"Look, I know the difference between how a person walks and how Bigfoot walks," he stated, feeling somewhat slighted at his wife's insistence.

"Honestly, you need to rethink what you just said," she laughed. She had always been a skeptic of Leon's obsession. Though he claimed to be an expert in all things Bigfoot, she would often argue that there is no such a thing and that for one to be called an expert in any field, there must be actual scientific evidence, proof of the phenomenon.

"Okay, maybe that did sound a little crazy, but I'm telling you, I know what I saw," he said.

"Leon, that ridge is so far away, it could have been anyone," Tammy said as she lifted the bar on the seat to prepare to disembark.

"Exactly my point. It is very far away, and just look at

the size of the thing!"

Tammy had already strapped her foot in on her board and was ready to slide off when Leon finally stuffed his cell phone back into his pocket, put the one glove he had back on and slid off the chair. They cruised down to a landing spot just below the lift station where they stopped to make sure everything was secure for the run. Leon pulled his cell phone out again to review his video one more time.

"I'll try to enlarge it where we can see it better, but I'm telling you, I know what I saw up there," he insisted.

The couple watched it several more times and finally, he trimmed the video to the segment that showed the figure on the ridge then insisted on uploading it to the internet. By the time the upload was completed, the ski lift had stopped, and no one else had gotten off.

"It's getting dark, we'd better get going," Tammy warned. "The operators are already gone, and it's going to be dark pretty quick.

"Yeah. You're right. Let's get moving," he said, shoving off down the slope with his wife following closely behind.

***

The diner was old and small, but it was clean. The tables and chairs were pure Art Deco straight from the '50s with a red pearl Formica finish wrapped with shiny chrome metal. The entire diner was themed in the bright red and white colors from the outside awning to the furniture and interior trim. It was small with three large plate windows in the front and a massive wood framed, glass inset door at the end, all framed in bright fire-engine red. Bright red letters on the glass spelled out, Greely's Diner. The door was littered with posters hawking everything from the latest

Pound class to local yard sales and movie night at Guthrie Green Park. No one ever bothered to remove them. A long counter with bar stools separated the dining room from the kitchen in the back. A long, narrow window served as the order station for the wait staff. A double-sided breezeway door made of gray metal with small windows near the top was one of the only items not painted red. There was no doubt in Troy's mind that everything about the place was original, including the black and white checkered floor. It looked as if it had seen its better days as black marks from thousands of pairs of shoes lay spattered in a weird mosaic pattern.

"Can I get ya anything else, Mister?" A tall, lanky kid asked as he refilled the nearly empty coffee cup.

Troy looked up from his tablet and smiled politely.

"No thanks, I'm good."

"Yeah, well - the thing is mister, it's almost eleven, and I'll be closing up soon. The only thing left is coffee, -" The young man let the sentence hang.

"Oh, wow. I'm sorry. I guess I lost track of time. Looks like I'm the last person standing," Troy laughed. "I'll just finish up and get out of your way."

"Oh, I'm not trying to run you off, just that I'm shutting the kitchen down and locking the front door in a few. It'll take me a bit to clean up so, you're more than welcome to stick around and finish your cup. Besides, I don't mind the company. It's been slow all evening."

"Thanks, I think I will," Troy said. "A unique place, considering the location."

"It is, indeed."

"By the way, names Troy, Troy Turner."

"Nice to meet ya, Mr. Turner. Leonard P Valentine at your service," he said, extending a hand.

101

Troy started to put his tablet away, but a sudden ding alerted him that he had a new email. He laid the tablet back down on the table. His OCD wouldn't allow him to put it away knowing there was a red dot indicating an unread email sitting there, waiting to be opened.

Leonard said, "Unique is almost an understatement when describing this little diner. Oh, the stories I could tell." The young man laughed.

"Do tell," Troy said.

The casual interest in the diner suddenly turned to curiosity. He listened to Leonard talk while he absently opened the email.

Leonard set the emptied coffee pot down and began wiping down a table nearby.

"Well, just a couple of years ago Commissioner William Wood was killed in that very seat."

"Seriously?" Troy asked, stunned. "I read about that. If I recall, they arrested the people behind the killing, right?"

"Yup, they sure did. They'll be behind bars for a long time. So, you aren't from around here, obviously," Leonard said.

"I'm that easy, eh? Troy laughed. "Actually, I used to live nearby several years ago. Out here visiting a friend now, but you're right, even then, I wasn't *from* here."

Troy had lived in the city many years ago, and had a lot of great memories, but also some that weren't so great. He had met his wife in college and after graduation she wanted to pursue an acting career in the Big Apple. At the time, Troy was perfectly fine with the idea of moving to a huge city. As a young writer, he was on board with the idea for the simple fact that was where all the publishing agents and major publishers were located. The newlyweds found the strain of new careers coupled with marriage was difficult at best. Though they tried hard at saving both, eventually they divorced, and Troy moved to Colorado.

"The island, huh? I've never been there. Spend most of my time right here in Tulsa."

"Nothing wrong with that, my friend."

Leonard laughed, "Sure, unless you've been here your whole life and have never seen the rest of the world except vicariously through my customers."

"That's better than being there sometimes. Besides, I could smell the cheeseburgers as I drove by." Troy said as he opened the email and glanced down at it.

A new YouTube video had posted with the keywords he had set as parameters long ago. He clicked the link and read the byline as the video played with no sound, drained his cup and quickly put the tablet away.

Leonard finished wiping down all the tables and then flipped the closed sign around and locked the door.

"Just locking up, so no one else tries coming in. When you're ready to leave just holler out, and I'll lock up behind ya." Leonard said. "I gotta few things to tidy up in the kitchen, and then I'm outta here myself. So, maybe you got five more minutes."

"Oh, I'm sorry. I don't mean to keep you," Troy said.

"No worries at all Mister. It's good to have company on a Monday night, the place is always dead."

"Pun intended?"

Leonard looked puzzled for a second then it occurred to him what he had just said.

"Oh, guess that was a bad choice of words. Sorry about that."

Troy laughed. "No worries, I've gotta get outta here anyway. It was a pleasure to meet you, Mr. Valentine."

"Same here, Mr. Turner. Have a good night."

Troy exited the diner and headed straight for his hotel room. He pulled his cell phone out, called the airport and moved his flight up to first thing in the morning. His mind was on the video and what the byline read.

Bigfoot captured on video in Hawthorn

12

Tammy leaned her skies on the rack and entered the hotel. Passing by a small group of skiers preparing to hit the slopes and several others that were milling about, she would soon be joining them on the mountain, but not before stopping for her favorite coffee. The baristas behind the counter seemed overwhelmed by the number of guests standing in line, but she was patient and didn't mind waiting. The waiting was something she was accustomed to at her coffee shop back home. The difference was, back home, she knew the baristas and several of the customers, but here, she knew no one, which gave her an excuse to people watch and eavesdrop on the conversation of a couple in front of her.

"It already has over a thousand views."

The man speaking looked to be in his late twenties wearing a red ski cap, a red jacket, and insulated pants. He was talking to a blond woman about the same age wearing a festive red sweater under a Sherpa-lined blue down vest.

"It's just a hoax. I'm sure it was done to get people

talking about this place; a publicity stunt," the girl replied.

"Maybe so, but remember a while back there were stories of a Bigfoot attack here. Now, a new video surfaces of one on the mountain. Of course, it's not real, but I can't believe anyone would want the kind of publicity that it would bring," he said.

"Excuse me, I'm sorry, but I just happened to overhear your conversation about a video?" Tammy asked.

"Yeah, everyone's talking about it. Someone uploaded it on YouTube yesterday. They say it's a Bigfoot that they spotted on the mountain. Or at least that's what they're claiming," the man answered.

He pulled up the video and let her watch it on his cell phone.

She recognized it immediately. *Just great*, she thought, *leave it to my husband to stir up controversy.*

***

Lisa Richards arrived at her office and set her leather briefcase on the desk, then opened the bottom drawer and dropped her purse in before turning on her computer. Mornings were never her thing, not until she had at least two cups of coffee. Opening the cabinet above the coffee maker, she grabbed a breakfast blend and dropped it in the machine and turned back to her desk. No sooner had she sat down when she heard the boiling sound the machine made just before the heated water poured through the pre-measured, plastic cups of coffee and into the waiting mug below. It was then she realized, she forgot the cup. The hot coffee poured out into the overflow tray and onto the cabinet.

"Damnit!"

She quickly grabbed a mug from the cabinet to catch what little, if any, of the breakfast blend that remained. It was less than a few sips.

"Ugh! Are you freaking kidding me?"

She collapsed in her chair dejectedly and surveyed the mess. A few seconds later, she heard a slight knock on her door. Her admin stood at the door with a disapproving look on his face.

"Don't give me that look, Lyle," Lisa said, cutting her eyes at him.

Feigning a look of innocence, he waved a hand in the air as if brushing the incident off. He entered the office with a, what she considered, much too chipper attitude for such an early hour.

"It's water under the bridge," he said. "Or on top of the cabinet. Tsk tsk. Either or. Well, one thing's for sure, you are not, and will never be a morning person."

"Ugh!" She said, sinking even further into her chair. "I need caffeine!"

"Among many other things, Honey."

Lyle Monroe had been her administrative assistant for three years. He was good at his job and kept her office organized better than anyone she could've imagined. He was quirky and had a somewhat disdainful outlook, was always quick with sarcasm, but was also loyal to a fault.

"Here, let me *not* get that for you," he said, waving off the coffee mess on the counter. "It's really such a simple thing - cold water comes in, hot water goes out. Usually, it goes out into a cup but to each their own."

"What do you want, Lyle?"

"Me? World peace, unbiased news reporting, my own island in the Caribbean, and an endless supply of grape snow-cones. Why do you ask?"

"Must you torment me so?"

"If simply letting you know that Stephen has been holding for you on line one since you came in this morning is *tormenting* you, might I suggest you let him go. He is a bit…brash, at times."

"Out!" She said, pointing toward the open door. Spinning her chair around, she picked up the phone. "Steve, Jesus, you're up early."

"Good morning, how are you? Oh, me? I'm well thank you," Steve replied sarcastically, feigning indignity.

"I'm sorry. You're right, that's no way to answer the phone. I've had a rough start this morning. Let me try again." She changed her voice. "Good morning, Steve. How are you doing on this fine, wonderful morning?"

Steve laughed, "That's much better. No coffee yet, huh?"

"Ugh! You don't even wanna know," she said.

"I know, much too early for my liking too, but we have a lot going on to get ready for this weekend, the grand opening, the party, the dignitaries, not to mention the Board of Directors."

She and Steve Slater, her assistant manager of the resort, had worked together for many years managing properties for the holding group. When Lisa had the opportunity to move to Hawthorn and operate the newest flagship properties for CGI, she jumped on the chance and was thrilled when Steve eagerly joined her.

Hawthorn itself was a small resort town, but its proximity to Denver made it an ideal location not only for business but for buying a home away from the busy city life. Urban sprawl was spilling into the bustling town.

"Yes, there certainly is a lot to do. But I think we have a handle on things. Chef has extra staff scheduled for the kitchen, and housekeeping is ready to go. We'll also have added security from the sheriff's office. I'm confident that we will get through it with nothing more than a few college kids that can't hold their liquor."

"I hope you're right. The board members have all rsvp'd, except for Martin. He's been in Europe for the last few weeks, but his secretary said he should be arriving closer to the weekend."

"That's good; I was hoping to see him this weekend. What about the mayor? Have you heard from him? I've been trying to avoid him," she chuckled lightheartedly.

Steve laughed, "You know I have. Our wonderful mayor checked in last night and hasn't stopped drinking and eating yet."

"Oh my," she laughed. "He means to take advantage of our hospitality all week long, apparently."

"Of course. Did you expect otherwise?" Steve said.

Mayor James Hennessey was a notorious mooch. He had been mayor of Hawthorn for several years. Nobody cared to run against him and his family legacy as founders of the town. It wasn't that he was a good mayor or a bad one. He was merely harmless and got along well with everyone. He was well-liked even though his behavior was somewhat peculiar at times. He never missed a chance to be the center of attention where he could use his gift of gab to charm and persuade people into his way of thinking. A bit on the portly side, his favorite vices were eating and drinking. He never missed a chance at a free meal, and when Steve invited him along with other dignitaries from the town, the board of directors of the shareholders, and other distinguished guests, he was sure to take advantage of the hospitality granted him.

"Well, one thing's for sure, he's entertaining," Lisa added.

"Yes, he is at that. Will you be coming up today?"

Lisa glanced at the clock on the wall. "I have some things to take care of here this morning, but I plan on coming up early this afternoon if I can get away."

Lisa kept an office at both the hotel where she lived in one of the suites and at the mountain lodge. She was always on the go taking care of both properties, not to mention the individual cabins located throughout Hawthorn.

"Sounds good. Not to change the subject, but I don't suppose you've heard the rumors flying around?" Steve asked.

"Concerning?" she asked.

Steve laughed.

"The video."

"Yes. Ridiculous. How could anyone believe such a thing? I'm sure it was just someone being somewhere that they shouldn't have been. That park has been off-limits for years. I think they found an endangered beetle or something. Who knows what the hell, but no one is allowed there, fragile ecosystem or some such nonsense?"

"Oh? I didn't know that, but there's still a lot about this town of yours that I don't know yet."

"All in due time, Steve, all in due time."

"Have you seen the video? Just a sec, I'll send you a link now."

Steve cut and pasted the link to the video and emailed it while they chatted. A second later, Lisa's email chimed.

"It's all abuzz on the mountain. Everyone's talking about it. Do you think we need to get out in front of it?" He asked.

"I'm not convinced that we need to do anything at all, to be honest. It seems that the subject is so controversial that the naysayers are doing the job for us. Either way, it's probably not hurting business. In fact, we've been turning people away all night that have been calling looking for rooms so that they can go searching for this elusive Bigfoot.

"That's just great!" Steve said. "That's all we need. Photographers and Bigfoot hunters. Sure, it's good for the local businesses, but it's not exactly the demographic we're looking for."

"No, it's not. But we, along with every other hotel in town, have been booked solid for months, well before that video surfaced. If people are coming to Hawthorn to go *Bigfoot* hunting, they'll have to pitch a tent," she laughed. "But I'll keep an eye on the situation, and if it changes at all, I'll let you know."

"Sounds good. Well, I better get busy. I just wanted to touch base with you, Boss and see if you needed anything."

"No, everything looks good here as well. See you sometime this afternoon."

13

Leon checked his pack and made sure he had the camera equipment necessary as well as his large hunting knife and survival gear before making his way downstairs to the hotel lobby. Even at the early hour, the place was already buzzing with excitement not just from those looking for a thrill on the mountain, but for the grand opening party coming up over the weekend that the hotel was throwing. The cold, brisk morning air hit him directly in the face forcing a shiver. He tugged the zipper on his coat tighter. The hotel's valet was standing nearby after handing the keys off to the owner of a red SUV.

Leon greeted him. "Good morning. Hey, I have a quick question, where is the nearest place I can rent a snowmobile?"

The valet pointed down the street. "Action Adventures, a ten-minute walk from here. They book tours all day. Can't miss it."

"Thanks."

Twenty minutes later, a young lady made a copy of his driver's license and handed Leon a waiver form to sign.

He signed the document and slid it back. Pulling out a map he had printed off, he asked, "How do I get to this ridge here?"

The girl looked at the place Leon indicated.

"Actually, that's Devil's Backbone. The entire area is off-limits. Sensitive ecosystem, endangered species. Besides, the trails are too dangerous. You have to stay on the marked path and have the unit returned by 4 p.m."

"Oh, I see. No problem. Was just curious."

She continued, "The fuel tank isn't big enough to get you there and back anyway. If you stay on the marked trail for *Action Adventures, Jackson Ridge,* you will have plenty of gas to get back safely."

"Even more incentive not to veer off," Leon laughed.

"Exactly. It's a long walk back, plus the extra charges for us to retrieve the unit."

He thanked her and exited the office. Once outside, he stowed his gear on the sled, cranked it up and put on his helmet. After attaching the tether strap for the kill switch, he zoomed out of the parking area. A few minutes later, he turned off the road and pulled into a convenience store, bought a five-gallon gas can, and filled it.

***

The dash panel lights blinked in a steady sequence illuminating the cabin of the overturned car once every two seconds as if it were a lighthouse beacon spinning its powerful beam through the pitch black of night. A steady, muffled buzz emanated from somewhere under the dash sounding like a small alarm clock hidden inside a suitcase. Upside down and more than fifty feet down an embankment beside the mountain road, the vehicle was hidden from view of any passersby. The car sat perched level on a large rock outcropping and lodged against a giant pine, teetering slightly. If not for the tree, the vehicle would have plunged another fifty feet straight down into the river below.

Cameron was the first to regain consciousness. He stirred slowly at first, but his subconscious was screaming at him to wake up. He sucked in a large breath in panic when his head cleared of the cobwebs. He realized he was trapped inside his vehicle when he heard his wife moan beside him.

Judith's seat belt held her tight with her arms dangling loosely, suspended upside down in the overturned Subaru. The burnt chemicals that caused the airbags to deploy mixed with engine coolant and left an acrid smell lingering in the frigid night air. The fuel leaking from the ruptured tank didn't help. A large bruise had already formed on her forehead in the shape of a baseball. The only thing that saved her nose from being broken was she turned to look at Cameron just before the car slammed into the trees. The airbag left small burns on her neck and cheek. She felt none of that now.

"Honey? Judy? Are you okay?" Cameron asked, reaching out for his wife in the cold darkness. His tone high-pitched and brittle, laced with guilt and worry. Hanging upside-down plus a thick coat made it near an impossible task to feel her. He grabbed for the seat belt buckle with one hand, sprang the latch while bracing himself against the fall out of the seat with his other hand. When the latch gave, he crumpled in a heap with a resounding thud though his legs were still trapped beneath the steering wheel and deflated airbag. Being as careful as possible under the circumstances, he oriented himself in the overturned wreck, peeled his legs from the airbag and rolled back out of the seat, onto the center console and scrambled to the area of the roof below the back seats. When he tried to get his legs under him and reach for Judith again, he winced in agony. His right ankle gave out, causing him to nearly pass-out again from the pain. He couldn't tell if it was broken or badly sprained. Cameron rolled to his knees and reached for Judith again.

"Honey, can you hear me? Are you okay?

The blinking dashboard lights illuminated the front seat area slightly, just enough for him to see her left arm hanging loosely. He reached for her face and touched her cheek softly. Leaning closer, he frantically whispered, "Baby, please be okay. Can you hear me? Wake up, baby. We need to get out of this car."

Judith stirred, moaning softly.

Cameron stroked her cheek again.

She came to with a start. She screamed and twisted, trapped by the seat belt, but not understanding why she was restrained.

"It's okay, calm down, you're okay, honey. Listen to me; it's your husband. I've got you!"

"Get me out, get me out," she pleaded.

"You're okay, baby, you're okay. I've got you. Stop struggling, and I'll help get you out."

"What happened? Where are we?"

"We had a wreck, and we need to get out of the car. I smell fuel leaking. Can you feel your legs? Is anything broken?"

"I...I don't know," she mumbled groggily. "I don't think anything is broken, but I'm hurting all over."

"Okay, good. The car is upside down, and you're strapped into your seat. I'm going to release your seat belt, but I need you to help hold yourself in place so that you don't fall on your head. It's going to be tricky."

Cameron wriggled around where he could push the button on the seat belt latch and help catch Judith once it was sprung. She fell into him and crumpled against the roof of the car, which was now the floor. Without much room to maneuver, it took a few minutes to help her move to the back-seat area with her husband. He helped her lie down so that she could catch her breath and he could check her out to make sure nothing was broken. He found his cell phone in his coat pocket and shook it to turn on the flashlight. He could see the bruise on her forehead. His first thought was a concussion, though he had no idea what to look for.

"I know you're hurting all over and sore, but can you feel your arms and legs? Does anything feel broken at all, baby?"

Judith moaned as she tried to sit-up, but was able to shift her body with Cameron's help and managed the task.

"I don't think anything's broken, just bruised. What happened?"

"I...I don't know. I can't remember everything. I remember you yelling at me, and I swerved. Next thing I know, I'm waking up upside down."

"I yelled?" She asked, still groggy and in shock from the accident.

Cameron thought a moment, trying to clear the cobwebs from his head. Suddenly he spun back to her, in a frantic voice he said, "You yelled when that...that thing stepped out on the road. We hit it, and I lost control of the car."

"What?" Judith asked, still groggy.

Cameron suddenly remembered everything. It was like a bad dream, surreal, but it happened, and it *was* real.

"That thing, that monster. It was covered from head to foot in long, black hair. It almost looked...human, but it wasn't. It was male, that's for sure. Not sure *why* I

116

remember *that*, but it was a male. It wasn't wearing any clothes or anything, just…hair. I think it was a - a Sasquatch. We hit it with the car. Oh my God, we hit a - a Bigfoot!"

"Oh, my God! What are we going to do? We need to call for help," Judith cried out. She was frantic. "Is it still out there on the road? Did you kill it?"

"No, I don't think so. I remember that it stopped and looked at us just as we came around the curve like we surprised it. I swerved to avoid hitting it, but I think we clipped it. Had to have injured it, but it was more than twice as tall as the roof of the car. It was huge."

"What are we going to do, Cam?" Judith pleaded.

"If I can get to my cell phone, maybe we can get a signal, but we need to get out of this car. I think I smell fuel leaking and we have no idea what else."

"But what about that animal, that…that monster?"

Cameron wriggled around and managed to get a hand in his coat pocket and grab his cell phone.

"I don't know," he said.

The moisture in his breath condensed in the cold mountain air creating small puffs of orange clouds refracting in the blinking dash light. The weather was already beginning to be a factor. Thankfully, they had on their thermal base layer and heavy down-filled ski jackets.

Fumbling with the cell phone and half-frozen fingers, Cameron was able to hit the buttons and open the dial app.

"Damn it! No signal."

"Oh, god, what are we going to do now? We can't walk out of here."

"I don't know. We've got to get somewhere closer to a cell tower or something. We need to figure out just where we are. Can't be far from the road. Someone will come along, I mean, we can't stay here."

As if to mark his words, sparks from the engine bay suddenly flashed across the snow-covered ground illuminating the steaming engine coolant still spewing from the ruptured radiator.

Cameron tried the passenger door on his side but it wasn't budging. He twisted onto his back and pushed hard with his feet. The door was crumpled but began to give-way. Just an inch or two at a time, but the loud creaking of the metal was a good sign. It meant the frame was bending, and with any luck, it would bend out enough for them to get out.

"What was that?" Judith asked.

"What was what?"

"That sound?"

Cameron brushed her off. "Just the door. It's starting to open. I'll have us out in just a minute."

"No, no. Not that. Listen!" She said, her voice a frightened whisper.

Cameron stopped pushing on the door and stayed still and quiet, listening for what Judith had heard.

Growling, deep low guttural growling.

"I hear it. It's that…thing. Oh my God, Cam, what are we going to do?" Judith trembled. "It's still alive, and it's here. It's right here with us!"

"Shhhh, stay calm, maybe it will leave," Cameron whispered. Desperately thinking about anything he could use as a weapon to fend off the monster in case it attacked. "We can't stay here, but we can't go out there."

They could hear movement just outside the vehicle but could see nothing in the darkness.

Suddenly a low-pitched scream erupted from nearby, piercing the cold night air and sending chills through the two trapped inside the overturned vehicle. The screams were relentless and terrifying, sounding furious as if a caged animal suddenly woke in a small confined space, going crazy with fear and hate, trying desperately to escape. The creature had been hit by the vehicle, tumbling with the wreck and ended up near the overturned car. The giant beast tried to stand, but the front of the vehicle clipped its legs, and the tumble down the embankment must have injured it. Though the car inflicted little damage to the beast, it was nothing more than flesh, bone, and muscle. It was hurt, but the extent was minimal.

Cameron could hear the Sasquatch clearly on the opposite side of the door he was trying to open. He kicked hard with his feet and with a final push, inched the jammed car door open just enough for the couple to wiggle out.

The car suddenly shifted and began rocking on the unstable ground it had come to rest on. Cameron reached back and helped his wife crawl out using the blinking dashboard light to navigate by. They could hear the frantic screams of the beast on the other side of the car as it thrashed about as if searching for something. They couldn't be sure. The only thing they were sure of is that they were terrified.

The Sasquatch grew silent though they could still hear it breathing. *Had it sensed their presence? Could it see in the darkness?* Cameron had put his cell phone back in his pocket but dared not chance the flashlight app as they lay on the ice and snow-packed ground.

"Be very still and stay as quiet as possible," Cameron whispered to his frightened wife. "Whatever that thing is, we don't want to mess with it."

"I'm scared, Cam," Judy whispered.

She huddled as close to her husband as she could. The

freezing temperature on the mountain was plummeting fast. Mixed with shock and the injuries sustained, she wasn't doing well, and he knew it. He had to get her out of there and get her medical attention.

The couple waited against the side of the car listening as the creature breathed heavily just on the other side. They tried to slow their breathing and remain calm in hopes the beast would not detect their presence.

Suddenly, the car moved. A creak of metal and a scrape of snow and ice, but it moved, rocking back and forth, slowly. A blood-curdling scream erupted from the Sasquatch sending chills through the couple as they held each other in fear. The beast shook the car violently, hitting it in pure savage rage, screaming, pounding huge fists into the metal as if it were a small toy. The shrieking was so loud the couple hiding on the other side shriveled into the snow-covered ground holding their hands over their ears, making themselves as small as possible, eyes squeezed shut, praying the beast would not discover them and rip them to shreds.

Cameron held his wife as tightly as he could, keeping his head down against hers. Tears streamed down both their faces as the adrenaline coursed through their veins to get them to flee, but they couldn't move.

Sparks from the engine bay flashed again and again as exposed wire touched bare metal. Suddenly, the interior dome light snapped on. Cameron glanced up but could see nothing other than a few things laying inside the car. The thought that it could expose them to the creature crossed his mind and the terror he *had* felt, suddenly doubled.

When the light flicked on, the creature hesitated and stepped back from the car. Cameron could hear its breathing grow deeper and longer until it took one deep breath and then blew it out as if exhausting its energy and rage against the machine that had hurt it.

The half-frozen couple held each other tightly, petrified with terror, huddling like rabbits in the snow for what seemed like an eternity. Shaking and trembling, it occurred to Cameron that it wasn't just the fear they felt; it was another enemy, the freezing temperatures. They couldn't stay where they were for much longer. They could die from exposure as the mountain air plummeted. They had no idea how long it had been since they last heard any sounds coming from the other side of the car, but they would have to move soon.

"Is it gone?" Judith whispered.

"I don't know. I don't hear any...wait, what's that?"

A low growl, a tone so deep that could only be emitted by a large chest cavity, was felt more than heard, and emanated from nearby, but not from the opposite side of the car.

Having heard or sensed the small humans cowering on the other side of the car, the beast crept towards them. How a creature weighing at least four to five hundred pounds could move with such stealth was a striking contrast to all that was sensible. The Sasquatch rose up, making itself as large as possible and screamed at the humans and pounded its chest. A sound like no other they had ever heard. The raging beast now stood at the corner of the car illuminated by the red blinking taillight. Its massive bulk encompassed the area and the night sky had suddenly been eclipsed by an even darker black mass. Its eyes shined just as red as the taillight lens. Its face, another three feet above the back of the upturned car, illuminated by the flashing signal light, was scarred and grotesque, matted fur covering its entire body including most of its head, chest, and arms. The legs of the beast were the size of oaks, and covered in the long, coarse black hair. The smell of the creature was nauseating, stinking of dead rot and decay. An ancient being, but one of flesh and blood, just as real as any other animal.

Judith screamed and fell back against her husband, nearly bowling him over, but he managed to push her hard enough to get her moving, back into the open door of the mangled car. Cameron scrambled in behind her, but he wasn't quite fast enough to escape the creature's grasp. A huge hand clamped around his leg and pulled him out.

The small car rocked against the large tree it rested on, the harsh roar of the creature seemed to shake the very roots of the pine. Deep, guttural noises mixed with an enraged shriek. Judith screamed hysterically and scrambled to reach for her husband and pull him back in. She grabbed at his hands, but couldn't find a grip. His hands were wrapped too tightly around the headrest of the front seat as the creature pulled on his leg.

Cameron kicked at the enormous beast with his free leg, but could not shake the grip. The car's interior light flicked off and on like a strobe light, and the buzzing under the dash only intensified the erratic light display. Cameron's left hand slipped off the seat's headrest, and he desperately grabbed onto Judith's coat sleeve jerking her toward the door. As she lurched forward, her hands blindly flailed about and caught the steering wheel and yanked on it. The action set off the car's alarm system somehow. The horn blared, and all the lights that remained intact flashed rapidly. The entire scene was chaotic and nightmarish.

The erratic strobe of the lights was brilliant against the pitch-black darkness of the mountain forest and worked to blind the creature. When the alarm system triggered, the beast suddenly let go of Cameron's leg and used its massive hands to cover its ears. It roared savagely and backed away from the car, stumbling on its shaken legs. It turned and crashed away into the brush leaving the two small and terrified humans alone.

The couple lay huddled inside the car for several minutes after the creature left. After catching his breath, Cameron finally spoke, "I think it's gone for good this time. We should try to make it back up to the road. I don't know how long this alarm system will keep going or how long that...that monster will stay away."

Judith whimpered but said nothing, just trembled in her husband's arms.

14

Sheriff Blaine walked into his office and poured a second cup of coffee and eased himself into the rickety, wooden-backed chair at his desk. Taking a sip, he set the mug on the brass framed leather coaster and flipped to the last page of the morning paper just as he heard Deputy Michelle Evers knock on the open door frame.

The deputy wore her medium-length, blond hair tucked up under a black baseball cap with the word, *Deputy* embroidered in large white letters. The brown and green uniform, complete with web gear and duty firearm, fit loosely, doing nothing to accentuate her figure, nor should it. The uniform was functional. That was all she wanted from it. She stood just over five feet ten inches tall and weighed one hundred-forty-three pounds with brilliant, blue eyes. That's what was printed on her driver's license. Most men would find her beautiful, especially attractive when she smiled, and the dimples in her cheeks showed.

"Come on in," the sheriff said as he folded the paper and tossed it down on the desk. "You read it yet? I'm done."

"Morning, Sheriff. No, not yet. Anything exciting in it today?" she asked.

"Nah, same old stuff," he laughed, adjusting the cushion in his chair, and sitting up straight. He reached for his coffee cup, rested his elbows on the old wooden desk, and looked over his reading glasses at the deputy.

Evers scoffed, "I did see that big front-page news about the grand opening celebration coming up this weekend?"

"Yeah, couldn't miss that. The mayor's been calling every day. Not sure what the hell he's expecting. Just a bunch of college kids getting hammered. Not our worry. That's up to Ned and his officers. His jurisdiction. He knows that, but I don't think those two see eye to eye on many things. Imagine that, a city mayor and a Chief of Police not getting along," he laughed.

"I know right," Michelle laughed.

"Reminds me, I have assignments for the weekend posted for everyone out in the hall. There'll be a couple of statey's at each check-point Friday night and at least two patrol units. You and Larsen will be running highway 82 at county road 1440 turnoff. The last thing we need is a carload of kids driving drunk and right off the mountain. We need everyone to get home safely."

"Suits me just fine. I don't envy *you* one bit though. I don't particularly care for the *upper-class* crowd that'll be up at the - *secluded* resort," she laughed as she emphasized her statement with a mock haughty, English tone.

The sheriff was one of the many dignitaries invited to the grand-opening celebration being held at the Buckhorn Lodge. The property's board of directors, city mayor, Chamber of Commerce and many other distinguished guests would be arriving all week for the special festivities set to kick off Friday night and extend through the weekend.

Nick laughed, "Trust me, I don't much care for it either, but at least I can wear my uniform instead of my Armani suit, Gucci shoes, and Rolex watch."

After an obligatory chuckle, Deputy Evers's face turned serious. "Being that I'm fairly new here in Hawthorn, is there any truth to the rumors about…well, you know… *Bigfoot?* Has there been a report? Are we investigating it?"

"You talking about that damn video?"

"Yes, sir."

Blaine stood and walked to the coffee pot, refilled his cup, and stared out the window a moment before answering.

"You see that ridge over there?" He began, indicating one of the highest peaks in the distance.

Michelle stood and walked to the window and stood beside him. "Yeah, sure. Devils Backbone? Where the guy supposedly shot the video. Everyone knows it."

"That's what the locals call it, *Devil's Backbone.* Ridiculous really. Mostly just one of those scary names that kids give something to add intrigue or mystery. Real name, of course, is Beckman Ridge. It's hard as hell to get to, not to mention off limits anyway. It's a National Park and closed to the public. Endangered species found there, beetle or some bs. It looks like a great rock to climb, but because of snow-melt and run-off, it's constantly wet. Climbers have tried it, but wet sedimentary rock tends to flake off and break. But, like I said, completely off-limits to the public."

Blaine rubbed his grizzled chin with an audible scraping sound of the two days of stubble he had collected. He was in his mid-fifties, and his silver hair was as much a badge of honor as the scar that ran across his left cheek - the result of a knife fight he broke up years ago as a young deputy. Without another word, he spun, returned to his desk, and sat. The chair groaned and squeaked under his weight as he pulled it closer to the desk with his boots.

Michelle had been with the department for a year and,

like others, heard all about the siege at Hawthorn Lake that happened five years earlier. It was also the one thing that attracted her to the town. Most people figured it nothing more than a bear attack that got embellished along the way and gained notoriety. Locals talked about it in whispers, embarrassed by the rumors, secretly doubting the stories that came from the ordeal. Michelle believed the rumors. She had her experience years earlier in Idaho Springs, a small town not far from Hawthorn. An experience she relived every single day. An experience that woke her in the middle of the night with sweat-drenched nightmares.

Confused by the way her boss stopped in the middle of the conversation, she cleared her throat, "Ahem, I think you need a new chair, Boss."

He laughed, "I've heard that more than once. Nothing wrong with this one," he said with a stern look over his glasses at the deputy. "Besides, if you saw the budget, you'd understand why this one will have to do."

He picked up his coffee cup in both hands and looked over the top at his deputy in silence. He took a long, slow sip.

Finally, it dawned on her.

"Ah, I get it. The ridge is off-limits to climbers, and this new video clearly shows something ...or someone walking on it. So, the whole Bigfoot thing could be a ruse to cover for someone that probably climbed where they weren't supposed to. Sounds like an issue for the Park Rangers?"

The sheriff smiled. "I knew you'd figure it out. Not our circus, not our monkey - or *Bigfoot.*"

The sheriff watched his deputy walk out of his office before turning his attention back to the window. His face contorted as his thoughts turned to the attack at Hawthorn

Lake just five years earlier. He would never be able to forget that night. He was lost in thought when the phone suddenly rang, startling him.

"This is Blaine," he answered.

"Have you read this garbage?" the lady on the other end of the phone asked. "Attention seekers I'm sure. Do you think it's legit? Or could it be someone just trying to get their fifteen minutes? Ahh, I can't believe it! *This* is the kind of crap that we don't need around here," the caller said stridently.

"You done yet?" Nick asked. His tone was sarcastic.

"Sorry, it's just that this Bigfoot stuff has me all worked up," Lisa Richards said.

"I don't think there's anything to worry about."

"My entire staff is talking about that damn video and this story on the front page," she said, perturbed.

"I think you're worried about nothing. Probably just some kook looking for his fifteen minutes."

"I don't have time for this, not now. They could have waited long enough for me to get through the weekend! Like I needed more stress."

Nick leaned back in his chair and took a sip of his coffee and listened. At one point he laid the phone down, walked to the file cabinet and retrieved some papers before picking the receiver back up. Lisa was still talking.

"I mean, seriously, what's wrong with people? What's the motive? A prank maybe? Attention? Is it to scare people off?" She took a breath then continued, "Every hotel in town is booked at capacity. This is the busiest we've ever been. Maybe it's someone trying to hurt business for the *new* hotel in town, but I can't imagine why? It could also be the opposite. You know, thinking it'll *bring* people to town, and I'm sure it will, but not the kind of clientele that we want."

"Could be," he replied.

"Either way, it's got people talking, and I don't like it. It's just not the image we need. Joe Dirt and his redneck buddies all out with shotguns and bloodhounds trying to track down Bigfoot?"

Nick laughed.

"I'm not laughing here!"

"Sorry, dear. I'm sure it'll blow over quickly."

Lisa sighed. "I hope so, but that's not the only reason I called."

"Yeah, I didn't think so." He smirked and leaned back.

"What's that supposed to mean?"

He could hear the frustration linger in her voice.

"Nothing at all. What else is on your mind?"

"Even though it may be official business for your department, I fully expect to see you in an actual suit and tie this weekend. You know, all spit-polished and shiny."

"What? Now, wait a minute," he started to protest.

"You promised. Besides, I really want you to be able to enjoy the party. Your staff can handle anyone that gets a little too tipsy. These people attending the grand opening gala at the lodge are VIP's. Besides, you know all the ones from Hawthorn. You'll be fine."

"I just don't see the need -"

She cut him off before he could finish his thought.

"Listen, you gave me your word, and I'm not about to let you go back on it. I want you looking as handsome as possible, old man. That also means shaving."

"Okay. Okay, I know when I'm licked," he laughed. "See you tonight for dinner?"

"Of course. Love you, Dad. Gotta run."

Click

"Love you too. Bye. Have a nice day."

Nick leaned back in his chair, sipped from his mug and chuckled. His daughter never said bye before hanging up.

***

The birch trees along the shoreline of Hawthorn Lake shimmered in the slight breeze that blew across the calm but icy water, dancing like millions of castanets on delicate fingers of the small branches.

The fisherman guided the small, red and silver v-bottom boat along the lake-shore of the pristine blue water, headed back in with a creel full of walleye. A large black and tan rottweiler lay on a blanket in the front of the boat soaking up as much of the sun as possible in the quiet afternoon hours. Ice had formed along the edge of the banks, but still thin enough not to present a problem for the aluminum craft. The small gasoline engine hanging on the transom was old, but ran well, and was powerful enough to push the little boat across the lake under most circumstances. If, however, the wind was howling down from the mountain passes, it always proved to be a struggle.

A glimmer at the dock caught the man's attention. Someone was there, waiting.

He waved from the boat and goosed the throttle. As he drew nearer the dock, Sheriff Blaine stood from the chair he had appropriated and walked to the edge to greet him.

"Any luck?"

Troy cut the engine and floated into the old rubber tires that hung on the side of the dock and tossed the tie-line to his friend.

Zeus stood, stretched, and jumped out onto the dock

before the sheriff had the boat tied off. He padded over and sat, waiting patiently for Troy to get out. Nick reached down and scratched the big dog's ears.

"Hey buddy, how ya been?"

Zeus nuzzled Nick's hands, not minding the attention.

"A little," Troy said as holding the wire-mesh creel up for the sheriff to take.

"Nice! Cedar Creek? Near the laydowns?"

Troy grinned, his steel-blue eyes shining brightly in the late morning sun. "Now, you know I can't tell you my secret honey hole, but nice try."

Nick laughed, "Can't blame a fella for trying, can ya? Oh, if Ol' Zeus here could talk."

Troy laughed. "Good thing, he can't. I have a feeling he'd tell all my secrets."

"Like I said," Nick chuckled. "can't blame a guy for trying."

"No, I suppose not."

Troy, now forty-seven years old, pulled his cap off, revealing a shock of dark blond hair and ran his hand through the locks before adjusting the cap back in place.

"How ya been, Nick?" He reached out and shook hands with his friend.

"Not bad. Arthritis acting up a bit, but that's expected at my age, I suppose."

"You're age? Hell, you're not much older than me. You're not old yet. All that silver didn't come from the years behind you," Troy laughed. "But, being that you're in uniform, I'm bettin' you didn't come all the way out of here just to see how the fish are biting today though, did you?"

Nick cleared his throat. His voice dropped to a more serious tone. "No. No, I sure didn't," he said with a glance toward the mountain.

Troy knew what that look was for. He grabbed his tackle box, rods, and reels and stepped out onto the dock.

"Let's go up to the cabin and talk while I clean these fish," Troy said then whistled to his four-legged companion. "Com'on Zeus. Let's go to the house, boy."

Zeus happily padded alongside Troy. The dog was a gift from a close friend who also had a full brother to Zeus named Hercules. Both dogs were brutes, but highly intelligent and well-trained guard dogs, not to mention incredibly loyal companions to their masters. Zeus was three years old and never left Troy's side, whether on the boat in the middle of the lake or resting in the afternoon sun on the front porch.

Troy's friend, Phil, had insisted on getting the puppies after the incident at the cabin those years ago. It was a good suggestion. The dog was very loyal and has an incredibly good sense of hearing and detection of unwanted guests. Not to mention he kept great company.

The cabin sat on a gentle slope of the quiet little mountain valley just a hundred yards from the edge of the water on the west end. From the upstairs balcony, the entire valley and most of the lake could be seen which made for a fantastic view. That's where Troy spent many hours working on manuscripts. As a writer, he enjoyed the solitude and worked best in peace and quiet.

"I heard you flew to Tulsa a few weeks ago. How'd that go?"

"Hmm, I thought I was flying under the radar these days? No pun intended."

"You know how it is in a small town, everyone stays in everyone's business but their own," Nick said.

"Apparently," Troy laughed. "Yeah, got back yesterday. Phil picked me up at the airport. Along with Zeus, here."

Troy said, patting his canine companion on the head. "I flew down for a conference. Wished I hadn't. They're always boring as hell."

Nick laughed, "I can only imagine."

When the two men reached the cabin, Troy stowed his fishing gear in the shop before leading his friend around back to take the fish to the small cleaning table he had set up. The sheriff knew the routine well. He and Troy had been friends for years and fished together often.

"So, what's on your mind, Nick? As if I couldn't guess. Probably the same reason that I cut my trip short and flew back home. The video on YouTube?"

The sheriff glanced toward the mountain again before replying. "Yeah. I'm sure it's a hoax. Most likely. Hope so anyway."

Troy stopped and turned to face the sheriff.

"Yeah, me too. I'd hate to have to put a lock back on the gate. The neighbors would consider that...well, rude."

"Ah, I think they'd understand though."

Being as remote as Troy's cabin was, isolated in a small valley with one of the most serene lakes in the area, a few of his friends enjoyed coming up to fish the mountain lake or just for the breathtaking views that photographers loved. The truth was, Troy didn't mind sharing a small piece of his Heaven on earth with friends and neighbors. They always asked respectfully if they could go fishing and never intruded. It was a courtesy Troy extended, and they respected that. It was the out of towners that just assumed they could trek all over his property hunting, fishing or whatever the hell else they wanted to do without asking permission. After the attack at the cabin several years ago many would be Bigfoot hunters tracked the location of his cabin down, and Troy was forced to put a gate up at the highway entrance. Some of the more determined individuals cut the fence and trespassed, but after a few years they eventually thinned to only a small trickle of passers-by. Someone had even had the gall to have a road sign made and stuck in the ground near his turn off. Troy dragged it down with his Jeep and tossed it in the woods.

"We've not seen or heard anything at all since well... since that night five years ago."

"I know. Was hoping we were past all that."

"Beckman's Ridge, huh? You think it's real?"

"Can't say for sure. Could've been a hiker," Nick acknowledged.

"On *that* ridge?" Troy scoffed. "Nick, you know better than I do that the entire area is off-limits to hikers because of how dangerous it is even when it's *not* covered with snow and ice. I watched that video a hundred times. I'm not seeing a human there, and it doesn't seem to be faked. What's park management saying?"

"Nothing. I talked to Fred when I first got wind of it. No one has checked in for hiking or climbing the trails, and if they had, they sure wouldn't list Beckman Ridge on their sign-in sheet. Ranger's would've stopped 'em flat."

The sheriff pulled his cell phone out of his pocket, and they watched the video together.

"I don't know. See that rock outcropping right there," Nick pointed out on the tiny screen. "I know that area. When we searched for Phil that time, we looked that entire area over good. Those rocks are huge boulders. I don't think a man could move like that. Not there, anyway.

"I have to agree. We flew the drone over it a hundred times after the incident. Seems like yesterday. But I've not seen or heard anything around here, and I've been." Troy was cut short when Zeus pushed up against his leg. "Sorry buddy, we've been *vigilant*."

"Whether it's real or not, it's got a lot of people stirred up again, and with the grand opening of the new hotel coming up this weekend it's just not something that we need. Nothing to be done about it though."

"Have you talked to Clance?"

Nick put his cell phone into his pocket.

"No, was heading over there after I leave here."

Troy glanced up at the mountain, carefully scanning it. He sighed heavily. "It's been what? Five years now? I dunno, maybe it is an elaborate hoax. Some brave idiots climbed up there and had another buddy shoot the video. Where was it shot at? Camera angle seems to be nearly level?"

"In the description on the video, it says they were on the Kerrigan's run ski lift."

"What the hell would make them return to the area?" Troy asked. "Encroachment was what caused the little war to begin with. I get that. We were pushing too far into their hunting grounds. They fought back, they lost and moved on. I assumed they moved further into places that no human has ever been. Lord knows there's thousands, if not millions, of unmolested acres in these mountains. And why now?"

"That's the million-dollar question."

"I honestly think the video is legit, but I'm hoping it's just a hoax," Troy said.

"Yeah, maybe. That's what I'm hoping anyway. Just…be careful I suppose and keep your eyes open. If you suspect anything at all, let me know right away. Your ham still in working order?" Nick asked.

"Yeah, it's working fine. So is the phone line, electricity, and satellite connection," Troy laughed, though it was restrained with a tinge of worry.

It took a lot of expense and work on his own part to get the electric and phone lines ran to the cabin, but it had proven to be well worth it. It was twelve full miles of unpaved road from the highway turnoff to the cabin. When the winter storms hit hard, it could be nearly impossible to get off the mountain by any other vehicle than the snowmobile he kept in the garage next to his Jeep. The cabin was intended to be off the grid and self-sustainable, but after the attack so long ago and no way of calling for help, Troy, along with Nick's help, was able to get the necessary updates in place. A diesel generator sat less than fifty steps outside and would supply enough electricity to the cabin to run everything in the case of a power outage. The phone line was working correctly, but if it ever went down, he would still be able to make calls via the satellite connection. He also kept a satellite phone for when traveling on the mountain. He left no stone unturned when it came to safety, not anymore.

Nick changed the subject, "So, are you going to the grand opening celebration at the lodge this weekend?"

Troy turned back to cleaning the fish.

"Undecided."

"Not telling you what to do, but everyone is expecting Hawthorn's very own famous author to be there," the sheriff said grinning.

"Everyone?" Troy asked with a hint of suspicion. He tilted his head and shot his friend a suspicious look.

Nick threw his hands up in a gesture of surrender.

"Hey, all I know is what I hear," he laughed.

"Is that the real reason you come out today?" Troy asked. "You know it was her that broke it off, not me?"

"Well, you know how women can be. She's my daughter,

but she takes after her mother. Very stubborn sometimes."

"Did Lisa ask you to talk to me?"

"No, she doesn't know I'm here at all, but she did ask about you. She phoned this morning. Was upset about all the Bigfoot talk. Thinks it might damage the reputation of the town."

Troy turned back to the fish. "You staying for lunch?"

"No, wish I could. I'm going to head over and see Clance, and then I've got to get back to town. It seems I am in need of a suit and tie for the weekend's festivities," he said, laughing. "I promised daughter of mine that I would wear one to her grand opening, so I suppose I better go buy a jacket and tie being that I don't actually have one." Nick turned back toward his truck. "I'll see you there."

"Don't be too upset if you don't."

Nick gave Zeus a scratch behind his ears, "See ya, big guy." He turned and walked to his truck.

"Keep an eye out and be careful. Just in case."

"Always am. I'll see ya, buddy."

"Yeah, see ya."

Troy watched the sheriff drive away. *Could it be real?* He thought. He went back to cleaning the fish, trying to concentrate on the task at hand. Flashbacks crept into his head that he couldn't ignore. Flashbacks of the night he, Nick, and several others fought for survival. One of his best friends had been killed on that mountain. After that, it was an all-out war. The sounds - snarling, growling, shrieking. The adrenaline ebbed and flowed all night as they fought off wave after wave. Some were huge, stringy-haired, evil-looking beasts, and others were thin and wiry. All were intent on breaking into the cabin and killing the occupants inside.

Phil had killed one of the Sasquatch earlier in the evening when he and the Denizen family trekked from the other side of the mountain to make it to Troy's cabin safely. He shot the beast point-blank in the chest from the seat of a snowmobile. The entire clan gave chase and lay siege on the cabin.

Most people don't believe in the creature's existence, but Troy had firsthand knowledge. They were real, and they were not to be messed with. He and his friends were lucky that night, and all survived inside the well-built cabin, but Clance Denizen had been brutally beaten, and his wife had suffered nasty bruises and sprains when one of the beasts grabbed her and attempted to pull her out a window. Troy could never forget that. None of them could.

Frustrated, he threw his filet knife down on the cleaning table and went inside. A few minutes later, he returned wearing his .45 on his hip and carrying an Ithaca Mag10 slung over his back. Zeus paid him no attention. He simply stretched and lay at his master's feet, waiting for scraps.

15

Tammy sat alone at a table for two near the entrance. The small café was bustling with energy. It was the time of day that most people were taking a break from the slopes or roaming the old shops of downtown Hawthorn. Agitated, she sent another text to her husband, who was supposed to meet her over an hour ago.

"Can I get you anything else, ma'am?"

She was startled by the waitress. A young lady wearing a powder-blue sweater, leggings inside fur-lined boots and a knitted hat stood at her table holding a tray of empty drink glasses.

"Oh, I'm sorry. Yes, could I get a refill on my coffee, please?"

"Sure thing," the girl said and trotted off through the crowd.

Tammy's cell phone buzzed.

"About time," she muttered.

When she opened the screen, she was disappointed to see that it was only a text from a friend asking about her trip. Frustrated and worried, she sent a quick reply, left a tip on the table before the waitress returned and exited the café.

***

The four-wheel-drive patrol unit was grimy from mud and snow. The wheels splashed through a slush-covered pothole as Deputy Evers drove along West Willow Street toward the Wolf Gap Brewery. One of Hawthorn's best-kept secrets. A small red-brick building with large plate-glass windows and bright yellow stenciling announcing the restaurant's hours of operation. Brats and brew, one of the most popular dishes, was her favorite, though while on duty unsweet tea was on tap for her.

"Have a seat anywhere you like. I'll be right with you," the waitress said as she scurried to the kitchen.

Michelle stamped her boots off and walked over to an empty booth by the front window and sat. A few minutes later she was joined by another deputy.

"Hey, Evers, how goes it?" Deputy Larsen asked as he all but collapsed into the seat across from her and slid over against the window. He stretched his left leg out into the seat and leaned his elbows on the table and the back of the booth.

"Eh, all is quiet on the western front...so far," she said, smiling.

"Yeah, but it's early," he said, blowing out a long sigh. "Just give it a little time. Full moon weekend coming up, packed hotels, lots of booze, we'll be busy. I'm sure."

"Can't wait."

Billy wrestled his coat off in the booth. "Never could get used to eating lunch this early, but then again, I could eat breakfast for lunch or dinner seven days a week. Can't beat eggs and bacon."

"I don't mind going on shift so early during the season. It's peaceful for the first part of it anyway."

The waitress stopped by the table to get their orders. She was an older lady with short brown hair wearing jeans, boots, and a brewery t-shirt with an apron tied around her waist.

Billy noticed Michelle's demeanor had changed when the waitress walked away. Her eyes lost focus as she stared into the distance. He said nothing. A moment later, Michelle turned to look him straight in the eye.

"I want to ask you something."

Larsen chuckled, "A little dramatic, but okay. For a minute there, I thought I had already bored another woman to tears. Ah, the story of my life."

She ignored his comment and leaned in closer over the table. "I guess, some time ago, four or five years is my understanding, you and the sheriff were both involved in a murder investigation that ended with a hell of a shootout. Made national news, something about a *bear* attack on the mountain."

She watched Larsen's facial expression change from confusion to something...more complex. Sinking back deeper into the booth, he stared down at his glass of water.

She waited.

Finally, he answered.

"So much for small talk, eh? Just business. Yeah, that was a long time ago. What about it?"

"Well, for starters, is it true? A *bear* attack? I mean, well...what about some of the things people say, you know...about *Bigfoot?* You were there. I want to hear the truth from you."

"Did you read the reports?" he asked.

"Well sure I did, but the reports all state that it was a bear attack. But I don't buy it."

"What makes you believe otherwise? And furthermore,

why is it suddenly a big deal? What are you poking around in old news for anyway?" he snapped.

"Jeez, cool your jets there, Turbo! I'm just curious is all. Have you seen the newspaper this morning?"

"No, I never read that gossip rag. There's no news in it that I don't already know about anyway," Billy said confidently.

Michelle looked around the restaurant until she spied what she wanted, a crumpled and discarded newspaper.

"Be right back."

She folded it back to the front page and handed it to Larsen.

"Here, read this."

A few minutes later, he folded the paper back to original as best he could and tossed it on the table nearest the booth.

"Total garbage. This is what journalism has come to in this country. Make up a bunch of crap just to sell newspapers. It's like a Jerry Springer or Dr. Phil show in print," Larsen scoffed.

"So, none of it's true then? I mean, what some of the locals are saying…about Bigfoot?" Still, her eyes fought to keep his in direct contact, searching for any sign he may be avoiding, or even outright lying.

"What do you think?" he asked.

"Don't deflect. Tell me the truth."

"Why? You're just going to call me a liar and that it must've been something else and that I'm crazy. Then you will laugh and mock me like any other sane person, and that's the last thing I want. I really don't want to hear it," he snapped.

"Listen, I would never accuse you of lying. I don't know you well enough for that. Besides, we're friends, right? I mean, I haven't been with the sheriff's department that long, but I've known you longer than anyone else and I consider us friends."

"Sure we are, but I've seen it all and heard it all before. It's best if we just leave it alone and not revisit the past."

"Look," Michelle said with a soothing voice to help get Billy to talk. "I understand that it's not easy to talk about, but I have a feeling that you saw something and it damn sure wasn't a bear."

Larsen leaned in closer to the table and stared into her eyes. Speaking in a low, ominous tone, he asked, "Can bears throw rocks? Boulders even? Do they mount full-blown attacks working in unison? Do bears walk on two feet the entire time? Do you think bears know how to knock out floodlights and stage a feint for others to outflank an enemy? Do bears carry off their dead?"

Michelle blew out a breath she had been holding. "Seriously?"

"Hey, you asked!" Larsen stated. He sunk back in the booth again and relaxed. He forced a smile when the waitress brought the food to the table.

"Can I get you anything else?" she asked.

"Nothing for me, I'm good. Just keep the coffee coming."

"Sure thing, Honey."

"I'm good. Thanks." Michelle smiled.

"Holler if you need anything," the waitress said as she walked away.

"Listen, Evers, all I know is this. The night we were attacked, it wasn't bears, but who the hell is going to believe that it was anything else? No way was I going to write up a report that said we were attacked by a goddamn clan of eight-foot-tall Bigfoots, Sasquatches or whatever the hell you wanna call 'em. I'd be laughed out of the state. We all would. So, officially, it was a bear attack, but I'll tell ya, that was the most terrifying night of my life!" He jabbed a finger at the table for emphasis. "And that's not something I'd wish on my worst enemy."

"I'm sorry, I realize a man was killed, and I certainly didn't mean to open up old wounds and upset you. That's the last thing I'd ever want to do."

Billy glanced out the window and stared at the sign across the street before turning back to Michelle.

"Why, exactly, are you interested in that night anyway?"

Michelle thought a moment before answering. Should she tell him the truth? Should she open-up her own old wounds that ate at her and kept her awake at night and when she did go to sleep, woke her in a heated sweat with nightmares? What if she poured her heart out to him about her own tragic experience and found that once she did, she would break down? Would she be doomed to repeat the months of anxiety and depression near Idaho Springs? Those months that she was unable to sleep, to rest or find any solace or comfort after the loss of her best friend. It was a tragic loss of life at the hands of those creatures. It took two years of therapy to come to grips with what happened. Then, one day, it all changed. She realized that her fear was turning to hate and loathing. She sought out help from a friend that worked in law enforcement and began training. It wasn't that she wanted to be a deputy, but it was a means to an end, a way to learn about weapons and how to use them, a way to learn survival skills. She found herself on the road to recovery with a new purpose, a burning desire to find the creatures responsible for the death of her best friend and punish them.

"Just curious is all. To tell you the truth, I find it

fascinating. I want to see one," she finally said, relaxing into the booth.

"No, trust me, you don't. You'll never be the same again. It's not something I'd wish on my worst enemy. You may think you do, but if you ever do, you'll regret it," Billy said.

He saw the serious look on her face, searched for something witty to say, but came up with nothing. Instead, he took a huge bite of his burger and smiled at her with both cheeks full as he munched.

She tried to keep a straight face, but after watching his chipmunk cheeks slowly chewing his burger, she burst out laughing.

"God, you crack me up."

"Um, thanks?" Billy said, swallowing with a loud gulp.

"But in all seriousness, I know they exist, and I'm going to find em!"

Larsen was surprised at his colleague's comment and studied her face as he took another bite and chewed slowly.

"Why would you want to do that?" he asked.

Michelle sunk back in her booth seat and glanced out the window a moment before turning back.

"You look like a chipmunk."

He laughed, "You had me going for a minute."

He thought back to that nightmarish night he spent with the sheriff fending off attack after attack at Troy Turner's cabin. A small group of men and women barricaded themselves in the cabin and held off the assault through the night. Even though the men had shot and killed several creatures, there was no physical evidence to be found when it was over. Nothing of the brutal siege other than photos and a short video clip the sheriff had on his cell phone. He claimed later must've gotten erased accidentally. Now it was as if that night never existed.

145

"I'm very serious. Can you take me there sometime? You know, where the attack happened, Troy Turner's cabin and introduce me?"

Billy thought about it for a moment before replying.

"Maybe. Will you have dinner with me sometime?"

"We're having lunch now," she said, choosing to ignore his implication. It wasn't that she didn't like Billy enough to date him, but she wasn't in the place she wanted to be to start dating someone.

"You know what I mean," Billy said, studying her face.

Michelle put her fork down and took a drink of water before facing him again, a line appearing between her brows as she creased her lips.

Before she could reply, Billy held up a hand and said, "Look, you're right, we are friends," Billy said, sitting up straight and held his coffee mug with both hands on the table. "I don't mean to jeopardize that. We've known each other for a while now, and I've never once disrespected you nor would I ever. You're a professional law enforcement officer, and I've always treated you as an equal."

"Of course, we…" Michelle said, interrupting.

"Please, let me finish," he asked. "It's taken me a long time to get the courage up to ask you out. This isn't easy, ya know?" he said with a lopsided grin. "I've wanted to for a long time, but you know how it is. Never the right time, so on and so forth. But, no guts, no glory. To be honest, I don't know where or how I got the gumption to do so now, but there it is. I'd like to take you to dinner sometime."

Billy's mouth clamped shut, and he slumped back in his seat again, his cheeks flushed bright red.

Michelle listened to every word, and once Billy had finished, she purposely relaxed her facial expression and softened.

"Okay. First, you don't know what I was going to say. Second, I'm sorry if I ever gave you the impression that I thought otherwise. Yes, you have always treated me as an equal, and for that, I'm thankful. It's just that I've been - well, single for a long time and…"

"Yeah, well it was a shot in the dark. I didn't really think…"

"Would you let *me* finish now, please?" she said, cutting him off. She gave him a mischievous laugh and smiled.

"Sorry."

"Now, back to what I was saying. I know how hard it is to get up the nerve to ask someone out, so I'm sorry I ignored you the first time you said it. It's just that I'm a little hesitant about dating someone right now and especially someone that I work with. I like you, Billy. I really do. Regardless if we go out or not, we will remain friends, but what would Blaine have to say?"

"Well, about that," Billy said. He had a squeamish look on his face. "I put in my notice just before my shift started. Laid it on his desk in a file folder. He was expecting it, though."

"What? What are you talking about?"

Billy laughed, "It's true. I've been offered a position with Parks and Wildlife, so even though I'm leaving the sheriff's office, I'm not going anywhere."

"Oh wow, that's short notice. You've been with the sheriff's department for years though. Why quit now?"

"It's what I went to college for actually, but the better pay and benefits, not to mention that I'll be stationed right here in Hawthorn. I couldn't pass it up, but we can talk about that later…like over dinner?"

"Oh, gotcha. Didn't mean to divert again. Tell you

what," Michelle said. A mischievous grin spread over her face. "I'll go out with you…one time. If it goes well then maybe a second and we'll see how it goes, but only if, and it's a big if." That same mischievous grin spread across her face.

"If what?" he asked, knowing what she would say.

"If you introduce me to Troy Turner so that I can see where the attack took place and get his permission to look around."

Billy leaned back in the seat and studied her face.

"You are relentless, aren't you?"

"I told you, I'm serious about it. I'm fascinated by it all."

Billy held his hand out, "Deal!"

Michelle laughed as she shook his hand.

"Not sure that I've ever negotiated a date in a manner quite like this."

"Me either, but what the hell. First time for everything."

16

Billy Larsen pulled onto the street, leaving Wolf Gap Brewery and maneuvered through the busy city streets. Winding down Clayborn Avenue, he turned west onto Aspen and continued out of town. The stretch of highway was busy the first few miles, but when he turned on County Road 4330, he found himself alone with nothing but the snow-covered landscape and the occasional vehicle passing by.

Though Larsen loved his work, patrolling the back roads of Hawthorn wasn't his idea of fun and excitement, but a necessary part of the job as a county patrol officer. Today was different. He wanted peace and quiet; he needed the time to think. It wasn't the fact that he had turned in his notice earlier this morning, and would be leaving the sheriff's office. Both he and Nick were on the same page as far as that was concerned. Billy had studied wildlife management in college and had been waiting on the right opportunity to come along since he had graduated. What weighed on his mind was his conversation with Michelle during lunch. Since then, he had been wound tighter than a two-dollar watch. Why was she asking all those questions about that night? Hell, it took him months before he was able to get past the night at Troy Turner's cabin. His eyes saw what happened, his body felt it, but it was surreal. In his mind, he couldn't fathom an attack of that magnitude from a creature that was only supposed to be a legend.

The siege at Troy's cabin at Hawthorn Lake lasted only one night, but the terror would live on forever in Billy's mind. A small group of people armed to the teeth barely stood off an angry attack by an apex predator who was smart, intelligent, and evil. Hell-bent on killing every person, Billy, and his cohorts found themselves trapped in the cabin with no phone or radio to call for help. The terrifying night resulted in several injuries to the small group, and several of the beasts lay dead on the ground. All the creatures were either dead or had retreated because the morning dawned with no signs of the horrible monsters anywhere to be found. Carrying away their dead and covering their tracks was something only a species of higher intellect could do. No other animals have ever acted in such a manner, except for humans. Billy would never have believed that Bigfoot existed had it not been for that night.

He drove slow following the county road that had recently been plowed. Though it wasn't used much, there were still plenty of people that lived in the area. The county crews did an excellent job of keeping the roads cleared and passable even in the worst of weather conditions. They were used to it. This was an environment they knew how to handle, a knowledge passed down through many generations. It was hard country and could test one's grit and determination, but it was also some of the most beautiful country one could imagine with its breathtaking views of snow-covered mountains, bright green pines, silver birchwoods, and shimmering golden leaves.

The road twisted and turned over the densely forested

mountain, but the four-wheel-drive had no trouble negotiating the snowy terrain. The outside temp was in the upper thirties, but the wind blowing at 15mph or better made it seem colder.

He reached over to grab a peppermint out of a bag he had laying on the passenger seat and turned on the radio at a low volume. He fumbled with the wrapper and finally freed the small candy, but the vehicle hit a pothole in the road, and it fell out of his hand. It hit the side of the console and bounced to the edge of the passenger seat. Leaning over, he deftly scooped it up and popped it into his mouth before it had a chance to slide off and into the floorboard. He straightened back up with a smirk of satisfaction. His quick reflexes had saved the fate of the red and white striped candy from an inevitable fall into the abyss between the seat and rocker panel never to be seen again. When he looked back up, he gasped and slammed on the brakes.

17

The snowmobile was well used with many miles and hours logged on it, but well maintained and fully capable of traversing the rugged terrain of Hawthorn's back-country trails. Bright green with white lettering, the powerful machine had plenty of room for Leon's camera gear, the snowshoes he had picked up and the extra fuel he carried. He passed several riders on the well-marked trails waving enthusiastically, content to stay on the path, enjoying the scenery. Leon had other plans.

When he reached an area marked Jade's Point, a scenic pull-off, he pulled over and killed the engine of his sled. There were a few people that had also done the same and were taking pictures of the view, but he, pulled out his phone and checked his position with the GPS coordinates.

Before he left town, he downloaded a topographic map to his phone's storage card, which allowed him to use his GPS even without having cell service in the mountains. He toggled the navigation app on and checked his coordinates. Three more miles would get him to the next waypoint. It was at that location where he would leave the trail.

In the early morning hour, the air was brisk as he rode along the snow-laden trail. The sky was overcast and gray, and it had begun snowing just as the weather report had predicted. He had plenty of time to scout the area he had in mind, and the trip to Beckman Ridge shouldn't take more than a couple of hours of riding.

For years, Leon had been fascinated with the Bigfoot phenomenon. He first became captivated with the legend of Bigfoot as a young boy after seeing the movie, "Legend of Boggy Creek" in 1972. Even if one didn't believe that a creature of that size could exist for so many years without a live specimen or more evidence, it was still an exciting hobby.

North American folklore often cited the beast for being ape-like, completely covered in hair, walking upright and seclusive. Many encounters have reported it to be upwards of six to nine feet tall, foul-smelling and nocturnal.

The term "Bigfoot" came into use when a bulldozer operator in Bluff Creek, California first discovered large footprints while excavating a site in a remote area. Almost a decade later, Roger Patterson and Jim Gimlin explored the area in search of the creature and successfully captured several seconds of film of a female. Though most sightings occurred in the Pacific Northwest, there have been documented encounters in every state except for Hawaii.

The night before, Leon had researched the area as best he could by using satellite views on his laptop. The image of the thing he saw on that ridge was not a person. He played it repeatedly studying as much detail as possible. The dark figure had long arms and moved at an incredible rate of speed and agility for it to have been a person on that rough terrain. Though the image was distant, he was confident that the creature was a Bigfoot.

He soon arrived at Guthrie Falls, the point where he was supposed to turn around, the last viewing area for the trail.

Several snowmobiles were parked with most riders getting photos of the falls. Leon pretended to walk around and take pictures of the area while scoping out the gate. Though the trailhead was clearly marked with a huge white sign with red letters indicating that access beyond this point was strictly prohibited, he fully intended to go past just as soon as he could without drawing attention.

After waiting for nearly an hour, most of the other tourists were gone from the area, headed back down the trail and into town to return their rentals. There were a few stragglers, but with any luck, they wouldn't notice as he slipped off down the Beckman Ridge trail.

The large ponderosa pines with their fan-like needles were sparse at this altitude and gave way to lodgepole pines, aspen, birch, and hawthorn. Underbrush was thick in most areas, but the trail was well marked though entirely covered in thick, heavy snow.

***

The rustic cabin lay quiet. The only sounds came from the fast clicking of the keyboard resting on Troy's lap and the occasional heavy sigh from Zeus. The big dog was resting comfortably at his feet. They sat in the living room, Troy working on an article for an outdoor magazine when the rottweiler suddenly stood, his attention drawn to something outside. The hackles on the back of his neck ruffled and a low growl escaped his throat. Troy stopped typing and focused his attention on listening and watching the dog. A moment later, he heard the distinct metallic clinking. It was an all too familiar sound. The aluminum boat tied at the dock had come loose on one end and the wind was causing it to bang against the metal ladder on the pier. Nick must not have secured the line. The bowline had come loose, and the wind had picked up since.

"It's okay big fella, just that old aluminum boat clanking around. Let's go fix it before the other line comes loose too," Troy said, calming the dog.

Grabbing his coat and hat, he hurried out before the second line on the boat gave way and allowed it to float out into the middle of the lake. Troy rushed down the front porch steps and was halfway down the path when he suddenly remembered he didn't have his handgun. He started to turn around and get it, but decided against it and continued down to the dock. Zeus was at his side. He wasn't worried. When he arrived, it was just as he suspected. The line had simply come untied. The line on the aft cleat was secure, but the bowline had slipped and caused the boat's nose to float out perpendicular to the dock. He sat on the edge of the wooden platform and pulled the vessel around with his feet before jumping in to tie it off. He grabbed the end of the line, wrapped it around the dock cleat and secured it.

"There, that should hold it," he said, admiring his handiwork.

Zeus sat on the end of the dock. He really didn't care.

The cleat hitch knot would keep the boat securely tied. Troy stood and looked out over the lake, admiring the serene valley when an old familiar feeling came over him. It wasn't something he could put a finger on exactly, just a sense he had that something wasn't right, an uneasiness, almost a foreboding. Something was just...off. He couldn't see anything out of the ordinary, and Zeus wasn't picking up on anything. It was just a sense of being watched. After a moment, he shook the feeling off as his imagination.

"Dammit, Zeus, I'm just making myself act foolishly

again over nothing."

The dog dropped his head uninterested in what Troy was talking about.

A moment later he gave a slight a chuckle, "Guess it's just my imagination trying to take off, isn't it, boy?"

Still, he couldn't quite shake the feeling.

It had been more than five years since his friend, Craig was brutally murdered on the mountain by a Sasquatch, a creature that was only supposed to exist in folklore and fairytale, but Troy and a handful of others knew better. When Craig's body was first discovered, all evidence pointed to Troy as the killer. It wasn't until the night of the siege that the sheriff, Deputy Larsen, and the Denizen family discovered that Craig wasn't killed by Troy, but by the Sasquatch.

After an all-night siege by the creatures at his cabin, they were lucky to have survived, but the cabin proved itself well built. The huge pine logs held off the attack of the intruders. Even though the people inside defending the cabin had shot and killed many of the Sasquatch, when daylight came. No bodies were found. The only the vehicles outside that were busted and shattered from huge rocks thrown by the creatures remained to tell the story.

Sheriff Blaine had taken photos and even a short video clip of the creatures, but in the end, the official reports were written up as that of a grizzly bear attack.

He walked back to the cabin to finish his article and send it to the editor before fixing supper. He had kept some of the fresh fish filets out but had put the rest in the freezer. That was one of his favorite perks of owning the cabin. It was on a beautiful lake chock full of several species of fish from catfish to Walleye. There was also the great hunting. Whitetail and mule deer were plentiful as were elk and squirrel. His freezer stayed well stocked no matter what time of year.

A radio dj talked excitedly about an upcoming release of a new song just before playing it. The small, black radio rested on the kitchen counter. It was mainly used as nothing more than background noise because the silence inside the cabin could get too quiet. Though Troy he loved the solitude of his home, he did long for company sometimes. The radio wasn't much, but it was at least a semblance of a connection with people, and that's all he really needed. The song playing reminded him of the sheriff's daughter, Lisa.

Troy and Lisa had dated for nearly six months when she suddenly broke things off. Her only explanation to him was that she had never intended to get so serious so quickly. She had her career that was extremely important to her. She had worked hard to get where she was and didn't want to jeopardize it with conflicting priorities. He never asked for anything more of her than the friendship they had so when she broke it off it came as a shock. She was the one that first asked him out when she moved back to the area. He merely resigned himself to the fact that no matter how hard he tried he would never understand what made people make the choices they made. He gave her what she wanted – space and room to breathe. He backed off completely and immersed himself in his work.

When Troy first bought the property more than five years ago, the peaceful valley and the solitude it provided were what enabled him to get as much work done as he had. Being a famous author came with an extensive workload. Not only was he a novelist, but he also wrote articles for various outdoor magazines. The research, travel, book signings, and visits with his editors, illustrators, and agent kept him busy. *It would be nice to see her again*, he thought.

***

Leon guided the snowmobile over the mountain trail headed for Beckman Ridge. He watched the tiny blue dot on his GPS move ever so slowly as he traversed the zig-zag path. The snowpack was higher than he expected and the ride was tedious, up and over large drifts, around one copse after another. At one point he had to turn around and ride back more than fifty yards to go around a large laydown of trees to get back on course.

The snow fell in large, gentle flakes that floated effortlessly to the ground. There wasn't much wind which kept the temperature balmy and comfortable. The gray skies wouldn't let any sunlight through the cloudy canopy, which made it difficult to know what time of day it was. If it weren't for the time on the cell phone display, there would be no way of guessing accurately.

1:27PM displayed prominently on his cell phone.

Damn, I was supposed to be back by now, he thought. Tammy was expecting him for lunch over an hour ago. No signal on the phone to send a text or a quick call either. He knew it was easier to beg forgiveness than ask her blessings to go off on a Bigfoot hunt alone. He would take her out to dinner tonight and make it up to her.

The snowfall was steady, thicker now than before. Leon puttered over the trail, which was clearly marked by the absence of trees and brush, winding through the dense forest. The snowmobile suddenly lost power, sputtered and coughed before catching again. When it happened the second time, he pulled up and stopped.

The tank was running dry. Before the fuel lines were emptied entirely, he got off and refilled the tank with the spare gas tank he had bought in town. He poured all its contents into the sled's reservoir, but it didn't fill it all the way up. He had ridden for the better part of the day on the one tank of fuel, and if he went any further, there wouldn't be enough to get back to town. That was a chance he wasn't willing to take. Not out here. Not in this weather.

The cell phone screen was wet from the flakes of snow that had found it, and he had to wipe the moisture away. He was near the area he had marked on the map and it was early enough in the day, so he decided to hike in the rest of the way. He grabbed the cell phone out of the holder, checked the pack for his camera then slung it over his shoulder and moved out.

18

Troy woke early the next morning and went downstairs to let Zeus out and put on a pot of coffee. He moved the large cross beam from the door and set it aside, unlocked the deadbolt and opened to door to a bright sun coming up in the east. The huge rottweiler bounded past nearly bowling him over. He crossed the porch, ran down the stairs and around to the back of the detached garage. He had a favorite place he always went to do his business.

"Okay, buddy. I know you have to go, but jeez. No need to run me down doing it," Troy called after the dog. "Let me know when you're back. It's too cold out here for me."

Troy closed the door and went back inside. Walking into the kitchen to get the coffee going, he noticed that he was running low. He had not been to the grocery store since flying back from New York. He pulled the magnetic note pad down from the refrigerator and started making a list. He would get dressed after breakfast and head into town.

The coffee was ready about the same time that Zeus scratched at the front door. Troy opened the door, and the dog went straight away for his food dish.

"I guess you're hungry, huh buddy? Not even a friendly, good morning mauling?" Troy laughed. "Can't say as I blame ya. We're going into town this afternoon and I'll need you on your best behavior. Remember last time? You almost got us kicked out of the store."

Zeus looked up from his bowl just long enough to see that Troy was speaking to him, but he didn't really care what the man was saying. He knew he wasn't in trouble, and he wasn't hearing any familiar commands, so he turned back to his breakfast.

The morning was filled with a few chores around the house and work on a manuscript. When Troy noticed the time on the wall clock was pushing near noon, he went upstairs and jumped in the shower. Fifteen minutes later, he toweled off and walked out of the bathroom into his bedroom where Zeus was curled up on his bed, patiently waiting. Once he was dressed, Troy turned to the large steel gun cabinet and unlocked it. Swinging the heavy door open, he reached in and pulled out the Ithaca Mag 10, grabbed a hand full of extra rounds and laid it all out on the bed.

"Never can be too careful, huh boy?"

Ten minutes later, Zeus jumped into the passenger seat of Troy's Jeep, and the two pulled out of the garage. Once outside, Troy hit the button and the garage door closed slowly behind them as the two drove off down the lane headed for town.

The road from the cabin to the highway was just over twelve miles. Once on the highway, it was still another half hour into town if the roads were all clear. During the summer months, it took less than half an hour to get to town, but during the heart of winter, it doubled easily. Troy had a tractor with a blade on it and would do his best to keep up with the snow on his road since it was his only way in or out. It wasn't particularly bad today, so the drive was moderate. About a quarter of a mile beyond the cabin, the road turned back and crossed the lake on an old trestle bridge. The span was less than two-hundred feet across, but each end of the bridge was a steep grade to allow for the rise in lake level throughout the year.

The snow-covered lane reflected the bright sunlight, creating a blinding glare on the windshield. Troy pulled his sunglasses off the visor clip and put them on.

"That's better," Troy said, speaking to Zeus who was whining at the passenger window. "Okay, okay, but only until we get to the highway, then the window goes back up. Got it?"

The dog loved riding in the vehicle but whined and pawed at the window until Troy rolled it down for him. He poked his head out to feel the wind blowing in his face. Troy knew the dog would tire after a while and curl up in the seat to nap until they arrived wherever it was they were going.

They crossed the bridge and settled in for the ride to town. He was in no hurry lumbering along in the Jeep, Zeus's tongue wagging in the breeze. Less than an hour later, they turned into the grocery store parking lot. Troy put a leash on Zeus and took him out to an area where he could stretch and take care of his business before putting him back in the vehicle. Zeus would have to stay while Troy was inside shopping.

Troy had just put the groceries in the back of the Jeep when his cell phone buzzed.

"Hey, Nick. What's up?" Troy answered.

"Hey, bud, where are you at right now? Are you inside?"

"Actually, I'm in town. Just walked out of Newmeyer's. Why? What's up?"

"Good. Can you swing by my office?"

"Sure, why? What's going on?"

"I'll explain when you get here," the sheriff said, and quickly hung up.

The drive across town took ten minutes. Troy parked between two Parks and Wildlife four-wheel-drive vehicles and climbed out with Zeus in tow. When he entered the building, he was greeted by the dispatcher.

"Hi, Troy. Oh, my goodness," Lindsey said when she saw the huge rottweiler. "Come here Zeus. I bet I have a treat in my desk for ya."

Zeus whimpered, but wouldn't budge from Troy's feet.

"It's okay, boy. You can go."

The dog trotted around the desk and made a beeline for Lindsey and certain ear scratches and petting.

Troy laughed. "I swear, Linds, you're going to make a wuss out of him with all the affection and treats. He's already spoiled beyond reproach."

"What can I say? I have a way with dogs," Lindsey said. "Sheriff's in his office. Said to send you in as soon as you got here. Zeus will be just fine right here, right boy?" she said, turning her attention to the dog.

"Thanks, Linds."

Troy walked down the hallway and rapped a couple of times on the door. Not waiting for an answer, he turned the handle and went inside. There were two men from Parks & Wildlife standing in front of a large county map on the wall, alongside Sheriff Blaine and Deputy Billy Larsen.

"Troy, glad you were in town. This is Sam Lazaro and Jim Braun with Parks & Wildlife. We have a situation. What we're about to talk about doesn't leave this room," Nick said. "An hour ago, Billy was patrolling County Road 4330 when he picked up a couple that had been in a car wreck and walked half the night."

"Seriously?"

"Yes, both were suffering from hypothermia and shock. He got them straight away to the hospital, but they were in no condition to give a statement," Nick said, turning toward Billy with a nod.

"Married couple, both to be in their mid-forties and from what I can tell, very fit, capable, up here for the week skiing. The woman never spoke at all. I got very little out of the husband. They're renting a cabin from the Buckhorn and were driving into town to see the manager. Obviously, they never made it. Not last night anyway."

Sheriff Blaine took over.

"On their way, they swerved to miss something and ended up going over the edge and totaling their car. I have deputies scouring the area now for the vehicle. Soon as they find it, we'll head up there. They have instructions not to disturb the site, but to call me immediately."

"Sounds routine enough. So, why am I here?" Troy asked puzzled.

Nick took a deep breath.

"It gets better. Sam?"

Sam Lazaro was in his mid-thirties, stood just over six-feet tall and wore his Park Ranger cap pulled down tight over his short-cropped black hair.

The ranger turned and cleared his throat. "We had a missing persons report come across the blotter this morning. City police took the report, but they called us as soon as they put it on the wire. A guy rented a snowmobile in town yesterday morning to go sightseeing and take photos. He never returned the sled, and his wife reported him missing this morning. Of course, the chief's more concerned about the missing property, but he looped us in since the last reported sighting was on the Jackson Ridge sightseeing trail. That's our jurisdiction. We left the Chief out of this conversation for a reason. Once again, this stays contained in this room. We have people out looking now, and we'll join them later. Right now, he's an adult. Not much we can do about it."

"Okay, so people get lost all the time. What's the connection here?"

"The guy that rented the sled was none other than the guy that shot the video of Bigfoot on Beckman Ridge and uploaded it to the internet. His wife claims he went sightseeing, but when we spoke with the owner of the rental, his employee said that the guy asked about Beckman Ridge but was told it was too far and off-limits."

Billy said, "Turns out that the couple who had the wreck...well, they didn't miss whatever it was they swerved to avoid. They claim to have hit a Sasquatch. Then to make matters worse, it was injured and terrorized them all night. The woman is still in shock and unable to speak at all, just mumbles. The husband...well, he was coherent, but just barely."

Troy said, "So, from our encounter with these Sasquatch, how is it that this couple is still alive?"

"Good freakin' question. When I asked the guy how they escaped, he said it finally left them alone. That's when they walked out of there."

Troy walked over to the map on the wall and studied it.

"That's interesting."

"What's that?" Nick asked.

"The video was claimed to have been taken here on Beckman Ridge." Troy pushed a red pin into the board. "The idiot rents a snowmobile and rides to Beckman Ridge. I think we can all agree to that. Jackson Ridge trail goes right up to the old trailhead for Beckman." He pushed another pin in the board. "Now, Billy picked those folks up on County Road 4330 which runs perpendicular to that ridge and goes up to the Buckhorn Lodge. Not sure where they hit the Sasquatch yet, but best guess would put it somewhere between the old Spencer Mine and the cabins. That would put the crash site somewhere north of here." He pushed another pin in place.

He stepped back to see the entire map. The red pins were in the shape of a triangle on the board. "Three pins, Sasquatch sighted here and here, and a missing man searching for Sasquatch...here. What's in the middle of that?" he said rhetorically.

"Exactly," Nick said.

19

Michelle heard the call come in when Billy found the couple out on the county road, but she was on the other side of the county. Wasn't much she could do anyway, Billy had them at the hospital before she could've made it halfway back to town. She was puzzled by the cryptic conversation. After reporting that he found the couple and transporting them to the hospital, the radio went silent. She would ask him about it later.

A few minutes later a BOLO was issued for a missing person on the mountain last seen at Jackson Ridge wearing a green parka, black beanie and riding a bright green snowmobile with Action Sports Rentals painted on the side. These two incidents on their own weren't a big deal. People go missing all the time just to be found a day or two later hungover from a party or hooking up with someone they met here, but Michelle had a hunch that somehow these two things were connected in some way. It wasn't anything concrete that she could put her finger on, but a nagging feeling in the back of her mind made her believe something different was happening here.

She pulled over on the shoulder, located a map and spread it out on the hood of her patrol unit. A moment later she pinpointed the Jackson Ridge trailhead and followed the route.

"That's it!" she exclaimed. She hastily folded the map back up and threw it in the passenger seat, whipped a U-turn in the road and headed back toward town. Her shift would be over in a couple hours, and she needed time to figure out her next step.

***

The sheriff's cell phone buzzed.

"Excuse me, fellas." A few seconds later, he hung up.

"They found it, went off the road three miles up from the old mine on 4330. Let's get up there. We should still have plenty of daylight to do a thorough workup of the site." Nick turned to Troy. "You're still a reserve deputy, mind if I call you up?"

"You couldn't keep me away," Troy said.

Troy and Zeus left the Jeep sitting in the municipal building's parking lot and rode with Nick to the crash site. As cold as it was, he wasn't worried about leaving his groceries, but he did take the time to plug the engine block heater into an A/C outlet and set the timer. The system also relayed power to the battery tender. He had no idea how long he would be gone, and he didn't want the cold weather to strand him when they returned.

The rangers followed closely behind arriving at the location in less than half an hour. The sheriff was the first one out of the vehicle and met the two deputies at their patrol unit.

"Noland, what do we have?" Nick asked.

"It's a mess, Sheriff. Looks like they left the road right up here, went off the embankment and rolled a couple of times before coming to rest against a couple of big cedars.

If it weren't for the trees, they wouldn't have walked out of here, that's for sure. They would've been ten feet underwater in the river. The car is literally half-way off the edge of a straight down drop off."

"Is that right?" Nick said, shaking his head.

"There's something else you need to see first, Sheriff." He cast a quick glance at the two rangers.

"It's okay, they know."

Noland waved with his hand to follow him. Just off the edge of the road, a yellow rain slicker lay spread out over the ground. The deputy kneeled beside it and pulled it back. A footprint lay underneath, clearly marked in the snow down to the moist earth beneath. No more than six inches away, a splattering of blood accompanied the track. Several others led down the embankment, but none as clear. The other prints seemed to be dragged through the snow and were too obscure, but the trail was more than obvious and easy to follow.

"There's lots more down by the car. We were careful not to get too close and disturb any evidence."

"Good. You two stay here on each of the vehicles. Make sure no one lingers. Keep 'em moving, no questions. Get a cast of this one."

"You got it. We tied off a couple of ropes to help you get up and down, extra harnesses in my Explorer if you need 'em."

Deputy Noland Chastain watched the team make their way down to the vehicle below while his partner, Tim Severs, retrieved the casting material for the footprint.

The embankment was covered with snow and ice, making the trip even more treacherous. The going down was the easy part, apart from sliding and falling several times on the slick surface even with the aid of the rope-line. The going back up was going to be the issue.

They carefully set about collecting evidence for forensics. Photos were taken, along with several castings of prints, blood and hair samples and all packaged in a large plastic tote.

On the road, Noland opened the back hatch of his patrol unit and grabbed the casting material. He used Snow Impression Wax to spray the footprint first and before they mixed the plaster.

A half-hour later a black SUV drove up the road, stopped and shifted into park across the road from the patrol units and just sat there.

"I'll take care of it," Noland said.

The deputy motioned for the new arrivals to keep moving. Nothing. The vehicle didn't move. He walked over to it and motioned for them to roll the window down.

"Let's move it along folks," he said, waving his hands.

Nothing.

He tapped on the glass, once, twice. "Come on, move it along. Can't block the road."

Nothing.

Frustrated, he pulled his baton and used the handle to tap on the glass. No response. The vehicle just sat there quietly idling.

"Troy, take a look at this," Nick said. He was using a pair of collection tweezers to pull a tuft of hair, flesh, and blood from a sharp piece of metal and put it into a plastic bag. "This didn't come from our two vics, that's for sure."

"I agree, that's more evidence in that one baggie than we were able to collect from the siege five years ago."

"Yeah, and I found tracks leading away, heading along the ridge and then straight up the mountain. Almost eighteen inches long and seven wide. Same as the track up by the road. I'd estimate something weighing in at a good four-hundred, maybe four-fifty. Good news is, there was only one."

Troy let out a long, low whistle. "Damn, that's not a small one by any means, but not as big as some."

"It's injured too. That's a certainty. I don't like that, not one damn bit. Nothing worse than an injured animal. Desperate and fearful of everything. Easily provoked and these damn things don't need provocation."

"What's that?" Nick asked. He was straining to hear something.

Troy listened and heard it too.

It was Zeus barking. He was usually very patient when given an order to stay, but he was in the sheriff's car waiting up on the road. Something was happening.

"Wonder what he's upset about?" Troy asked. He was unable to see the vehicles due to the trees and the slope.

"Well, we're almost done here. Let's get wrapped up and climb our asses back up. Not much more we can do," Nick said.

"What about the car? Are you going to have it pulled up?"

"We've got all the evidence we need. One vehicle crash. No crime. I'm not in a hurry to get it pulled up today. I'll find out what the owners want to do as far as towing. I'm sure they have insurance to cover it all as long as it doesn't take more than a few days."

The three men inside the SUV watched behind the pitch-black tinted glass in silent amusement. The deputy wouldn't

171

have been able to break the glass even if he tried. It was bulletproof.

Finally, Noland gave up and stepped away to assist the team below as they scrambled up.

The going was difficult, and it took them a good while to pack up all their gear and scramble up. When they arrived at the top, they spotted the source of Zeus's consternation, the large black SUV parked near the cruisers.

"Get that vehicle out of here, Noland," Nick growled at the deputy.

"Sorry, Sheriff. We tried. They're not budging. Won't even roll the windows down. Just sitting there."

"We'll see about that."

The driver wore a plain black suit, white shirt, black neck-tie, and expensive sunglasses. His hair was as black as his suit, neatly cut in a French style brushed forward and then up. The man riding beside him could have been his twin brother had it not been for the blond hair accompanied by black eyebrows that stuck out above the rims of his dark sunglasses.

It was the man riding in the back seat that gave the orders. The one in charge. He was tall and lean with a firm-set jaw. A jagged scar starting at his right temple trailed down like a lightning bolt to the corner of his mouth. His red hair cut short and trim. He wore an expensive well-tailored suit, gold sub-mariner watch and a gold ring with a USNA emblem on it.

The three men inside watched in silence as the sheriff walked toward them. When the sheriff was within a few feet of the vehicle, the red-headed man in charge gave the order. "Drive."

Nick watched the vehicle disappear up the mountain road. The plates were government issue. He made a mental note of the numbers and turned back to the team.

"Well, that was easy," Noland said, watching the vehicle drive off with a puzzled look. "Damn rubberneckers!"

"What the hell was that all about?" Troy asked. He walked over to the sheriff's cruiser and let Zeus out. The big dog padded alongside him, and they joined the others.

"No idea. Government plates though," Nick said.

"Rubberneckers," Noland chimed in. "Just nosey, probably taking video or pics to post to Facebook."

"So, what do we do now?" Troy asked, looking around at the group.

"Gary?" Nick said, looking at the ranger. "Your call, but my suggestion is to issue an alert to be on the lookout for an out of hibernation grizzly in the area. Close the back-country trails. At least until we know what we're dealing with here."

"I concur," Gary said.

"What d'ya mean?" Troy asked. "We know exactly what we're dealing with, Nick. That thing is a killer! Could be more than the one."

"I know that as well as every man here, but we can't very well issue a *Sasquatch* alert, can we?"

"Wait a minute, seriously?" Deputy Severs asked. "I mean, I never doubted you when all that went down before, I saw the pictures but isn't it possible that this is exactly what you just said though, a crazed Grizz out of hibernation? These tracks could be a bear, right? They do tend to step into the front track with their back foot?"

The men just looked at him.

"I've seen them," Ranger Braun said looking at his partner. "Fact is, we both have. Years ago, even before the deal with the sheriff and Billy went down. What was that, six years ago or so?"

Gary nodded in agreement. "Several years ago, before I joined the park service. I was camping with some buddies one summer near Jones Summit, a fairly popular place. Late one night, when we were all asleep in our tents, something came into the camp. I was the only one that heard it. I grabbed my flashlight and poked my head out. When I clicked on the light, it was standing no more than twenty feet away, just looking at me. It covered its eyes with a forearm, but I saw its face. Its eyes were big and red. They didn't glow from eye shine. They were just - red, menacing. After a few seconds, it huffed and snorted, I dunno, kinda like a bull when you get too close. It dropped its arm, slowly turned away and walked off into the woods looking over its shoulder at me the whole time."

"What'd you do then?"

"I was terrified, couldn't move, but finally I was able to get enough gumption to step out and build the fire back up. I just sat there the rest of the night, jumping at every little noise I heard. Next morning my friends said I was as white as a ghost. I never told them what I saw. They wouldn't have believed me anyway. Hell, I didn't believe me. Never saw it again, but I'll never forget it, I'll tell you that!"

Nick shifted his look from one ranger to the other and jammed his hands into his pockets. He felt the familiar plastic bag of evidence he had collected from earlier. Without mentioning it, he said, "You weren't there, Noland. If you were, you would never doubt what happened and what these things are. It's hard never have seen one for yourself, but trust me, you never want to. My office in an hour?" he asked with a stern, unwavering look at his deputies.

"You bet, Sheriff."

Gary said, "We'll meet you there once we stop at the office and issue the warning. We'll have to file a quick report to get it across the wire."

"Sounds good, Gary. See you in a bit." Nick turned back to Billy, "Stop by the hospital and check on that couple. If they're able to, talk to 'em and find out everything you can. Get a statement. Hopefully, they're not telling everyone within shouting distance what happened. Maybe we can contain it."

"You got it, Sheriff."

"Tim, soon as we get back, get all of this evidence loaded in the van and sent to the lab in Boulder, and tell them it's a code-9, gotta have it back as quickly as possible."

The men scattered and disappeared, leaving the scene of the wreck to allow the forest to drift back into silence.

It was dark by the time Nick turned the 4X4 around and headed back to town. The two park rangers followed them with Noland and Tim bringing up the rear.

"So, what now?" Troy asked.

"Now, we go hunting."

20

"What are you saying? I brought them in myself. A man and woman in their mid to late forties. Car wreck, hypothermia, half-dead, ring a bell?" Deputy Larsen said.

He was speaking to the emergency room attendant as the lady looked through the computer. The sheriff had sent him over to follow-up on the couple from the car wreck.

"I'm sorry, Officer. I don't have any record of a couple brought in this morning from a crash. Nothing even remotely resembling this. Do you remember who was on duty when you brought them in?"

"No, I don't remember who was on duty. Why would I remember who was on duty? I brought them in, they were in bad shape, and you people took them back right away. They had no ID on them, but that wasn't a concern then. I really didn't think you would - *lose* them," Billy said, "Especially billing it to the county."

"I'm sorry, sir, but as you can see, we have lots of patients coming in during ski season. Broken legs, arms, collar bones, you name it. This is like Grand Central Station here, so finding two people in this madhouse is like winning a lottery. But you're more than welcome to ask around."

When Billy reported back at the sheriff's office and delivered the news, Troy and the two park rangers were there to hear it too.

"How is that possible?" Troy said. "You did take them to Hawthorn Memorial Hospital, right?"

"Of course, where else would I take them?"

"Okay, so what happened to them?" Troy asked.

"Well, that seems to be the million-dollar question. Maybe someone made a mistake and just haven't filed any paperwork on them yet, and they're in a room somewhere?" Nick said.

"Nope, I checked with the duty nurse, doctors and anyone else I could. Nothing. It's like they never existed!" Billy said. He paced across the room and blew a huge breath of air he had held. "I dunno, I just don't know what the hell happened to 'em."

"Wait a minute, you said the man told you that they were staying at one of the cabins. If that's the case, then they would be in the hotel registry. I'll give Lisa a call."

Nick opened his cell phone and dialed his daughter's number.

"Hey, Dad. What's up?"

"Listen, I need a favor. You have a couple in their mid-forties or so staying at one of the private cabins on the mountain near the old Spencer Mine," Nick said before looking toward Billy with a questioning nod, covering the receiver he asked, "Got a name?"

"First name only, Cameron," Billy said.

"Only have a first name, Cameron. Nothing else."

He heard the clicking of a computer keyboard.

"Actually, a group of college kids rented the only empty cabin we had out this evening. Before that, it was empty, which is odd. We've been booked solid for months. Let me check a few things out and call you right back."

When the cell phone rang five minutes later, she had no further news. There had been no couple checked into the nearest cabin to the old mine. She checked the other cabins as well, but no couple matching the description had ever shown as checked in.

"Goddammit!" Nick said. "How can we lose two people? Even as busy as it is, there should be a record of them somewhere. Do we even have their names?"

Billy stammered, "Well, the woman wasn't able to speak at all, and the man barely was." Billy pulled out his note pad. "I remember him saying the word camera a few times when I asked who he was and what happened. At first, I thought he was saying camera, but then I figured out he was telling me his name, Cameron. But no last name. I figured I'd get to talk to him once we got to the hospital."

"So, what do we do now?" Troy asked.

"Billy, run the plates on the car and let's get a name."

"I called them in on my way back from the scene earlier. I'll check with Lindsey to see if anything is back yet," Billy said. He hurried out of the office and returned a moment later.

"Sheriff, you're not going to believe this. Apparently, the plates are bogus, not registered in the system at all."

"What? How the hell can that be?"

"No idea."

"Stolen? I could buy, but bogus altogether, sounds ridiculous. In all my years in law enforcement, I don't think I've ever come across bogus plates that don't even show up in the system. Most of the time, thieves simply steal an out of state plate, quick and easy," Nick said, pacing toward the window again. "Okay, get Earl on the phone and have him get that car out of there, now! I don't care what he has to do to make it happen," Nick said. "Work through the night, but get that vehicle out of there."

"You got it."

"And Billy…"

"Yeah?"

"You get back up there and meet him there, and take Noland with you. Do *not* let that car out of your sight. We need to get the VIN, but there's got to be more to it than that."

"On it boss."

The sheriff pushed the intercom button for the dispatcher.

"Lindsey, any word from Mountain Patrol on the missing man?"

"Nothing yet, Sheriff," she replied. "They found the sled, but he wasn't with it. They're still searching the surrounding area."

He stepped back around the desk, took his coat off, and hung it on the rack.

"Okay, so now we have three missing persons. What the hell else can we lose today?" Nick asked.

The others had all left the building leaving the sheriff alone with his thoughts. He stood and walked to the window and gazed across the town. The lights from the buildings shimmered off the bright white of the snow. Hawthorn was a beautiful town during the day but at night it sparkled.

He hit the intercom for the dispatcher who had relieved Lindsey earlier.

"Clark, I'm heading home. Forward any calls to my cell, but please use some discrepancy."

"You got it, Sheriff. Just the important stuff," the dispatcher said.

Nick stood, walked across the room, and grabbed his coat and hat. He flicked the light switch off and started to step out of the office when he felt the plastic collection bag in his pocket. It was already too late for anyone to run it to Boulder for forensics, so he locked it away in an empty file drawer and made a mental note to have it delivered in the morning.

***

Troy opened the door of the Jeep, and Zeus jumped in, scrambled over the console and settled in the passenger seat. Troy got in, tugged his seat belt around, started the vehicle, and pulled out of the parking lot. The plan was simple. Go home, get some rest and meet back at the sheriff's office the next day. The group of six men would pair up on snowmobiles beginning at the Buckhorn Lodge and work their way outward, looking for any sign of the creature and, of course, the missing man.

First things first, Troy thought as he carried his groceries into the cabin, *supper!*

Zeus waited patiently by his bowl until Troy told him it was okay to eat, then the dog ate ravenously. He finished well before Troy, padded over by the fireplace and laid down.

"Yes, you may be excused," Troy said, laughing at the dog. "You want me to turn on the TV for ya, big guy?"

Zeus didn't pay Troy any attention, just stretched out and closed his eyes.

After supper, Troy set about getting his things ready for the next day's search. He couldn't help but have that same old familiar feeling of foreboding that he had felt so long ago.

Troy had only had the cabin a short while when he invited his two best friends, Craig Morton and Phil Jackson up to stay for a couple of weeks when the creatures attacked them. The Sasquatch had killed Craig on the mountain when they were searching for Phil, who had gotten lost. Troy was badly injured but made it to town for help. When Craig's body was found, Troy was arrested on murder charges. He was released shortly after, but Phil was still missing. Upon his release, the sheriff escorted him to his cabin where they found Phil, who had been severely injured and convalescing at a neighbor's house several miles away. The creatures attacked at that point, leaving them with no way out, but to fight. The remote location offered no communication, completely cut off and no way to get the word out.

Troy would never forget that night or the sounds. It was a savage, brutal attack. The shrieking, growling and pounding, the giant rocks and limbs hurling against the sides of the cabin still filled his nightmares. The beasts were huge, powerful, and relentless.

When it was over, Troy and Phil traveled to Oklahoma to bury their best friend and see to his affairs. It was a time of great sadness and reflecting. When he returned, Phil came back with him. They wanted to make sure that none of the creatures ever came back. It was Troy's place, and he would defend it. It was pure rage, hatred…revenge!

Together with the sheriff and Billy, they searched the mountain weeks. No other sign of the Sasquatch was ever found and, eventually, things got back to as close to normal as possible.

Even though the official reports said to have been a bear attack, word leaked out about possible Bigfoot activity in the area. Troy had to put up a gate with a lock on it and no-trespassing signs to keep out the wannabe Bigfoot experts and camera crews. Even that eventually waned, and he was able to stop locking the gate.

Phil had been seeing a local girl named Irene Denizen, the daughter of Clance Denizen who had experienced the assault with them. Two years later, the couple was married and living just outside of Hawthorn.

They had seen the last of the Sasquatch, until now.

Zeus was fast asleep at the foot of the bed when Troy got out of the shower. He watched the big dog's chest rise and fall as he toweled off. Zeus was only a few years old but well trained and disciplined. He was there for a reason.

After setting the alarm, Troy flicked the light switch out and lay down. A moment later his phone buzzed on the nightstand. He was surprised to see who it was.

"Hey, Nick, what's up?" he answered.

"You'll never believe this. I hope you're sitting down."

"Actually, I just got in bed."

"Good, because you may pass right the hell out when you hear this."

"What's happened? Another attack?"

"No, nothing like that, but get this. The car is missing. I sent Billy back up to the site to wait on Earl. When he got there, he said he waited at the top of the road for Earl. It hadn't been more than a couple of hours since we had left. Billy waited another half an hour when he arrived. When Earl got to the site with the tow truck, they went down to the car but it wasn't there."

"Could it have fallen into the river?"

"No, they looked around. Apparently, it was dragged out probably just minutes after we all left."

Troy was sitting on the edge of the bed, and Zeus had padded over to see what all the talk was about.

"Who the hell would've taken it?" Troy asked.

"No idea. We checked with every wrecker service in the county and the one over. Just doesn't make any sense."

After a few more minutes of conversation, Troy lay back down, staring at the ceiling. The sky was clear, so the moonlight shined into the small half-moon windows at the top of the door that led out onto the upstairs veranda. He had the double-doors closed and locked, but he also had large wooden doors reinforced with iron, and a heavy crossbar closed over those. The massive doors were built to keep bears out. The entire cabin was built with security in mind. Troy had always assumed it was to keep the bears out like any other cabin in bear country, but since the siege, he suspected the previous owner built such reinforcements with the Sasquatch in mind.

Along with the fortified doors and windows, he kept an arsenal of weaponry. He had an Ithaca Mag 10, a Berrett M107 A1 and, his personal favorite, the Super Redhawk chambered in the .454 Casull. The caliber was first developed as a wildcat cartridge in the late fifties and didn't find mainstream commercial production until the late nineties, almost forty years later. The big-bore Ruger revolver with a seven and a half-inch barrel had more than enough stopping power for anything that he would come up against including an eight-foot-tall bipedal beast that weighed upwards of four to six-hundred pounds.

21

Sheriff Blaine rolled out a large map onto a conference table just as Troy and Zeus walked into the office. Troy unzipped his coat and hung it on the stand near the door and joined the group at the table.

"The sightings, events or whatever you wanna call 'em happened here, here and here," he said, marking the same positions as the wall map from the previous day. "At the very center of this activity lies the Buckhorn Lodge. The plan is to pair up and begin a search pattern on the ridgeline just due south and above the lodge. If we fan out making a large sweep of the area working our way in clockwise and meet back on the slope above the lodge at Beeman Trailhead, we should be able to cover a massive area before nightfall."

"And if we don't find anything?" Noland said.

"That's exactly what I'm hoping we find," Nick said. "Nothing."

***

Michelle wasn't scheduled to work that day, but she needed information about what was going on. Everyone was tight-lipped at the station house, but when the men left, she poured two cups of coffee and made her way over to her friend.

"Good morning, Linds, how are you?" Michelle said, handing her one of the cups.

"I'm good, Chel. Thanks for the coffee."

"No problem. Just came in to finish up some paperwork."

"Gotta love the administrative side of the job. The part you never seem to get caught up on, eh?" Lindsey said.

"You're right about that. Hey, what's up with the Rangers this morning? Where are they all headed out together, packing all that heat?"

Michelle made note that the men were all were carrying Mag 10's and heavy gear bags.

"Officially," Lindsey said, "They're going to assist Mountain Patrol in the search for the missing person."

"And...unofficially?"

Lindsey looked around the office. Seeing no one within earshot, she leaned closer.

"Unofficially, they're going hunting alright, but not for the missing person."

***

Troy opened the back door for Zeus to jump in, and then he climbed in beside the sheriff.

"Any further news on the vanishing car?"

"Nothing."

"The missing couple?"

"Not a word."

Troy turned to the window and stared out in thought.

"This is strange as hell. Who or why would anyone kidnap the couple, steal their car, and delete their records at the hotel? Why would anyone need to hide a car wreck?"

"Because it wasn't just a simple car wreck," Nick replied. "Think about it. Remember the black SUV that stopped when we got back up yesterday?"

"Yeah, sure."

"It had government plates. I made a note of it at the time, but I should've written the numbers down."

"Have you been reading those Facebook Groups again? You know, the ones that believe that the government has known about the existence of Bigfoot all along, but they're covering it up. Conspiracy theorists unite!" Troy laughed.

"Oh, hell no, those are the same people that believe that Bigfoot can teleport, fly in spaceships, and control your mind. I don't believe any of that low-brow stuff. If the only explanation someone can come up with defies the basic laws of physics, then that is a simple mind that will never understand or accept the more reasonable answer. It either doesn't exist or one hasn't been captured. It's as simple as that. We both know it's a flesh and blood creature; it's real. Real as hell, and I've never believed in government conspiracies either, but what other explanation is there in this particular case?"

"Great! Black helicopters will come for us in the middle of the night. This is good stuff for my next novel."

Nick laughed. "Well, at least there's no *Bigfoot erotica* in that."

"Oh, dear lord," Troy said, rolling his eyes. "I've seen that crap too. People really need to get a life!"

***

The two park rangers followed the sheriff's team to the designated area near the lodge, parked their vehicles and unloaded the snowmobiles.

"We radio in every half hour or if you see anything at all that doesn't look, act or feel right. Got it?" Nick said.

When everyone acknowledged, Nick rolled the map up that he had spread out again on the hood of his patrol unit.

"Troy, you're with me. Let's get moving."

Sixty seconds later, the six men were buzzing over the trail in single file on snowmobiles. The sleds were the only way they could cover the hundreds of acres of mountainous terrain.

The air was cold and crisp, but the sky that was clear and blue earlier was beginning to darken. Visibility on the mountain would be good for now but could deteriorate rapidly.

***

Leon scrambled over the boulder, hopped down to the next smaller one, and then down to the game trail below. The path was covered with snow and ice, making the trek even more stringent under the given conditions. He ran out of energy bars long ago, but an unlucky hibernating marmot would make an excellent meal. He had food. What he needed were water and fire.

Two days earlier, he had gone in search of the elusive creature that he had read about for so many years. He was fascinated by the stories and watched everything about Bigfoot that he could find. When he made the video a few days ago, it only fueled the fire for more. It also made him take chances that he never should have alone.

In his mind, he replayed everything that happened, leading up to this point. In retrospect, he should have told someone where he was going, what he was doing and what to expect. He should have found someone to go with, a partner, a believer, but someone with more experience. Not particularly with outdoors experience, but a tracker. He knew there were no experts in the field, mainly pseudoscience practiced by amateurs. No discoveries have ever been made other than circumstantial evidence, most of which could easily be refuted by anyone that was raised in the woods and grew up hunting. Not the suburbanite middle management guy that drove an expensive jacked up truck and came to the woods with their pretty new sporting rifles only a few times a year to hunt deer.

No, not those guys. He was thinking about the ones that lived off the land. The ones that weren't out just to hang a trophy on a wall, but to put food on the table type of folks. The ones that spent hours in a tree stand after weeks of scouting. Folks that were in the woods before sunup and after sunrise, quiet sentries watching and waiting fifteen or even twenty feet high up in a tree-stand for the right deer to come along. People like that, they had patience to sit in those stands for hours every day. They watched everything that went on in the woods; they became a part of the forest. They saw the wind blow trees every which way, felling giants into one another, crossing trunks over, twisting limbs into shapes that looked unnatural, only they *were* natural. Those are the ones that know that when they see one of these creatures, they are without a doubt flesh and blood. There is no supernatural woo science happening. Simply a creature that has yet to be identified. No bodies have ever been recovered. No bones. No DNA. Nothing, regardless of the thousands of eyewitnesses around the country.

Still, it was a fascinating hobby, and that's all it was to him. He was a definite believer. He was very young when he had an experience with the creature. It was on a camping trip with his parents. He was playing down by a lake when he first smelled a powerful, foul odor. He looked around thinking it could be a skunk or dead animal somewhere nearby and that's when he spotted it. It was mostly hidden in the woods, but he could see its face, shoulder, and arm as the creature peered out from the tree it hid behind. He would never forget that moment. The creature didn't try to hurt him but simply disappeared into the forest. His parents didn't believe him.

How could there not be something out there, he would ask himself. Real scientists were making new discoveries every day all around the globe. There are literally millions of uninhabited acres of forest scattered across the continent. It is entirely conceivable that any number of areas were more than adequate for sustaining a population of large primate type bipedal creatures. He would go so far as to even say it was not just possible, but likely.

He lost his way two days ago when his cell phone with the map on it died. He knew his best chance at survival was to stay put until searchers located him, but he had to move to find shelter. One unfortunate mistake after another left him tumbling and sliding down the side of the mountain. The fall left him beaten and bruised, but nothing was broken except his pride.

The fall was a blessing in disguise. He found a small cave of sorts in the rocks, an animal den not more than eight feet deep and just high enough to sit up inside. It wasn't much, but it was dry and kept the brutal winds at bay. The mouth faced west and gave him the last waning rays of warmth of the day. He had found enough dry wood and woodfat to keep the den warm, but he needed to scavenge for more. Under snow and ice of winter, that was a feat in and of itself.

Leon had only a small amount of the fatwood left in his pocket. He had passed by some dead pine trees earlier, and there were some old, decayed stumps near. With any luck at all, he could find some more and get a fire started. His foot sunk deep into a snowdrift. He stumbled forward banging his elbow on a rock. His heavy coat helped cushion the blow, but he still felt the pain shoot through his half-frozen body.

Growing up in the woods and spending much of his youth running the backwoods of Oregon, deep snow, rugged terrain, and harsh conditions weren't new or particularly scary. His dad taught him at a very young age how to make a fire even in the toughest environments. What he didn't understand at the time was his father was teaching him survival skills. He taught him how to locate and use fatwood from pines. He would use a machete and start chopping on dead trees and stumps. On his own, he found little that was usable as fire kindling. With practice, he eventually became very adept in finding it.

His body ached, and his stomach felt as if it were collapsing on his spine. He was hungry and becoming desperate. His cell phone battery had died long before. It was useless. Leon slogged his way through the snow, over the rocks and into the clump of trees. Rotten stumps were his goal. Mushy, rotten pine stumps.

The wind had picked up on the mountain, blowing through the treetops and stirring up loose snow from the tops of drifts that swirled up in small eddies. It was colder than the last few days, and the sky was getting grayer. A winter storm may set in soon. He had to get a fire going soon.

He spotted a likely stump and set about digging out

more fatwood. His dad taught him to look for these types of rotten stumps with several spires rising. Many times, those spires are filled with fatwood. Most fatwood will be in the bottom of the stump where the sap hardens over time. He pulled his pocket knife out and hacked in to it. Ten minutes later, he found what he was looking for. A large sliver of mushy pink wood. He dug deep into the soft fleshy part until he hit solid wood and dug it out. It had a very distinct odor of turpentine. He started shaving it out into small slivers.

It was nearly dark when he finished on the stump. He was able to slice several bits of the tinder out. Enough to fill the entire backpack. He would need it.

***

Nick pulled up on the sled and came to a stop just at the edge of a tree line overlooking a large bare, flat area. He pulled his goggles off and rubbed his eyes as Troy pulled up beside him. Zeus was riding comfortably on the large back-seat area designed for canines. The department didn't have a full-time canine officer now, so Zeus lucked out. He loved riding with Troy on his property.

"That's the old Miller Pond. That's why it's so flat. I'm sure it's frozen over solid, but I hate taking chances. We'll skirt around and head back to the checkpoint. We're losing daylight," Nick said.

"Yeah, we've not seen anything anyway. I'd think that we're tilting at windmills if it wasn't for the evidence at the car wreck. Maybe Severs was right that it was just a bear. Maybe it's nothing more than some form of Pygmalion effect, you know, self-fulfilling prophecy, or something like that," Troy said, "Where we see what we tell ourselves we'll find."

"Could be, but that doesn't explain the disappearing couple or the vanishing car?"

"True enough."

Just then, a helicopter painted red, white and black could be seen over a distant ridge. The men could hear the blades whirling even at the great distance.

"Still searching for the *other* missing person. I have some deputies working on the search party alongside Mountain Patrol. They've been read-in on what to expect. No one goes out alone, and no one goes unarmed. They're to let me know as soon as they hear anything at all, but no word yet."

Nick called into the others on the radio. Same thing. Nothing.

"Let's head to the last checkpoint."

"You got it."

22

The Buckhorn Lodge boasted one of the best restaurants in Hawthorn. With a world-class chef creating extraordinary dishes and a large menu to serve even the most finicky of diners, it was no wonder that the Ponderosa Grill was always busy from morning until late in the evening.

The centerpiece of the restaurant was the large horseshoe-shaped bar. It was masterfully created to resemble a log cabin minus the top half of the walls. Tall cedar bar stools surrounded the sides and seated up to forty guests on the three borders. Leather backed booths with intricate hand-carved wildlife scenes surrounded the outer edges of the restaurant with beautiful views through large plate windows. The night sparkled in a snow-covered winter wonderland that reflected the soft yellow glow of Edison bulbs encapsulated in wrought-iron sconces along the exterior of the walls. The interior seating featured the same Edison styled bulbs hanging from round wrought-iron chandeliers high above the common areas. The effect was one of rustic elegance.

Michelle sat at a table near the entrance that gave her a view to the lower parking area. She sipped on a steaming mug of Earl Gray, patiently waiting to see headlights from the snowmobiles returning to the law enforcement vehicles.

She had followed the other officers to the lodge earlier. Once she saw them leave on the snowmobiles, she left and went back home for a few hours. She figured the men wouldn't go to all the trouble of hauling and unloading the sleds if they were only going to be gone a short time. She was right. Several hours had passed, and they still had not made it back. But it would be dark soon, and the snowmobiles would need refueling. She waited.

***

"There's one other place I'd like to check out before we head back," Sam said. The corners of his eyes crinkled from the balaclava held tight by the goggles he had pulled up on his forehead. "Remember the old surveyor's cabin near Pronghorn Gap?"

"Yeah, we used to hunt muley's up there. It's not far from Beckman Ridge. The old cabin's probably fallen in by now," Jim said. His breath floated on the condensation of the cold evening air.

"Oh, I'm sure it is. I've not been there in years, but that's a nice choke-point for game. If you were a…somewhat intelligent being and had to hunt for survival, wouldn't you use the land to your advantage?"

Jim's eyes lit up. "You're right. It's not far from here."

Sam yanked the cord on the snowmobile, and the engine roared back to life. He hit the throttle lever and moved forward zig-zagging through the pinion pine and cedar. The snowdrifts were piled high in the areas directly surrounding the trees, but the sleds had no trouble negotiating the undulating terrain.

Sasquatch, Bigfoot, Yeti. All names for the same type of

creature. Where did it come from? Where does it live or better yet, *how* does it live? It's said to be a large, bipedal beast with apelike features that lives in remote wilderness areas. Some say it's an ancient beast leftover from the last ice age. Some believe it to be pure myth, folklore designed for bedtime stories to keep children from acting up, the boogie-man will get you. Those in the scientific world have routinely dismissed the entire idea of the existence of such a being and consider most eyewitness accounts as misidentification or hoaxes. For those that have had firsthand experiences, the beast is real, flesh and blood, intelligent enough to be a cunning and skilled hunter. Also, terrifying, brutal, and dangerous.

Sam guided the snowmobile over the snow-packed mountain pass, through a stand of cedars and out onto a ridgeline free of trees. Lots of small shrubs dotted the landscape, but visibility was clear for quite some distance. From their vantage point, they could see down into the arroyo below and how the ridgeline traced the outer rim. There was an old logging road hidden somewhere in the trees far below that hunters would use from time to time, but it took horses or snowmobiles to navigate into the back-country area now. It didn't take long for nature to reclaim the land.

The wind was much stronger up on the ridge, and colder. The sun was hidden behind the blue-gray sky, but there was still enough daylight to continue the hunt. Once the sunset, it would get dark rapidly. They would need to be back on the trail to the north ridge above the lodge within the next half-hour if they wanted to make it back before dark.

Jim raced up beside Sam and shouted, "The trail turns down into the gap just up ahead by that overhang. We should be able to get down there just fine, coming back up will be the hard part. Probably have to circle back around near the falls to be on the safe side."

"Okay, you lead us down," Sam shouted back.

Jim saw the familiar landmarks and guided his sled down the treacherous slope with expertise. He grew up, as most did that lived in the area, riding snowmobiles over the rugged countryside. Though it was beautiful with magnificent views all around, the mountains were also very dangerous. One wrong move could cost someone their life.

When they arrived at the base of the slope, the terrain smoothed out and led into the forest. They once again found their way through the maze of trees. Soon, they came upon a small clearing where a small cabin stood in the middle of the natural wind-break of pinyon pines. The cabin was a small one room with a rock chimney on the east side. The structure was still standing, which was a remarkable feat considering its age. The chinking was missing in several places, and the only door of the cabin lay rotting on the inside floor, hinges busted by wind or animals. The roof had given way long ago, and the structure was slowly being overtaken by nature.

The rangers split up and rode the outside perimeter looking for tracks or sign of recent activity before stopping at the open doorway.

"I didn't see anything at all, but then again, it's snowed what…at least six to eight inches in the last week. Could've covered anything before then," Jim said.

Sam killed the engine on his sled and stepped over to the door and tested the wooden flooring.

"Yeah, I didn't see anything either. Doesn't look like anything but raccoons and squirrels have been in here for a while," Sam said, standing in the doorway.

Jim stood, pulled out his binoculars, and scanned the area around them. "Too dark to see anything." He breathed in and out, his breath hanging in the night air. "And to be honest, I've got a weird feeling about this place," he said, pulling out his SureFire flashlight and shining it all around. As powerful as the light was, it did little to penetrate the thick forest.

Sam looked around at the forest, scanning for anything out of the ordinary. "Yeah, I have to agree," Sam said. "Gives me the heebie-jeebies!"

"It'll take us the better part of an hour or more to get back to the rendezvous spot. Guess we should call in and get going."

Sam took one last look around the inside of the cabin. When he turned back to the doorway, he froze in his tracks. The hairs on the back of his neck spiked.

It started as a soft wail that sounded halfway between a shriek and a roar. It lasted several seconds before trailing off. A few seconds later it came again, but this time it sounded more like mountain lions fighting, snarling, growling and gnashing at one another.

"Dear lord, what the hell is that? Cougar?" Jim said.

"Doesn't sound like any cat I've ever heard," Sam said, instinctively reaching for his sidearm for reassurance. "Sounds like it's coming from the ridgeline further west, but can't be sure with this wind."

"Therein lies the bad news. That's the direction we need to go in order to get back up."

"I don't wanna jinx us, but that may very well be what we're out here for," Jim whispered, scanning through the trees more intently with the binoculars.

"I'll radio the others." Sam keyed the radio mic on his shoulder, "Sheriff Blaine, do you copy?"

Static

"Sheriff Blaine, do you copy? This is Ranger Lazaro, come in Sheriff."

Static

Sam rubbed the back of his neck, a worried look on his face.

"I bet being down here in this canyon the ridge is blocking the signal. Probably have to get back up top before we can get through to 'em."

"It's already dark, and I'll be honest, whatever the hell *that* is, I don't want to tangle with it at night. Let's get back and get the others, make a plan for tomorrow. Make sure you have your sidearm ready."

Jim put the powerful flashlight away, straddled the sled, and gave the rope a quick pull. The engine pinged to life.

"I'm with ya," Sam said, following suit with his machine.

***

It was dark when Michelle saw the lights. Four bright white headlamps with four dull red taillamps shined brightly on the snow-covered trail and made a beeline for the four by fours that had been parked for most of the day. The sleds came from behind the lodge. She had moved over to a comfortable sofa in front of one of the huge fireplaces with an open book, pretending to read while she waited. She still had a good view of the trucks and trailers at the far end of the parking lot. She knew the men must have circled the lodge because they left in the opposite direction this morning. *They must be doing a perimeter search*, she thought. *No other reason for them to have circled back like that. Surely the damn things aren't coming this close to a heavily populated area.*

The hardware she saw the men packing suggested that

what her friend told her this morning was accurate. Ithaca Mag tens have more than enough stopping power to bring down anything, and the Benelli M4's were beasts. They were armed for war. There were six that went out this morning.

She walked down to simply inquire as to what brought them out and see if they would clue her in. She wanted in on it but wasn't going to bust Lindsey out by telling them how she heard about it.

***

The fatwood caught fire quickly, and Leon began building the fire up bigger by adding dried pieces of driftwood he found in the den. It became apparent why the den was uninhabited once he began looking around. It wasn't a den at all; it was a cut-out fissure in the rocks from the thousands of years of snowmelt from the mountain. Snow and ice had covered the top area and created a nice dugout in the rocky mountainside. Leon was able to use a long stick and poke a hole through the ice above. The smoke from the fire drifted lazily out through it and quickly dissipated on the cold wind once it reached the surface. He had dressed in layers the morning he left and had removed a yellow shirt, stuck it on a stick and stabbed it into the ground above the dugout. With any luck at all, anyone searching for him would see either the smoke from the fire or the shirt.

Leon watched the smoke rise to the top of the fissure, out through the hole above and disappear. The iced-over roof made for an eerie skylight casting crazy shadows over the cut-out granite. The mouth of the small den was just big enough to allow him to crawl inside, but he ripped his coat on a sharp jagged edge of rock when he scrambled through. He wasn't too worried about surviving the weather out in the wild, his thoughts were more about what his wife, Tammy, would be going through. *She must be worried sick*, he thought. But she was smart, and if the snowmobile rental place didn't report him missing, she would have by the time the first evening rolled around and he hadn't come back. The only problem was he didn't tell her what he was up to or where he was going. They had no idea where to search.

The last of the strained sunlight faded, turning the dull gray sky into inky blackness. No moon or stars could penetrate the overcast leaving Leon feeling more alone and isolated than ever before.

Leon lay with his back against the cold wall and stared into the fire. The glow from the small yellow flames danced on the stone floor, and tiny sparks popped and sizzled as pieces of the partially wet wood dried. His abode for the evening wasn't necessarily warm and cozy, but the small fire staved off the issue of hypothermia, and the small cave opening kept the bitter cold wind from reaching him.

He tried sleeping, but it was no use. The best he could do was doze for a few minutes at a time. The wind, brutal and relentless, passed over the mountain picking up more chill as it swept along, and whisked down into the darkness like a sharpened blade of ice cleaving off pieces of earth on its way. He had to stay out of it during the night, but he was restless. He looked over at the small opening and let his eyes adjust to the black. He was drawn to the cave mouth like a person nearing a cliff's edge had to peer over knowing exactly what was below. He crawled over to it and clambered out. He wanted to look around. His small flashlight was bright against the pure white snow, but it didn't shine very far. It would be no use trying to use it to signal for help unless someone was very nearby. He hunkered against the rock face and stared out into the night. It took a few minutes, but soon his eyes adjusted to the night sky and he saw a soft orange haze in the distance. His heart felt like it jumped into his throat. He smiled. He would be okay now because he knew which direction the city of Hawthorn lay, and it wasn't as far as he first suspected.

I can make it, he thought. *Soon as daylight comes.*

At one point, he thought he heard a snowmobile, but he couldn't be sure because of the wind. Leon stood and stretched before he had to get back inside the cramped quarters of the cave. That's when he heard it. A shrieking howl lasting for several seconds repeating twice more before dying away, followed by *whoop whoop.* The hairs on his entire body stood, shrinking his skin even tighter than the freezing temperature did. It wasn't a sound like anything he had ever heard. He couldn't tell how far away it was, but it was close. Too close!

He put a few more pieces of wood on the fire, saving one long stick about four feet long. He didn't have much wood left other than the snowshoes. Using his knife, he whittled the end into a spear point. It wouldn't be much protection, but it was better than nothing. Looking around, he found a couple of rocks that he used to help cover the entrance. When he was done, there was a small opening about the size of a basketball left. He emptied his gear bag and shoved it into the hole before scrambling to the back of the cave. He kept the short spear on his lap with his hunting knife at his side. And he waited.

23

The fire burned low, and the temperature had dropped even more. Leon shuddered awake and put the last few sticks on the small flames along with the snowshoes. He had no way of knowing what time it was or how long he had dozed this time. For that matter, he had no idea what it was that woke him. Perhaps the cold chill of the small stone cave.

He heard something just outside the entrance. He held the short spear in one hand and reached for the hunting knife laying beside him.

He heard it again. Rocks tumbling away as if pitched aside. A low guttural growl followed by what sounded like sniffing or panting. He was beginning to second guess going out alone. Whatever it was, wanted in.

***

Michelle drained the last of her hot tea, tugged her coat and beanie on and exited the restaurant via the parking lot entrance. When she arrived at the trucks, the sheriff had just ratcheted down the snowmobiles on the back of the trailer and jumped down.

"Hey Evers, what brings you up to the lodge?" he asked.

"Just having a little dinner and enjoying the day off, Sheriff," she said. "What's up? Apparently, no word on the missing person?"

"No, nothing yet. We just finished a perimeter search. Turned up nothing."

"Wasn't the sled he rented found over near Beckman Ridge?" she asked.

"Sure, but if he was staying at the lodge, I figure he may have tried to make his way back. Mountain Patrol is covering the other areas. We'll keep searching 'til we find him. Matter of fact, when you come in tomorrow, prepare to work a double."

"You got it."

Billy walked over and joined them as they talked.

"Hey Billy," she said in greeting him. She smiled at him. When the sheriff turned away, she gestured with her eyes at Troy, who was just walking up.

Billy knew what she meant.

"Oh hey, have you met Troy Turner?" Billy asked.

After Billy made the introductions, he found an excuse to turn away. Something about the snowmobiles.

"So, you're the writer, right?" Michelle smiled as they shook hands.

"Sometimes. I'm also a reserve deputy so I guess that makes us co-workers," Troy smiled. "It's very nice to meet you."

Michelle could hear the sheriff on the radio trying to raise the rangers that still hadn't made it back in yet. Zeus had pounced over the snow, ran behind the trucks and came out on top of the trailer where he jumped back on the warm platform of the snowmobile that he had ridden all day on.

"It's nice to meet you too. I've seen you around the

office before, but haven't had a chance to say hi yet," she said. She desperately wanted to steer the conversation to the hunt. "So, did you see anything while you were out today?"

"No, no sign of the guy at all. At least not once you get some distance away from the lodge in the more remote areas. We made a sweep of the entire area, but came up with notta."

"That's too bad," she said.

"That sidearm you're carrying, that looks pretty big for a search party, Mag 10's, the Benelli? Awful lot of firepower for a search party."

Troy paused a moment before replying.

"Never can be too careful up in the mountains. I've ran across mountain lions the size of a horse. If you'll excuse me, I need to check on my dog."

Michelle found Billy, who was standing beside the open door of the truck racking his gear inside and securing his shotgun. He turned to her when she came over.

"That was a quick conversation," he said.

"Yeah, but it was long enough." She grabbed his elbow. "What were you really doing out there, Billy Larsen? I know you weren't out looking for a missing person on this side of the mountain. What gives?"

Billy shook her hand off and spun back to his gear bag in the truck.

"No telling where the guy is. You know as well as I do, he could be anywhere."

"You're lying through your teeth," she whispered emphatically. "I know better. I know what you were doing. I know *what* you're hunting. I told you before. I want in!"

Billy spun around. "No way, no way in hell, Michelle. It's too dangerous."

"Bull! I can handle myself out there, and I guarantee you I can shoot as well as any man here!"

"I'm not trying to be sexist for Pete's sake. I'm just trying to be realistic."

"What's going on?" Sheriff Blaine was standing at the back of the SUV.

"Nothing, Sheriff," Billy said squeamishly.

Michelle turned to the sheriff and looked him straight in the eyes. With a hardened look, she said, "Bigfoot? I want in."

Blaine stomped over the snow to stand in front of the two deputies.

"How did she find out?" he asked glancing at Billy.

"Don't look at me, Sheriff, I didn't say a word."

"It doesn't matter how I found out; I just want in on it."

Blaine turned back to the deputies and repeated what Billy had said.

"Too dangerous. You have no idea."

"The hell I don't!" Michelle flared. "If you won't let me in on it officially, then I'll have no choice but to do so unofficially."

The sheriff's direct gaze told her she had gone too far. He was angry, but to his credit, he held his temper at the young deputy. It had been a long stressful day, and he needed to calm down before he spoke.

Michelle stood quietly but defiant. She knew she had pushed on his good nature and went too far. She shouldn't have spoken that way to her boss, but she was adamant about going on the hunt.

Nick never turned around, he walked away and over his shoulder, said tersely, "My office at seven sharp. Don't even think about being late."

***

Leon held his breath and waited. He could see his gear back stuffed into the hole in the rocks from the firelight. It wasn't much light in the darkened den, but it was enough to see that he had nowhere to go.

More growling and heavy breathing. The creature, whatever it was, was near the mouth of the den. Leon prayed silently that it wouldn't find the hole. He had done his best to plug it to keep any of the light from the fire from being seen from outside. The heavy breathing and grunting sound suddenly stopped. Leon held his spear tightly and flexed the muscles in his legs that were cold and stiff from the cramped quarters. He had no idea if he would be able to fend off anything, but he was determined to fight no matter.

The backpack moved. It was slight, but he was sure it had moved. He stared at it hard. Nothing. Maybe it was the weird shadows playing on the rough granite walls. Then, it moved again. It was sliding out of the hole. His breath caught. If it fell out, it would expose him to whatever it was out there hunting him. He had to shore it up. He put the spear down, and tucked the hunting knife into the sheath at his side, and slowly crawled to the entrance. It was no more than ten feet away, but it seemed to take forever to get there.

He heard more grunting and heavy breathing, but it seemed to have moved a little further away though he couldn't be sure. Still, on his hands and knees, he reached up to the pack to push it back in place. The canvas ruffled when he pushed on it making a scraping noise. It wasn't loud, but it was loud enough to make his stomach churn a bit more. He tucked one of the straps behind a rock to help hold it in place against the wind, then dropped back to his hands and knees. The sleeve of his coat caught on another strap dangling from the bag that he didn't see, and when he dropped down, he dragged the bag out of the hole altogether. He panicked and froze.

A loud screeching roar, unlike anything he had ever heard before, shattered the night. A huge arm completely covered in long coarse hair reached inside grabbing for him. The screaming continued at an ear-piercing level like a pack of wild snarling dogs, ferociously attacking its prey.

Leon, finally able to move, scrambled to the back of the small granite cave. The extra padding in his outer-layer ski pants wasn't much protection against the rough edges of the rocky cave floor, but he didn't notice. Fear and adrenaline wouldn't allow him to feel the pain in his knees. He grabbed for his spear and saw how useless it would be trying to fend off the beast.

The fire had consumed most of the wood, and the little glow flickered with just enough light to see the creature's arm. It was huge, the size of an eight-inch steel pipe. The long, sinewy muscles were powerful, and Leon could feel the strength of the beast each time it pounded against the stone walls grasping at a way in.

Fortunately for Leon, the opening of the cave was far too small for the giant beast to get inside. The granite wouldn't give, and Leon was just out of range of the long arms.

The beast pulled back, and Leon thought it may be leaving, giving up, but it screamed again and pounded on the outside of the opening. The rock didn't budge. Looking around the cave floor, there was nothing left to use if the rock gave way, the beast could easily kill him. The fire was but a small flicker now, and with no ambient light from the moon or stars, the darkness would soon engulf him. The creature pulled its arm out. Leon watched the hole carefully. He thought he could see movement just outside, but couldn't be sure. He inched closer. A loud, ferocious scream reverberated off the granite walls inside the cave, and the ugly, grotesque face, appeared at the opening. The mouth of the beast seemed as wide as its face lined with viciously sharp teeth-gnashing and grimacing at him. The eyes were large red orbs set deep under a prominent low ridge brow line.

The wooden spear seemed minuscule and could barely be considered a weapon against the Sasquatch. The backpack had nothing left in it. He had emptied its contents to carry woodfat and dry sticks for the fire. *The contents? The camera!* he thought. *The flash!*

The camera lay against the wall, nearer the opening than the back of the cave. If the Sasquatch could see it and want it, it could easily grab it, so Leon had to use the spear to reach out for it and pull it to him with the strap.

The screaming roar of the beast was terrifying, reverberating off the cave walls, and the look of pure hatred on the grotesque face was petrifying. Using the spear, Leon reached out for the strap of the camera trying to stay out of reach of the beast. He couldn't see the strap very well as the light of the small fire wasn't much help. He would be plunged into complete darkness any moment now. The long powerful arm reached through the entrance grabbing for him. Leon felt a heavy resistance on the stick and dragged on the camera. After a few attempts, he was successful and fumbled with the switch on top and pushed it to the on position. The screen powered on, He quickly moved it to night photography, aimed it at the creature and waited for it to look inside again.

He didn't have to wait long. The last flickers of the firelight illuminated the entrance just enough to see the beast. Leon clicked the button, and the strobe flashed a blinding white light several times as the shutter opened in rapid succession. The creature roared and rubbed at its eyes, staggering backward. Leon pushed forward and clicked the button again aiming the camera at the entrance, closing his own eyes as he did. The beast screamed in rage but shrunk away in fear of the flashing light. One more click, and finally, the creature fled down the ridgeline trail. Leon fell against the cave wall and exhaled.

He woke disoriented in the pitch dark of the cave. He didn't know how long he had been asleep. It could've been a few seconds, a couple of minutes or even an hour or two. Leon felt the cold and his entire body trembled. The wind had changed directions blowing across the wide-open entrance of the cave, making a low-pitched whistle. He waited a moment to let his mind clear before moving. Not that moving was an effort easily carried out. He was stiff from the cold.

He lay next to the fire in a fetal position, but all that remained were a few small embers glowing in the darkness. A buzzing noise from outside grew in pitch, but he was much too exhausted to care. His mind couldn't fully register it. He closed his eyes and slept.

***

"Hey Sam, hold up a minute," Jim shouted. "What's that over there?"

Sam pulled up on the throttle, coming to a stop. Jim pulled his machine up next to his. They had been riding for fifteen minutes skirting the bottom of the ridgeline looking for the trail to lead them back up when Jim spotted the lights.

"Looks like sleds, but pretty far off," Sam shouted over the blat of the engines. "That's gotta be the trail out of here. Let's check it out."

"I'll lead," Jim said.

***

She never should have spoken to her boss like that, but she was impassioned about the subject. Hopefully he would understand and by the time she reported in tomorrow, he would have forgotten all about it. The last thing she wanted to do was to have to explain herself and why she was so adamant about going with them.

She unlocked her car and got in. She started it, shifted it into drive and pulled out of the parking lot. When she got to the road, she noticed two sets of lights coming from a different direction from behind the lodge. *Must be the others coming in*, she thought. *I'll plead my case in the morning. He's gotta let me in. Or at least feel sorry for me.*

***

He felt his body being lifted and moved, but he couldn't say or do anything. He was much too weak and exhausted. He could barely keep his eyes open. Everywhere the hands touched him, it hurt. The pain was sharp and intense, but there was nothing he could do to stop it. Then, he was floating.

***

The lights had disappeared over the ridge by the time they found the trail. The night air was cold, and their breath billowed out through their balaclavas like thick clouds of fog. Jim maneuvered his sled up and over the jagged terrain until he spotted the tracks and pulled up short.

"This is definitely the trail they followed up. Whoever it is knows their way around these parts. I might've missed it."

Sam stood on his machine, looking around with the aid of his headlights and flashlight. "Looks like there were several of 'em."

"I'd say there were at least six sleds from what I could count, but they were a long way off."

"Surely it wasn't a search party all the way out here," Sam said incredulously.

"Nah, no way. But they were stopped here for a long time. They had to have seen us coming. Why wouldn't they have waited?"

"No idea," Sam said. He turned off his engine and dismounted.

Jim also killed his engine and got off. The men searched the area for any clue. Ten minutes later, they returned to their machines. Sam tried calling the sheriff on the radio again but only received static.

"I just don't get it. Whoever they were, they were doing something right here, but what?"

"Hey check this out! That's blood!" Jim shouted.

Dark crimson stained the rocks nearby, and several boot prints had trampled the snow down. Sam hurried over to see. He was shining his light looking for more when he spotted the opening. He climbed up on the rocks and shined his light inside.

Jim watched as his partner disappeared inside the small opening.

"I've got something," Sam shouted.

Sheriff Blaine sat in the truck beside Troy when the call came in.

"Sheriff Blaine, this is Ranger Lazaro, do you copy?"

"This is Blaine, go ahead."

"Sheriff, we found something. On our way now. ETA twenty minutes."

Billy heard the radio call. "Sheriff, I'll run up to the lodge and grab some coffee for everyone. I'm sure we could all use it."

"Thanks, Billy," Nick said.

It took the rangers nearly half an hour to get back to the trucks.

"Sorry, it took so long. We're practically on fumes now. We lost radio contact down in that canyon, but Jim wanted to check out the old surveyor's cabin before we circled back in," Lazaro said. "Good thing we did."

Nick looked at his watch. It was nearly 9 p.m.

"What'd ya find?" he asked.

"This," Jim said, holding up a camera bag. "Didn't want to say anything over the radio, but the missing guy's name's on it. Leon Souter, right here on the leather tab. Found this and a camera laying in a corner of a small cave. Looks like he had been holed up there for a while. Had a fire in there at one point. Tried to power up the camera, but it's dead. Not sure if it's broken or just dead, but get this…"

The rangers relayed the events of the evening to the sheriff and the deputies. They all came to the same conclusion. Search party must've found Leon, but the sasquatch wasn't far behind and probably tracking them.

"No way we're going back out tonight, but we need to find that damned thing before it kills someone," Nick said.

"Let's get some sleep and get back out in the morning. Sounds like that canyon is the place to concentrate our hunt."

"Your office in the morning Sheriff?" Lazaro asked.

"You bet, let's pack it up, fellas."

Nick closed the door to the truck, buckled his seat belt and pulled out of the lodge parking lot. Zeus had climbed into the back and was already fast asleep while Troy examined the camera the rangers had found.

"This thing's dinged up a little, but it seems to be okay. I'm sure it's just a dead battery. I'm curious as to what's on it if anything."

"When we get back to the office, we'll see if we have anything to charge it. It's a Nikon, so I'm sure we do," Nick said.

The sheriff reached for the radio and called in to dispatch to let them know they were in route back to the office, then asked to be patched through to Mountain Patrol. A voice answered on the other end a moment later.

"Patrol, station three, go ahead, Sheriff."

"Can you give me an update on the BOLO for one Leon Souter?"

"Not much of one. Just got word that he'd been located safe and sound and reunited with family. BOLO was lifted not more than fifteen minutes ago."

"Just got word? It wasn't your patrol team that found him?"

"No sir, BOLO was canceled at State. That's all we have right now. You might try back in the morning. Maybe we'll have more information by then."

"Roger that."

Nick hung the mic back up on the dash.

"Well, that's interesting."

"Why's that?" Troy asked.

"Why would the BOLO be canceled at the state level when it was Mountain Patrol that initiated it?"

"Who knows," Troy said, reclining back in the seat. "I'm exhausted."

24

Leon Souter was sedated and immobilized for the ride over the mountain. He wouldn't wake anytime soon. The six men he was with were all dressed in black fatigues and cold weather gear. They wore automatic weapons strapped to their backs along with night-vision equipment and FLIR cameras.

The leader of the group studied the mobile data terminal mounted to his snowmobile, made an adjustment and uploaded data with a punch of a few buttons then motioned his team to move out.

***

Michelle lay in bed, staring at the ceiling. She couldn't sleep. When she looked at the alarm clock on the bedside table, it glowed a bright red, 1:27 A.M. She punched her pillow, released a heavy sigh and rolled over to face the wall. It wasn't the meeting with the sheriff in the morning that worried her. It was missing an opportunity to join the hunting party.

As Billy had suggested during their lunch a few days before, she had read the reports submitted by the department of the incident that happened nearly five years ago. It wasn't bears that had attacked them. She knew better, knew first hand what these creatures were capable of. They were bloodthirsty, evil beings. She had no doubt that their habitation had been encroached upon, but given a choice, a typical animal would seek deeper recesses in which to hide, not band together and create an all-out frontal assault. No, these are not simply animals, they are much more than that, they're apex predators, bigger, stronger, and much faster than anything she had ever seen or heard about.

The sheriff and all those with him were lucky that night. They had the protection of a well-built log cabin to withstand the siege. They also had numbers. From all accounts, they had a minimum of five excellent marksmen, hunters that knew how to handle firearms, and they had plenty of guns and ammo. When the Sasquatch attacked her and her friends, they were sitting ducks. Only one person had a gun. They were no match for the beasts. Michelle's best friend, Jennifer, was killed that night. Michelle could never forget that night of terror. Her mind drifted away to that event as she lay in bed staring into the darkness.

It was a beautiful day in late spring when Michelle and her best friend, Jennifer, chanced upon three men while hiking near Idaho Springs. The men had been searching for signs of an old gold mine when their GPS was broken, and they became lost. It was pure luck that Michelle and Jennifer found them. After hearing their story, they all decided to give their adventure another shot and set out to find the lost mine. That's when her whole world exploded into a nightmare that she would relive every day of her life.

The group found the campsite in the remote wilderness. The setting was pristine, a beautiful valley, a long, meandering river running through it, and a gold mine. It was too perfect. They set up camp and that very night is when the Sasquatch attacked. The small company had found a cave behind a waterfall and thought they could hide from the beasts in there. Little did they know that the creatures used the cave as a den. It was dark when they attacked, ripping Jennifer's throat out before she could scream. One of the men got off several shots with a pistol, but it was no use. There were too many of them and not enough bullets. The screams of that terrifying night echoed through her head now. The evil rage of the beasts along with the cries of panic and terror of her friends were numbing.

Michelle survived when she was knocked into the falls. The rapid churning water below pushed her far below the surface. Being an excellent athlete, she swam as hard and as fast as she could. For some reason, the sasquatch never came after her. She was quite some distance down the fast-flowing river when she spotted two of the creatures on the far bank. At that point, she was clinging to a floating log without the strength to swim to shore, and after seeing the creatures on the banks, she preferred the water. The Sasquatch was huge with long arms and powerful shoulders and stood at least eight feet tall. They were heavily muscled, which is why she believed, they never entered the water to come after her. They paced her as she floated down the river, for how long she had no clue. She woke sometime later lying on the gravel shoreline not far from a public camping area where she was found by other campers. Though rescuers had searched for days, her friends had never been seen again. That was seven years ago. It was only two years that she learned of the attack at Hawthorn which was not far from Idaho Springs. It had to be the same clan of Sasquatch. There was no other explanation. She wanted revenge plain and simple. Revenge not only for her friend but for the mental scars they left her with.

Michelle endured nightmare after nightmare, unable to eat, sleep or function normally. Professional therapists never believed her story, and neither did any of the authorities. They eventually said that they must have been killed by bears. No bodies had ever been discovered.

At first, she resented the therapy, but now she was thankful for it. She had learned ways to cope, to deal with her fears and anger. She learned to control it, to focus. When she was strong enough, she took lessons in martial arts, survival, and even weapons training. She trained extensively with several master instructors. She could shoot any gun with expert marksmanship. She was more than ready for the task at hand. Her mission was to overcome her weaknesses. Now her new goal was to find the source of those fears, face it down - and eliminate it.

Regardless of whether the sheriff would let her in on the hunt, she knew for certainty now that the Sasquatch was in the area. That's what she was waiting on. The sheriff had to let her in on it.

The alarm clock buzzed startling her. She rolled over and slapped the button on top to turn it off then dragged herself to the shower.

***

Sheriff Blaine walked out of the hotel lobby, got in his waiting cruiser and drove back to his office. He dialed the number for Mountain Patrol. It was answered before the first ring ended.

"Mountain Patrol, this is Stan."

"Good morning, Stan, Sheriff Blaine here. I called and talked with your dispatch last night. I understand you found the missing person, or *someone* found him anyway. Is that true?" Nick asked.

"I couldn't tell ya, Nick. Matter of fact, I thought it was your guys that found him when I got the call to stand down yesterday."

Nick could hear Stan breathing on the other end and the fast typing on a keyboard.

"BOLO was canceled around noon," Stan said. "You sure it wasn't one of your boys that found him?"

"No, it wasn't us," Nick started, "Wait a minute. Did you say the BOLO was canceled at noon yesterday?"

"Yeah, I called off the search soon as I got the word."

"Stan, we were out on the mountain all day yesterday, there were two birds flying the whole time. Are you saying those weren't yours?"

"Hell no, I have one that I can barely afford fuel for, let alone two. We were grounded all day."

"If it wasn't MP and it wasn't my guys, then who the hell was it? The state didn't have anyone on the mountain that I'm aware of."

"Damn good question, but I honestly have no clue. Sorry, Nick. There's nothing on the system other than the cancellation of the BOLO. Nothing at all."

"I'm just leaving the hotel now, and apparently he and his wife checked out late last night. What the hell is going on, Stan?"

"Another good question to which I have no plausible explanation for. But to be perfectly honest, the guy was an adult, wasn't any kind of skiing accident or car wreck, avalanche or anything like that. I'm not too worried about it. The only thing that bothers me is the fact that my

BOLO was canceled by another agency."

"I tend to agree. Well, I'm going to wash my hands of it. Good talking to ya, Stan."

"You too, Nick. Talk to you later, buddy."

The sheriff hung the phone up and leaned back in his chair, rubbing the back of his neck. Suddenly, a thought occurred to him. He stood and walked to the filing cabinet and pulled the missing person's report. He flipped through the pages and found the phone number for the wife. A moment later, a woman's voice answered.

"Hello?"

"Good morning. Is this Mrs. Souter?

"Um, Yes, it is. Who's calling?"

"I'm sorry to bother you this early in the morning, Mrs. Souter but this is Sheriff Blaine of Hawthorn County. I understand that your husband was found last night? I just wanted to give you a call and check on him. How is he doing?"

"Good morning, Sheriff Blaine. It's no bother at all. Yes, he came in late last night and is perfectly fine. He ran out of gas and got turned around when he tried walking back for help. But he's back now and resting."

"That's great news," Nick said.

"I appreciate you following up, but I'm afraid I'm terribly busy now. If you'll excuse me, I really need to get back."

"Yes, ma'am. Oh, just one more thing if you don't mind. Rangers found his backpack and some camera gear on the mountain, has his name on it, shall I have someone drop it at the hotel? I'm afraid it appears busted, though."

He knew she had already checked out. He heard her hesitate a moment.

"No, no that's alright, Sheriff. It's not a big deal. You

have my permission to dispose of it. We've already left town, and the equipment was old anyway." the woman said.

"Whatever you wish, Mrs. Souter. Thank you for your time."

Nick hung up the phone, then flipped through the report. The sled was found with nearly a full tank of fuel. The man had bought an extra can of fuel. Things were not adding up. Why would she lie about that?

His office door was closed, but he heard the outer door open, feet stamping off snow and the thud of it closing behind the person. He glanced at the clock, ten minutes past seven. He turned back to the map he was studying. A soft knock came on his office door. He didn't hear it. The second rap on the door frame was harder and the door opened slightly.

"Oh, sorry Tim, guess I was lost in thought," Nick said.

"No worries, Sheriff. Lindsey said you wanted to see me first thing?" Deputy Severs said.

"Yeah, have you heard back from forensics yet about any of the evidence we collected at the car wreck?"

"Actually, no, I haven't. Should be someone in the office now. I'll go give 'em a call."

"Okay, let me know as soon as you hear back."

The young deputy closed the sheriff's door and walked to his desk and sat down. A few minutes later, he didn't bother knocking on the sheriff's door. He barged right in.

"Uh, Sheriff, you're not gonna believe this, but the lab is saying they never received the evidence. I swear to you, I tagged it correctly and sent it straight away the other day!"

"Who did you talk to?" Nick asked.

"The lady I just talked to was Dr. Karla Everett. She said she never received anything from our office. I know for a fact that it was bagged, tagged, and recorded properly. I put in on the van and dropped it off myself at the front desk."

"Go pull the receipt and let's see who signed for it."

The deputy turned and hurried away to retrieve the paper. Nick picked up the phone and dialed the number for the state police headquarters. He hung up just as Deputy Severs returned with the piece of paper.

"Here it is. Can't really make out the signature, to be honest. You know how doctors are, can't take enough time out of their *busy* schedules to sign anything legible," Tim said, handing the paper to the sheriff.

The sheriff studied the paper then picked up the phone and dialed the number to the lab himself. After a brief conversation with the same lady that Severs spoke with, he slammed the phone down in the cradle.

"Dammit! What the hell is going on?" Nick growled.

"Should we come back?"

The sheriff looked up to see the two Rangers standing in the doorway, accompanied by Troy.

"Sorry fellas, come on in. We seem to have a serious issue going on," Nick said.

"What's the problem?" Troy asked.

"First, the couple that was in the car wreck disappears from the hospital without a trace. They just vanish into thin air. The hospital never even heard of 'em apparently. Then the car vanishes right out from under us within a matter of hours."

Just then, Deputies Chastain and Larsen stepped in and closed the door.

"Come in. Close the door, Billy."

Michelle parked her car, looked in the rearview mirror, and with an exasperated sigh, shut off the engine. She practiced her argument all the way to the office. She would apologize for her outburst first thing, but then make her case by explaining why it was she felt she should be allowed into the *inner circle* as she liked to call it.

When she opened the door, the cold north wind blew frozen snow off the top of the car. The tiny pellets found their way down her open coat and melted on the exposed skin of her neck and shoulders. She shivered, zipped her coat up, and pulled on a beanie. She grabbed her bag out of the back seat and slowly made her way into the front door of the sheriff's office.

"Good morning, Linds," Michelle said as she closed the door behind her.

"Good morning, Sunshine," Lindsey said.

"Sheriff in yet?"

A serious look came over Lindsey's face. "Yeah, but he's not happy. The others are in his office with him. I can't hear what's going on, but I can tell you that I wouldn't wanna be a part of it."

"Great, just freakin' peachy," Michelle said, glancing at the office door. She looked at the clock on the wall. She was supposed to be at his office in three minutes.

"You planning on going in there?" Lindsey asked.

"Yeah, 'Fraid so," Michelle said, biting her lip. "Guess I better get it over with."

The good news was the fact that the other deputies were already in there. Maybe he would be hesitant to come down on her too harshly. Or so she thought. As she neared the inner office door, she could hear the sheriff, and he didn't sound happy.

"Now, we have a missing person that's been found, which is great, but who the hell found him. I went over to the hotel this morning where they were staying. They checked out yesterday morning. Here's something else, the BOLO was canceled yesterday just before noon. Now, tell me, if he wasn't found until last night, why the hell would anyone cancel it eight hours before he was found?"

"What?" Billy said.

"Yeah, I just got off the phone with Stan at Mountain Patrol. He's pissed that someone canceled his BOLO without going through him. It wasn't us; it wasn't him," Nick paused, his hands on his hips. "So, who the hell was it?"

"Well, maybe it's not such a big deal after all. I mean, the guy was found safe and sound, that frees us up to hunt. Right?" Deputy Chastain said.

"No, it doesn't. Here's another damn problem with this whole scenario. Tim drove the evidence over to Boulder and signed it in, only when we called this morning to check on the progress, they claim they never received it. So, now, there's no evidence of what we're dealing with. Fellas, there's something going on, and I want answers!" Nick all but shouted, slamming his palm down hard on his desk.

A knock at the office door silenced the men.

"What?" Sheriff Blaine growled.

The office door creaked open slowly.

"Sorry to interrupt," Michelle said.

Nick eased up and waved her inside. A few minutes later, she was caught up with everything that had transpired over the course of the last few days. Not a word was said about last night.

"So, now what?" Lazaro asked.

"I don't think we can afford to let all this drop. That damned thing is still out there, and for all we know, it could be stalking its next victim," Nick replied. "Regardless of anything else, our first priority is to protect this town!"

A half-hour later the group had all parked near the Buckhorn Lodge and were in the process of unloading their snowmobiles when Lisa Richards pulled into the parking lot. She parked near the sheriff's patrol unit and got out.

"What's all this about, Dad?" she asked. "They already found the missing man."

Nick gave his daughter a hug. "Well, we're going to do some scouting around. The missing man may have been found, but we still have a bear possibly still prowling around a little too close. We just want to make sure everyone's safe and having a good time. No need for alarm."

"Oh, okay. Makes sense I suppose, but when's the last time we've had a bear sighting this close to the slopes?"

"Exactly," He laughed. "No need to start now."

"Well, happy hunting. Too cold for me," she said, holding her arms and stamping in the snow to stay warm. "I'm headed to the office. I need to get ready for the big grand opening celebration tomorrow night. Hope you have your suit pressed," she said with a wry smile.

"You know I do," he grinned.

Troy revved the engine on his sled, backed it off the trailer and pulled around to say hi to Lisa before joining the others.

"Don't wanna keep ya, just saying good morning," he said.

Zeus wasted no time jumping on the carpeted back seat of the black and green snowmobile. The cold didn't bother the big dog unless he had to walk in the snow and ice too much. Troy wouldn't let that happen.

"Good morning, Troy," Lisa said. "Good luck on your hunting trip...or, should I say hope you have no luck at all?"

"That's what I'm hoping for," he said. He smiled at her.

She smiled back but then turned serious. "Hey, do me a favor. Keep an eye on the old man, would ya? I worry about him."

Troy gave her a reassuring look. "You know, I will."

"Good, and you be careful too."

"I always am," Troy said.

"I was talking to Zeus," she laughed as she petted the big dog on the head.

Lisa got back in her car and drove off. Troy hit the throttle of the sled and joined the others.

25

"We'll split up into two teams," the sheriff explained. "Team one will take the northern route above the lodge before meeting up at noon with team two taking the southern route below the lodge at the old surveyor's cabin in the canyon. That ridge is where the missing man was *possibly* found so stay sharp. If that damn thing is still out there, it's possibly injured and damn sure dangerous."

Unit one consisted of Troy, Sheriff Blaine, Michelle and Deputy Severs. Unit two was led by Billy and Rangers Lazaro and Braun, and Deputy Chastain would follow him. Unit two would take a southern route encircling the lodge, but also over Dyer's Pass before moving into the canyon. The trail would also take them near the old mine where the car accident took place. The creature was last known to have been through that area.

"Comm check every hour. Let's move out and remember to keep your eyes open. What we're hunting is most likely already hunting us," Nick said.

The morning was cold, but the sun was bright, and the skies were clear. There wasn't much wind, so it was a rather pleasant start to the day. Traffic was moving with skiers heading for the parking lots nearest the ski lifts. The

Buckhorn Lodge had only one lift for the slopes near it, but it stayed busy from the time it opened until it closed. One of the more popular trails, the lodge parking lot teamed over with guests and non-guests alike.

Billy led his team across the road then down through the tree-dotted landscape of the southern slope. Several skiers were in line at the lodge's ski-lift for one of Hawthorn's favorite black diamond runs. Billy was never much of a daredevil, though living in Hawthorn he learned to ski and snowboard at a young age. He preferred snowmobiles to back-country skiing, though, and often joked that he was simply too lazy for all the hard work that went into it.

Rangers Lazaro and Braun brought up the middle while Deputy Tim Severs was last in the lineup. They moved quickly beyond the public areas and reached the more rugged terrain of the heavy forested mountain by first communications check-in.

***

Nick took the lead heading his team up beyond the ski slope and over the ridge, slaloming through the shimmering birch and aspen trees. Towering pines dotted the hillside and tended to grow more on the western side of the mountain. Cedar thickets grew randomly and abundantly all over. The bright red ski beanie he wore along with the red 'Sheriff's" coat made an interesting contrast against the yellow snowmobile he rode. Troy commented earlier that he looked like a tomato riding a banana. Nick didn't seem to find it amusing, but the others laughed.

The group fanned out to cover more ground but always stayed within sight of one another. When they reached the apex of the ridge an hour later, Nick pulled up and radioed the other team.

"Team one to team two, you got a copy?"

A moment later, a static-laced reply came back.

"Uh, roger that, Sheriff. Team two here."

Troy thought the voice sounded like Billy's but couldn't be sure. He parked near the Sheriff and scanned the area below with a pair of binoculars.

"Coming up empty here," Nick said. "Have you seen anything?"

"Nothing yet, Sheriff, but we've not made it to the canyon yet. Should be at the pass in the next fifteen minutes or so. ETA to canyon is probably an hour from now."

"Roger that," Nick said, looking at the time on the GPS screen. "We should be there before you if the trail down isn't blocked."

"You got it, out."

Troy put his binoculars back inside the case on the side of the sled's gas tank. "Maybe that thing's gone, Nick?"

"I hope you're right, but sure would like to be certain of that, but who knows?"

Michelle pulled up on her sled in time to hear the conversation.

"Maybe if it's still around, it's hiding down in that canyon, injured from getting hit by that car. Maybe it even died of its wounds," she surmised.

Nick thought about that for a moment. "That's possible, but just when you think these things are down and out, another one takes its place. Hard to believe there's only one."

"I, for one, don't believe there's only one," Troy said.

The sheriff and Michelle both turned to him to elaborate more.

"Think about it, Nick. The whole time during the siege at my cabin, we might drop one, but then it immediately disappeared. Another one was right there to pick it up and drag it away out of the line of fire. They don't leave any of their - *clan*, behind. It's like they're freaking Navy Seals or something." Troy shook his head slowly from side to side, "No, I don't think this one is alone either."

Zeus jumped off the sled, relieved himself near a few select trees then trotted off on his own while the others sat and talked.

"We should find the trail down over the ridge at that big outcropping just below that peak there," Nick said, pointing out the craggy boulder. "Did quite a bit of hunting in the area along with half of Hawthorn, I'm sure. I know it well. Won't be easy, but it's passable. Just keep tight, and we'll be at the bottom of that canyon within the hour."

"I'm ready," Michelle said.

Troy whistled for Zeus who trotted over and gladly took his seat on the warm carpet behind his master. Troy pulled out following Michelle, who was just behind the sheriff. Deputy Severs rode drag as the troupe made their way along the crest before Nick steered his machine down the sun glistening embankment.

The going was slow, but the trail was solid, and the sleds had no issues traversing the terrain. Michelle was a good rider, and Troy wasn't worried about following her. He was more than certain she grew up riding all over the backcountry of Colorado. He stayed close behind and kept the group tight. When the sheriff reached a fixed midway point, he stopped the sleds and called in for the radio check. It only took a few minutes before Billy responded with an all-clear.

"Shouldn't be long before we make the cabin. We kinda

got slowed down a bit back there when I had to backtrack a bit. Ready?"

The team was tired and more than ready to get to the bottom of the canyon and get off to stretch their legs. Though the riding wasn't difficult, the continued strain and stress of constantly looking for tracks or other signs of their quarry was fatiguing. They had ridden for the better part of the morning, and the sun had begun stretching west. The wind picked up and blew loose, frozen snow off a nearby boulder on Troy's face, stinging just a little. He wiped at it with the back of his glove and pulled his neoprene face shield back up to the bottom of his goggles.

The wind was even more brutal on the open face of the ridge with no trees to block it. The rim ran in a large oval, curving from south to north of the arroyo below. Craggy rock outcroppings covered mostly with snow dotted the entirety of the landscape. The bright midday sun glistened off the white frozen landscape. Though it was picturesque. the riders couldn't enjoy the scenery due to the nature of the mission.

Nick goosed the throttle on his sled, steering the rudders carefully over the rocky terrain of the trail leading down into the tree encrusted valley below. The machine rocked over a boulder, straight up, then gently down on the other side hugging the edge of the cliff. The sheriff had a black balaclava covering his face, but he could hear the wind whip the tiny ice and frozen snow pellets against it sounding like a rainstorm against a tin roof. He was thankful for the cold weather gear, including the tinted goggles that kept the blinding sun at bay.

***

Lazaro pulled up beside Billy and pointed out a game trail that led away from the main trail they were following. "That goes up to Eagle Bluff because of the nest area in the cliff. Wanna check it out before we get to Dyer's Pass? Should be able to see for miles in any direction. Won't take much time and should get a good bird's eye view of the canyon."

"Sounds good, lead the way."

***

Troy watched Michelle Evers follow along behind the sheriff expertly guiding her machine over the same trail. He was no expert himself, but he was a fast learner, and in the last five years since he's lived in the Rockies, he'd learned a lot. He was more than confident on the sled, and Zeus had no trouble trusting him. The big dog rode comfortably behind him, somehow knowing to be still with no sudden weight changes during delicate maneuvers. From time to time, when Troy drove slowly, the Rottweiler would jump off the machine and run beside him, but for the most part, the dog enjoyed riding on the warm carpeted area just behind Troy.

Deputy Noland Chastain rode drag on the expedition and stayed close behind Troy. He had grown up in Hawthorn and was no stranger to snowmobiling, skiing or anything to do with the outdoors of the Rocky Mountains. He was an avid hunter and outdoorsman and had been with the sheriff's department for several years. He suddenly stopped his machine and looked around. Thinking he heard something he shut the engine off. There it was again, but the sound was so faint it was difficult to make out. He thought it sounded like gunshots. He gunned his sled and caught up to the sheriff and stopped the team.

"Thought I what sounded like gunshots!" he said.

The sheriff stopped his machine on an area wide enough that the others could pull alongside. They were about two-thirds of the way down.

"Could've been hunters, I suppose."

Nick picked up the radio microphone hanging on his shoulder. "Team one to team two, you got a copy?"

Radio static.

"Team one to team you, do you have a copy?" the sheriff asked again.

More static, but no response.

"Could be out of range. No way of knowing. We'll keep trying to raise 'em, but they know to meet up at that cabin. We should make a bee-line straight there."

"Lead the way."

The sheriff hit the throttle on his snowmobile, picking up the pace. The trail wound down the ridge in a zig-zag pattern, curving around the contour of the millions of years of weather-beaten mountain range. Nick suddenly pulled up sharp and grabbed his binoculars to scan below.

"What is it?" Troy asked.

"Thought I saw something just off the trail below. See where the trail juts down in a switchback just before disappearing in that thicket of evergreens?" He pointed near the bottom of the ridge trail. The wind was still blowing at a good clip and branches from the trees whipped back and forth, making it hard to see anything that far away.

"Yeah, just under that old dead-looking birch?"

"That's it. I thought I saw someone or something standing there, but it may have just been limbs moving, shadows or something, can't be too careful though. That old surveyor's cabin isn't far from here now, maybe a couple of miles once we get to the bottom of this canyon. That's when we all need to really be on the lookout. The trees can really tighten up, and I have no idea how the trail is beyond what we can see now."

"I'm ready," Noland said.

Michelle stood up on her machine and peered closely at the area the sheriff indicated. "I don't see anything now, but I'll keep a close eye out. We'll be ready."

"How's everyone doing on fuel?" Nick asked.

"I'm good. Shouldn't have to refill for a while," Troy answered.

"Yeah, me too," Michelle said.

"I'm good to go," Noland said.

Troy settled back on his machine. "Lead the way, Sheriff,"

"Roger that. Once we get down to the bottom, we'll move faster and make the rendezvous, but keep your eyes peeled."

Nick eased down the ridge trail once again, this time even more slowly than before. They reached the bottom within minutes and were able to ease into a steadier pace.

The brightly colored snowmobiles reminded Troy of the Jagdgeschwader 1; a unit of the German Luftwaffe nicknamed the Flying Circus due to the various colored planes flown by the German aviators.

The unit reached the switchback where Nick thought he saw something earlier and they fanned out to check it out more thoroughly. The evergreen trees were clumped in pockets, but the forest floor opened with scatterings of birch and aspen. Visibility was good for only short distances. The group still felt the necessity of keeping a close eye out for anything out of the ordinary. Literally, anything could be within a few feet away and they would never see it.

Troy kept pace beside the others as they zig-zagged the snowy carpet of the forest floor, twenty to thirty feet apart. Zeus jumped off the machine and ran along beside them for a few minutes but soon disappeared. Troy wasn't worried, the big dog could take care of himself and did this sort of thing all the time. Zeus liked to run on his own and check things out. When he tired, he quickly came back or he came running if Troy called for him.

Michelle goosed the throttle on her sled and spurred alongside Troy.

"Cabin is just up ahead," she shouted over the blat of the engines while pointing it out. "Sheriff said to make a wide sweep before we get there."

"You bet," Troy shouted back, glancing over at Noland who acknowledged the instructions and veered off.

Each person turned their machine to make a wide swath of the area and scattered to move apart. They had only gone a short distance more when Troy saw Noland, who was on the outside perimeter, slide his machine to a snow flying halt. Troy slowed and then hit the throttle to make a beeline for him. He had something.

Troy was the first to arrive and drew alongside Noland's sled and killed the engine. When he climbed off, he saw what had stopped Noland in his tracks.

A trail led from the forest toward the cabin only a hundred yards away. The path was evident in the foot-deep snow. Whoever or whatever made the trail was broad, or there were several individuals. The broken trail was trampled down and wide.

The sheriff and Michelle pulled up beside the two and

jumped off their sleds.

"Can you see any tracks? Bear or mountain lion maybe?" Nick asked.

"None that I can make out. Trail's been trampled down, but new snow has covered most of it." Chastain said. "Whatever made it is big, leads right to that cabin."

The others turned their gazes to follow the trail and then stopped at the cabin. They could make it out through the trees, but couldn't see any detail.

Sheriff Blaine reached for his radio.

"Unit one to unit two, do you have a copy?"

Static

"Unit two, come in. Do you have a copy?"

"Maybe they're still out of range," Michelle said. "Could be nothing."

"Maybe, but I don't like it."

"Listen," Troy said, indicating for everyone to be silent.

Zeus could be heard deep in the forest.

"Sounds like it's coming from that direction," the sheriff said, pointing the way they had come in.

Troy jumped on his machine and gunned the throttle. Snow churned behind him in a high arc as the sled lurched forward, spewing the white powder like a rooster tail.

"Noland, stay with him. We'll wait here!" Sheriff Blaine shouted.

"You got it," Chastain said, jumping on his machine and following close behind.

Troy rode hard in the general direction he heard Zeus barking, but it was difficult to tell precisely where the sound was coming from in the woods, especially with the wind blowing like it was. He thought he saw movement out of the corner of his eye and leaned into a turn around a small pile of brush. Just as he cleared it, he saw the big black and rust dog. He slid to a stop near Zeus, pulled his goggles off with his left hand and snatched his sidearm out with the other.

The Rottweiler trotted over to Troy, barked a few times in a low, gruff half-hearted alarm more as a greeting than warning.

"Zeus, buddy, what's gotten into you?" Troy asked, looking in the direction the dog came from.

Chastain pulled up beside the two and pulled his binoculars out and scanned the area.

"I'm not seeing anything in any direction," Noland said. "Hey, what the hell is that?"

Troy noticed it at the same time Noland did. Zeus had blood on his feet and snout. Troy pulled his field glasses free of the case and scanned the area. "I'm afraid to say, Noland. I'm sure your guess is the same as mine. I got a bad feeling about this."

"Yeah, me too. We can get back to the others and let them know. We probably need to check it out," Noland said, goosing the throttle on his snowmobile.

***

The team reached the peak of Eagle Bluff and stopped long enough to scan the area below. The canyon lay stretched out for as far as the eye could see. The sun sat low in the eastern sky, reflecting off the snow and ice that covered the arid landscape. Granite escarpments surrounded the peaceful arroyo forming a bowl filled with tall evergreens, aspen and birch trees stretching like tall spires competing to see which one could get more sunlight than the others.

Billy pulled his goggles up on his forehead and put the binoculars to his eyes. He scanned everything below but saw nothing out of the ordinary.

"The old surveyor's cabin should be straight across the canyon on the western edge. Dyer's Pass will get us there within the next couple of hours," Ranger Lazaro said.

"Yeah, I don't see anything. Who knows, maybe the thing isn't around anymore," Billy said.

"I hope to hell you're right."

"Let's get going, don't wanna make the others wait too long on us," Billy said just as a howl echoed through the canyon from somewhere below.

"What the hell was that?" Tim asked.

"I dunno, coyote maybe," Billy replied, looking at Sam.

"I've never heard a coyote sound like that," Sam replied. "Could be though. Whatever it is, it's a long way away."

"Agreed, let's just keep our eyes open and be ready," Billy said. "Let's get going."

The team moved out single file heading back down the same trail that brought them to Eagle Bluff. Navigating down was much easier than the trip up. The ridge was nothing but solid rock with a wayward tree sprouting up at various locations. Dodging the giant boulders and cutting a new trail took a little longer than they wanted, but it was still a good idea. Following the trail back down was easy going.

26

The Sasquatch was at home in the mountains. Though its usual habitat was much further away and higher up, it came down at certain times of the year when the game became scarce. It was nomadic by nature and moved with the changing of the weather and the migratory movement of the big game it hunted for survival. Its origins were unknown but ancient. The species lived in clans, mated for life and watched out for each other, protected one another. They had their own way of communicating through grunts, whistles, and motions. The females were generally smaller than the males, but just as fierce and capable hunters.

This one, a large male, was injured, angry and hungry. Separated from its clan, a self-imposed exile of sorts, it knew all about the small, frail humans, but had no fear of them. It feared nothing. It was an apex predator and more than a capable hunter. It was intelligent and capable of rational thought. Under normal circumstances it avoided contact with people. There was nothing in it for the Sasquatch. But that was under normal circumstance. It had been injured by people, attacked. It didn't know the difference. And when one is attacked, the only defense is a stronger offense.

The beast waited until the group of riders wound

through a tight funnel that ran through the pass near the top of the canyon. Its breathing labored and jagged, its rage built as the humans and the machines got closer. Its muscles tightened and released to get the blood flowing. It sprang out of nowhere and with a blood-curdling scream leaped into the middle of the group knocking Severs off his sled and crushing him into the rock wall of the canyon trail before anyone could get off a shot. Not that anyone could have taken a shot in such tight quarters. It was too dangerous. No one had a clear opening at the creature without a team member being in the way.

Sam pulled his hunting knife from his boot and jumped off his sled to help Severs, who was now pinned by the creature against the rocks. The ranger sunk the blade deeply into the creatures back. The Sasquatch roared in rage, spinning and thrashing about, grabbing for the knife lodged in its back, but the knife was just out of range of its grasp. The beast screamed again and again while grabbing at the object causing the intense pain. The violent movement was so swift that the ranger was knocked backward and he tripped over the snowmobile. He went down on the other side of the sled, off balance and grasping at anything to scramble back to his feet.

Billy, who was riding drag behind the group, aimed his handgun at the beast, but couldn't get a clear shot. He hesitated. The others were in the line of fire.

Sam clawed at the sled desperate to escape the beast, but when the creature saw him get to his feet, it grabbed a large rock, pried it loose from the frozen ground and threw it. The rock hit the ground with an audible thump before bouncing against the snowmobile.

The creature shrieked in fury and sprang for the downed ranger. Lazaro made it back on his feet and scrambled to get back on the snowmobile. The pass was only ten feet wide at the choke point, leaving little room to maneuver the sled. Lazaro swung a leg over his machine and grabbed at the kill switch. The sled wouldn't start unless the strap was attached. He yanked off his gloves and grabbed for the end of the strap to reattach it. His hands shook from adrenaline and he struggled, unable to focus on the action. The beast was enraged by the knife still lodged in its back, but the knife seemed tiny in comparison to the size of the creature. Lazaro knew he only had a few seconds before the monster turned on him.

The Sasquatch's enraged roar sounded deep and guttural but ended in an ear-splitting shriek. It was huge, at least eight feet tall and massive. Its shoulders were as broad as a door, and its incredible strength came from muscles bound tight and covered in long reddish, coarse hair from head to toe. Its face was also covered in the thick red hair except for around the eyes and cheeks which were a deep red under a thick brow. Its skin was dark, almost black and seemingly as thick as leather, hardened by the elements.

Sam never seen anything that looked as evil as the terrifying beast. He tried not to look at it but concentrated on getting the safety strap reattached to the machine. Finally, he got it. He hit the throttle and blasted through the frozen snow back the way they had come just as the creature slipped in the snow and fell to a knee lunging after him.

Jim Braun was leading the team when the huge hairy beast leaped into the middle of the group and knocked the deputy off the snowmobile. He was surprised by the suddenness of the attack. At first, he thought it was a huge grizzly bear, but a moment later he realized what he was seeing and hearing.

The creature was enormous and unlike anything he had ever seen before. He pulled his handgun, but his partner was between them and he had no clear shot. The trail was blocked by the other sleds and the beast, no way around through the tight quarters. Braun watched as his partner scrambled to his feet and back on the sled. The Sasquatch roared in protest and flung its arm in a wide arc attempting to hit the vehicle or the man riding it. Jim saw the opening he needed when the creature fell. He twisted the throttle hard and aimed his sled to the opposite side hoping to pick up Severs while the beast was distracted by Lazaro.

The Sasquatch roared and spun, looking straight at the ranger making eye contact. Jim froze momentarily, but it was long enough that Sam was able to get to the other side of the pass and near Billy.

The beast was bigger than anything they had ever seen before, and the sheer look of hatred and evil in its eyes was terrifying. Its features resembled that of a man, but much more primitive. Its teeth were huge, and the mouth seemed too big for its head going from ear to ear. A dark black tongue could be seen behind huge jagged and yellow teeth. Its lips were long, flat and jutting outward under the large bulbous nose. It grabbed the knife in its back and yanked it out, looked at it and then threw it down with a roar and stepped straight at Sam.

When the creature turned away, Jim grabbed the badly injured deputy and hauled him onto the sled behind him. He hit the throttle and kicked snow high into the air as he took the injured man out of the tight passage and away from the beast behind.

Billy, seeing that Jim had Severs safely on the other side of the trail, hit the throttle on his machine.

"Let's get out of here, no clear shot. We'll have to hope the radios work, and we can meet up with them once we get clear of that damned thing. Looks like they made it out of there, but not sure how bad Tim is hurt."

Sam heard what he said and understood. He too hit the throttle and sped out behind Billy.

Billy looked back over his shoulder to see if the creature was giving chase, but it had disappeared as quickly as it attacked.

Sam also slowed only long enough to look behind him, searching through the trees for any sign of the others. He was out of breath from riding hard but elated to be clear of the pass.

***

Troy and Deputy Chastain returned to the sheriff and Michelle, who waited on the trail.

"Anything?" Nick asked.

"Something, but we didn't see it. I think Zeus did and whatever it was is bleeding," Troy said. "Thought we should regroup before we checked it much more. I don't think it's still around in the area though or Zeus wouldn't have come back to me so easily. He was waiting on us when we got there."

"Could be the Sasquatch," Michelle said. "We know it was injured when the car hit it. Maybe Zeus scared it off."

Troy turned around to examine his canine friend and patted him on the head.

"Whatever it was, it's gone now. It may have been what made this trail," Troy said. "Had any luck raising the others?"

"No, still nothing. I say we make our way to that cabin

and find out what the hell's waiting on us. Trail doesn't look old, but I can't find any tracks or telltale signs of what or who made it."

"Do you think we approach together or spread out in case something tries to run? If it's the Sasquatch, maybe we can trap it inside," Michelle asked.

"We cover the front and the back. We stay in pairs. From this point on, nobody goes or does anything alone. We know exactly what we're dealing with and it won't go down without a fight. Better to have backup. Noland, you and Troy, cover the rear. Michelle and I will circle around to the front. Be ready, but do not shoot unless you have to and only then with a clear line of site."

"You got it," Chastain said.

***

Nick and Michelle rode off to circle around to the front of the cabin. When they were in position, Troy and Noland pushed in on the back. They had about eighty yards to cover before they had a clear view of the cabin.

It was a small, two room cabin. The walls and doors were still standing though part of the roof had collapsed. The trail led up to about twenty feet from the cabin and then disappeared. The entire area around the cabin had been trampled down and was mostly covered with pine needles. They couldn't see any footprints leading to the back door.

Troy dismounted and pulled his rifle from the sheath. Deputy Chastain pulled his sidearm and stood ready as well while Zeus remained on the back-seat bench, He was surrounded on three sides by baggage compartments attached to the sled. Troy heard Sheriff Blaine call out from the front of the cabin.

"Hello! This is Sheriff Nick Blaine. Is anyone inside?"

He got no response. He called out again.

"Hello! County Sheriff. We're coming in."

Nick looked over at Michelle, "Cover me."

She nodded and stood ready with her handgun up and away from the sheriff as he prepared to breach.

Just as Nick stepped onto the front edge of the porch, they heard a thump on the wooden floor inside.

"Hello? Someone there?" Nick called out.

Nothing

Sheriff Blaine looked back at Deputy Evers who stood ready. In one smooth motion, he kicked the door open and quickly moved to his left, arms extended brandishing the Ruger revolver. The old boards gave easily, and the door splintered off the top hinge and fell back against an interior wall.

Evers sidestepped the busted door and paralleled the sheriff's move, covering the right side with flashlight in one hand and weapon drawn in the other.

The cabin was small so they covered the entirety of it in seconds. At first, they saw no sign of anyone or anything in the room but then something caught the sheriff's eye. There was something in the back corner. It wasn't big enough to be the creature they sought, but it was big enough to worry about. He pulled his own flashlight and trained it on the object and slowly moved toward it. His boots echoed on the hollow wooden floor with each step.

Deputy Evers trained her firearm toward the object and stood ready.

Nick moved closer. The thing was partially obstructed by the pieces of the roof that had collapsed. Upon closer inspection, he could tell it was a crumpled canvas tarpaulin weathered by age. He could see the tattered threads and a dark-colored grommet of a corner.

The sheriff reached down, grabbed a corner of the worn tarp, and yanked it clear. It took only a moment to realize what lay beneath.

Ranger Jim Braun and Deputy Tim Severs lay crumpled together, both out cold. Their clothes were shredded and in tatters and their faces bruised and bloodied. A makeshift splint was on the leg of Severs from the knee down.

"Give me a hand here," Nick called to Michelle.

"All clear, Troy!" Michelle shouted to the men outside before jumping beside Nick to check on the men.

Nick felt for a pulse on Severs.

"Weak, but there," Nick said.

"Jim's coming around," Michelle said. "What the hell happened, and where are the others?"

"Damn good question."

Troy and Noland entered the back door and quickly jumped in to help.

"I'll grab the first aid kit," Troy said, hurrying out. He came back a moment later followed by Zeus.

"Let's get these wounds cleaned before they get infected. Can you tell if they have any broken bones or internal bleeding?"

"Neither appears to have any internal bleeding. Severs' leg is broken, but it looks like they were able to set it properly. We need to get them to a doctor as quickly as possible. There's a rescue toboggan attached to the side of my sled."

"I'll grab it," Chastain said.

Michelle looked up at the sheriff. "How'd they get here."

"I don't have a clue. Didn't see either sled anywhere around. It had to have been them that made the trail."

"We can do a perimeter sweep and see if we can find em," Troy suggested.

Chastain returned with the portable toboggan and placed it beside Deputy Severs who seemed to be the more critical of the two. A moan escaped the throat of Ranger Braun.

Troy grabbed his thermos, poured a cup of hot coffee. "He could probably use this. Help warm him up."

Braun's eyes suddenly flew open wide, and he tried to speak. Nick reassured him that he was safe and offered him a sip of coffee. The ranger tried to gulp but choked on the hot liquid.

"Easy now, small sips buddy. Can you tell us what happened?" Nick asked.

The ranger was able to gain his composure but was still weak.

"It - it attacked us. Caught us off-guard at Dyer's Pass. It came out of nowhere. We never saw it coming until it was right on top of us."

"What was it? What did it look like it?" Michelle asked.

"It - it was huge, covered with dark hair from head to foot. Massive! We never had a chance." The ranger was getting worked up and shaking, trembling from shock.

"Okay, take it easy buddy. You're still in shock. Deputy Severs is here. You got him to the cabin. You did good, real good. Do you know where the others are?"

"I…I don't know. We got separated when it attacked us as we came through a narrow pass on the ridge. It came out of nowhere, knocked Tim off his sled and pinned him against the rocks. I think his leg is broken. I remember grabbing him up on mine, and we tore out of there as fast as I could."

Michelle checked Deputy Severs' weapon.

"He never got off a shot," Michelle said, holding up the

handgun. "Mag's are still full."

"None of us did. I don't know if it got lucky, or it knew that we wouldn't be able to shoot at it if it were between us?"

Nick looked at Troy, "You and Chastain go ahead and make a quick parameter check. Make sure the others aren't out there. They could be injured too. Maybe the blood that Zeus found was theirs."

"Roger that," Troy said.

***

Billy Larsen rode his snowmobile at breakneck speed followed closely by Ranger Lazaro. The machines raced along the forest floor jumping undulations of snowdrifts and dodging trees and boulders. When they reached a clearing near a small frozen stream, they slowed to a stop to take a breather.

"Think Severs and Jim are okay?" Lazaro asked.

"Sure hope so. Tim didn't look so good. Jim had to drag him on his sled, but it looked like they got away. That damn thing was frikkin huge! I've never seen anything like it."

"I couldn't get a shot at it."

"Yeah, I know. It split us up perfectly and stayed in between us like it knew what a gun is. It's smart."

Billy took out his binoculars and scanned the area.

"We don't have any cover out here, and we're a long way away from the cabin," he said, reaching for his walkie mic. "Sheriff, this is Larsen, do you have a copy?" Billy said, pausing a moment before repeating his call.

"I know they're expecting us at the cabin, but it looked like Severs was hurt pretty bad. If that's where they ended up, the sheriff is probably going to get him out of there as fast as they can."

"They saw us get out of that pass so, I wonder if we should keep going and circle back around to the cabin and hope to run into 'em, or do we bug outta here and get somewhere closer so we can call in backup, maybe a chopper?"

"Good question!"

27

The two deputies returned to the cabin after making a wide sweep of the area. Nick opened the door for them.

"See anything?" he asked.

"Nothing I'm afraid."

"We need to get Tim to a doctor, PDQ," Michelle said. "We've dressed the wounds, but he also has a broken leg."

The deputy was secured on the toboggan. It was made to drag behind the snowmobile, but the ride wouldn't be smooth in the terrain they would have to cover. Jim Braun was on his feet but looked exhausted.

"I agree," Nick said. He stood and walked to the open door of the small cabin to look around. The others watched him in silence. "But the others are out there somewhere and supposed to meet us here. They could be making their way here now. We need a plan."

"What do you suggest? He needs to get to a doctor quick. He's lost a lot of blood, and Jim isn't much better off," Troy said, looking at the ranger.

"I'm good. I can ride and shoot," Jim said. "Besides, I really want another crack at that thing!"

"The question is, did it track you down and attack or did you happen upon it and spook it?" Sheriff Blaine asked. He looked around the room at the team. "It could have

251

attacked you because you startled it. It may be gone for good now."

A wind gust suddenly whipped through the open doorway of the cabin, and the propped-up door slid to the floor with a loud bang. Everyone in the room jumped at the sudden noise.

Noland chuckled, "Damn, that scared the hell out of me."

"Me too," Troy said, smiling.

The group enjoyed a moment of levity and relaxed.

"Okay, we won't be able to move fast, but we still have plenty of daylight left," Nick said, walking to the door and peering up in the sky. He turned back to the others but he was suddenly stopped in his tracks by a sound he was all too familiar with coming from the forest.

Whoop! Whoop!

"We're too late," Troy said. "It's here."

"Dammit!" Nick said, turning back to the door. "This cabin doesn't give us much protection."

"We have to get Tim to a doctor. He can't wait," Noland said.

Nick turned to look at his deputies. Each person could be counted on. They were a good team.

"Evers, I need you and Chastain to lead the team out of here, get Severs to the hospital as quickly as possible."

"Think it's a good idea to split up?" Noland asked.

"We're not. Not exactly anyway. Troy and I will give you a head start. It'll probably give you some room and try to follow you or cut you off somewhere. We won't let that happen. We will flank you and stay between you and the Sasquatch, keep it off you and give you a chance to make it."

Michelle pulled her handgun out, popped the mag into

her free hand, and checked her rounds. She slammed the mag back into place then slid the semi-automatic back into the leather holster. She then felt along her belt and reassured herself she had plenty of spares.

"I'm ready," she said.

"If you hear us shooting, don't turn around. Just get the hell out of here and don't turn back. We can take care of ourselves as long as we know you're not in the way."

"What about Larsen and Lazaro?" Jim asked.

"I'm hoping that they don't have plans to come here, but if they do, we need to leave them a message and let 'em know what's going on," Nick said.

"I've got it," Michelle said, hurrying out the back door.

A moment later she back carrying a can of orange spray paint.

"It was in the toolbox of my sled. Been in there for long time, just hope it's not frozen. We can put an 'X' on the door letting them know it's been cleared. Maybe that'll warn 'em away?"

"Good thinking," Nick said. "Let's try it."

Noland followed Michelle outside and watched her mark the wall of the cabin. The hair on the back of his neck stood up, and chill bumps covered his body. It wasn't from the brisk winter air.

"We'll have to take the long way out, but it's the easiest trail. I don't think Tim can handle going over the ridge," Noland suggested.

"I agree. Safer for him and us," Nick replied. "It's more open and less likely for an ambush. Let's help get Tim outside and you guys, get moving."

Evers pulled away from the cabin with Chastain following closely behind towing the lightweight emergency toboggan with Tim Severs buckled in tightly and covered. Jim Braun was right behind with his rifle ready in the scabbard beside the tank of his sled.

The sheriff watched the group leave then turned to back to Troy. "You ready?"

"Ready as I'll ever be. Do you think it'll follow them or wait us out?" Troy asked.

Nick walked across the room to the tiny back window of the cabin, his boots thumping on the wooden plank floor. He pulled the balaclava up to cover his face, zipped his coat and pulled the revolver from his holster. The cylinder popped open with a metallic click. He gave it a fast spin, flipped his wrist and snapped it closed.

"We wait five minutes to give them some room, then we fall in behind them and close the gap. That damn thing is smart, but it's also injured. I'm hoping it can't move as fast. If it tries to follow them, we take it out."

***

The mat-black helicopter circled the clearing before descending. Six men dressed in black BDU's complete with black balaclavas and tinted goggles waited with rifles slung over their shoulders. When the chopper set down, the redheaded man with the scar jumped down and made his way over to the men.

"We need it alive!" He shouted over the whine of the helicopter's engine. "Tranq' it and bring it in. We'll provide air support."

"Yes, sir!"

"Another thing - we spotted local LEO's out there. They're hunting the damn thing. They've split up into two teams and one of which made contact with the Sasquatch.

They all made it through the encounter, but two got through the pass, and the other two went back up and over the ridge. Those two could be headed out, possibly going after backup. I have bravo team in route to intercept and will pick them up. The other team is still four strong and holed up in an old cabin, but doubt they'll be staying long. The big man is closing in on them as we speak. He doesn't like them being in the canyon and will protect the valley. We have to get to it before they do, tranq it and get it moved," the leader said.

"What happens if they get in the way or get to it first?"

The redhead leaned closer to the man, leaned down to look him in the eyes, "Don't let that happen, we've had too many people already get in the way. You need to get to it first so that we can get it out before further civilian contact. One or two people disappearing in the mountains is one thing, but not a half-dozen local cops. Get moving and don't let them see you!"

"Yes, sir!"

The soldier on the sled waved his arm in a circle indicating it was time to move out. Each man carried a rifle slung over the shoulder loaded with large tranquilizer darts loaded and had a tracking radar unit mounted across the fuel tank. The men were all experienced military special-ops and a tough crew. They had worked together in the Navy. The only way to become a member of the elite team was to be handpicked by the team.

They still worked for the government in what was hastily called the Bureau of Land & Wildlife Reclamation and Natural Resources Enforcement. The title and accompanying acronym were simply too ridiculous and vague to be of any use. They referred to themselves in more humorous terms as the *G-Team* or *Unicorn Chasers*.

They were put together at the very top level of the Department of Interior and just as mysterious and unknown as the NSA or CIA. The general public had no idea the office even existed or if they did it was only rumor and speculation.

The soldiers rode out single file, but once they reached the forest, they split into three groups and followed the tracking signal.

***

Troy followed the sheriff to the sleds while scanning the area for any signs of the Bigfoot in the area. They hadn't heard any more whoops since the first group left the cabin. Troy called quietly for Zeus who had no trouble jumping up behind him and settling in. The dog was always willing to follow his master, his friend, and was not afraid of anything. Just a few months back, the dog backed a brown bear down when they happened upon one while fishing near a stream. The bear made a bluff charge at them, but Zeus wasn't having it. The two squared off, but the bear soon changed its mind about a confrontation and scooted off into the woods.

Sheriff Blaine climbed on the bright yellow snowmobile, his eyes continuously moving, leery of the creature's proximity. There had been no indication that the beast was still close, but nothing would be surprising. After the encounter during the siege at Troy's cabin, he knew all too well how quickly those things can move. It could be on top of them in seconds. His deputy was lucky to be alive. He unclipped the radio mic on his shoulder and called to the team.

"Evers, do you have a copy?"

A moment later he called again, "Evers, do you have a copy?"

"Yeah, I copy, Sheriff. All clear so far. No contact."

"Copy that, we're not far behind you and covering your six, will check in later. Out."

"Copy that. Out."

The men started their machines and followed the tracks of the others. They would be no more than half of a mile ahead of them which should give them enough space to keep an eye on their back trail in case the Sasquatch tried to follow the slow-moving rescue team. The once clear sky was now overcast, and the wind had picked up. The tops of the tall pines bowed and swayed causing loose snow to fall off the bending limbs. The gray sky did little to illuminate the forest floor, but there was still plenty of natural light to navigate by. Visibility at greater distances, however, was a bit more difficult at ground level. They had plenty of time to make it back to town, providing there were no obstacles in the way.

The trail was easy to follow in the virgin snow. Both men kept their eyes moving for any sign of the creature. The two men wearing black were concealed against the dark forest background where they waited as the group pulling the toboggan rode past. They were no more than fifty yards away, and if they didn't move, the group of riders wouldn't notice them. The tracking radar on the screen showed the Sasquatch moving steadily along with the group but hanging back just slightly. The men lay crouched low against their own machines, each one with a tranquilizer gun steadied over the top of the seat waiting on the beast to appear. With any luck, they could put the Sasquatch down without alerting the deputies.

"Red Team in position and holding. Our target is

following the LEO's. Waiting for clear shot."

"Roger that, Blue Team in forward position. Ready to back up."

"Red Team, we have a visual."

***

The Sasquatch was injured. The car that hit it in the road so many nights ago had cut it badly across the left thigh, and it hurt. It was not merely an animal. The Sasquatch was an ancient being and was intelligent with a rudimentary knowledge of healing. It had to in order to survive. The creature had made a mud poultice and put over the wound, but it was not healed. It still bled. Its long coarse fur was matted down against its bulging muscles, and he was weak from the loss of blood. It felt anger as it paced the group of humans just ahead. It waited for the right time and place to attack. He wanted to kill them all for the pain their kind had inflicted on him. The Sasquatch's concentration on the group of humans and the pain from the injury, however, made it vulnerable.

Troy saw the creature at the exact moment Zeus did. With a tremendous bark that came from somewhere deep in its chest, the big dog leaped from the seat of the sled and ran at the Sasquatch. Troy hit the throttle and shot forward with a burst of speed throwing a huge rooster tail of snow behind.

"There!" Troy shouted.

The sheriff, who had been scanning the opposite side of the trail heard the dog then saw Troy speeding after it. He hit the throttle on his sled, splitting away to try and flank the creature while still paralleling Troy.

Surprised by the second group, the eight-foot-tall

Sasquatch stopped running and turned toward the new threat. It had seen dogs before. It wasn't afraid. The humans racing its direction angered it. It was caught off guard, and its instincts took over. It was a predator not designed for fright and flight. It felt the adrenaline rush through its veins shutting down pain receptors. It crouched, knees bent arms out. It would kill the dog. Then it would kill the humans.

Zeus rushed at the creature, barking and snarling, drool from his muzzle splattering the ground as he ran. Just before he was in striking distance, the dog stopped and squared off with the strange beast. Deepthroated growls came from its chest and escaped through its bared teeth. The dog weighed upwards of one-hundred pounds but was tiny in comparison to the huge Sasquatch.

The Sasquatch was ready for the dog to attack, but it was confused when it stopped out of range of its long arms. The beast had other experiences with dogs, and they always ended the same. The dogs would nip at its feet, never suspecting just how quickly the huge bipedal creature could move. It would simply grab the dog in one of its huge hands and break its neck. They were nothing more than an annoyance. The Sasquatch growled back at the dog and swiped one of its huge paws at it, but the dog easily moved out of the way and attempted to bite the hand. The creature shrieked when it saw the two snowmobiles getting closer and turned to run. It was caught out in the open. It needed to move, for right now anyway, and find a better place. Higher ground perhaps. Just as it turned to run, a loud explosion reverberated through the woods, then another. It heard a streaking of air pass by its face. The beast let out another roar and ran for a large clump of trees further up the trail.

***

"Red Team, check-in. What the hell is going on?"

"Red Team here. Seems our LEO's had split up. Two were following the first group out, apparently covering their retreat. They spotted the big guy and took a couple of shots. Don't think they hit it though. Your orders, Sir?"

"Hang back. Don't intercept. Let it play out no matter which way it goes. Keep a visual."

"Blue Team, coming your way."

"Roger that, we're ready."

***

Michelle's group heard the gunshots. She pulled up hard on the brakes and came to a sliding stop.

"That's close!" she shouted.

"Yeah, can't be more than a few hundred yards back, but I can't see a damned thing," Noland said. He stood on the sleds running boards to get a better look but could see nothing.

"Sheriff, this is Evers, you got a copy?"

Static was the only sound she heard.

"Sheriff, are you there?" she called again over the radio.

"I'm going back," Michelle said. "You've got to get Tim out of here and to a doctor!"

"Sheriff gave us orders that if we hear anything we're supposed to high-tail it out of here," Jim Braun chimed in. "I think we better do exactly as he said."

"I know, but I'm not staying out of the fight. I'm going back. You guys get the hell outta here!" Michelle said. "Go, I've got this."

Chastain looked at Braun who just shrugged his shoulders and motioned at Severs lying on the toboggan.

"Your funeral," Chastain said. "But be careful."

Chastain sat back down on the sled and hit the throttle.

Michelle watched them pull away, towing the wounded deputy. They were moving much faster now. She felt good about her decision. She had their back.

28

The Sasquatch moved faster than anything Troy had seen before. He knew the creatures were fast and nimble for being so incredibly huge, but he had never seen one dart through the forest like this. At first, it ran in the direction of the rescue team, but then it circled back around. The beast moved too fast to get another clean shot at it.

"Zeus, come!" Troy shouted. "Zeus, come!"

The rottweiler was well trained to follow commands and was loyal to a fault, but the heat of battle caused difficulty in persuading the dog. Finally, Zeus stopped running after the creature and jumped back on the snowmobile.

Nick had raced off after the Sasquatch, so Troy had some ground to cover to catch up.

The Sasquatch raced back toward the ridge. It dodged in and out of trees like a shadow dancing across the ground. It was amazing at how fast the creature could navigate almost as if it were running on top of the deep snow.

The sheriff hit the throttle and tore out after the Sasquatch, jumping over mounds of snow that beneath the surface was probably large rocks and downed trees. The sled seemed to be in the air just as much as it was on the ground. Rooster tails of snow flew behind him as he accelerated out of turns as he mimicked each move that the creature made. He caught a slight movement out the corner of his eye but was too consumed following the creature to give it much thought.

Troy and Zeus raced to catch up to the sheriff quickly. The bright yellow snowmobile the sheriff rode was easy to see even in the gray gloom of the isolated canyon. When he saw the semi-circle the creature was making to head back toward the ridge, he cut straight across the forest floor. He closed the gap within seconds and moved up alongside the sheriff.

"There!" the sheriff shouted over the screaming engines. He pointed to a break in the trees leading up the side of the steep ridge.

The fleeing beast burst through the opening crossing perpendicular to their path and leaped with surprising agility into a huge pine before catapulting over the incline and disappearing.

The area was a boulder-strewn cliff side and steep. The snowmobiles weren't designed to navigate over those conditions.

"Damnit," Nick shouted angrily. "We lost it."

Zeus barked so loudly that Troy had a hard time hearing, and his ears were still ringing from gunshots.

"Zeus, quiet," Troy said calmly. After he repeated the command a couple more times, the brute settled but whined that he wasn't allowed to go after the beast.

"I don't know how I could've missed it! I had it in my site the whole time. I could've sworn I hit it at least once."

Troy stood on the running boards of his machine and scanned the cliff face. "We're sitting ducks down here. We need to get up there."

"Agreed," the sheriff said. "Let's head this way and see if we can find a way to get up." He gunned his engine and shot forward angling away from the cliff face to give enough room to react in case the Sasquatch tried to attack them from the higher ground.

The two sleds raced along the forest floor zig-zagging around trees and rocks while the two men kept a close eye out for the Sasquatch. They were cautious but also relied on the senses of the dog to alert them to anything out of the ordinary. It didn't take long to find a slope they could climb and they shot up and over the smaller ridge. The trees were spaced out wide enough that navigating the hillside wasn't a problem.

The sky was beginning to lose any hint of sunlight behind the gray overcast, and the wind was much more intense on the ridge than below in the cover of the trees.

Nick stopped his sled and pointed to the ground, "Hey, look there!"

Troy saw the blood trail and the tracks left by the Sasquatch. Its stride was significantly shorter than before.

"Looks to be walking now, not in a hurry."

"Yeah, and that looks like a lot of blood. No idea why it just started bleeding out like that," Nick said.

"Maybe you did hit it after all, and the running from us finally moved the bullet around, I dunno," Troy said confused.

"We know it's definitely injured, could be from a bullet, could be from previous injuries. No matter, it's wounded and it knows we're hunting it. It won't like that, so we'd better be careful. It could be anywhere."

Troy looked around, cautiously, "Yeah, I have an eerie feeling."

The tiny hairs on the back of Troy's neck were standing. It was a primeval sensation buried somewhere deep in the back of his mind. The sub-conscious receptors understood and fed back to him a warning of danger.

Zeus must've felt it too. The big dog jumped from the sled and sniffed the blood trail. A low growl escaped his snarling muzzle, and his hackles were fully raised.

"Zeus, come," Troy said.

Zeus obeyed Troy's command and leaped back on the sled, but not before hiking a leg and urinating on the tracks to mark his territory.

"I don't think it's very close or Zeus would've lost his mind again, but we should still be careful. He doesn't like it any more than we do."

"Let's get moving before we lose what light we have left. I'd rather not be out here at night."

"Hell no," Troy said. "Lead the way."

Nick opened the throttle on the sled and eased forward. The terrain of the area began to change with the contour. The small ridge they climbed to get to the flattened area was lined with huge chunks of granite and few trees. They progressed northward toward the rim of the canyon, which was still a few miles away, more trees dotted the landscape making visibility of more than a few yards at a time difficult at best. The snowpack on the slope had been blown by the winds and frozen solid in places. The sleds had no trouble over the terrain, but there were areas where large granite rocks and outcroppings covered the ground.

The creature was still losing blood but it was slowing down. The tracks disappeared again over another rocky patch, and they lost the trail. Zeus wasn't trained to track. The men tried coaxing him, but Zeus didn't know what they were asking of him.

"Maybe I should've gotten a bloodhound instead of you, buddy," Troy said, patting the dog on the head.

"Let's spread out a little and see if we can pick it up

again," Nick said.

A gnarly scrub tree of sorts covered with thorny limbs stood alone next to a large boulder. It was barren of any leaves. The sheriff spotted something hanging from one of the limbs and steered the snowmobile under it. He stood on the seat of the sled, reached up and pulled the object down to examine it.

"Check this out," Nick said as Troy rode up beside him. "It's fur. Had to be seven feet high on that limb."

Troy lifted his goggles and pulled his face mask down to breath in the cold air. The sheriff handed the tuft of hair to him to examine. The hair was coarse and long with a reddish tint to it. Troy brought it closer to his eyes, but as he did so, he nearly gagged from the smell.

"Oh, dear God, that's atrocious!"

"Tell me about it. Look there, more blood," Nick said, pointing to a large splotch of blood on one of the rocks close by. "Looks like it understands tracking because it's sticking to the rocks instead of snow."

"Yeah, I don't think we're dealing with a simple-minded animal here at all," Troy said.

Just then, a crackle came over the radio and startled them both. Nick turned the volume up just a touch more, but the sender's voice was buried in the static.

"Tried...the pass...back...opper."

"This is Sheriff Nick Blaine. Can you repeat?"

Nick tried a few more times, but could not raise the other team.

"That sounded like Chastain," Troy said.

"Yeah, but I couldn't make out what he was saying."

Troy shook his head and pulled his balaclava back up to cover his face. "Me either."

"Wait, what was that?" Nick suddenly asked, spinning

around on the seat of his sled while pulling his revolver out with the same move. "There!" He pointed.

A small tree, about fifty yards away swayed back and forth as if something or someone moved it intentionally. A low gravelly growl came from Zeus's huge chest, and the hackles on his back were standing straight up.

Troy grabbed his binoculars and scanned the area, one hand reaching for his own gun.

Another tree further away moved. It was slight, but Troy picked it up through the field glasses. "It's moving away from us in that direction," he said.

"Let's go," Nick said, holstering his weapon and easing the throttle open. "Remember, it's injured and mad as hell. It'll put up one hell of a fight."

Troy said nothing. He shivered from the cold and zipped his parka up tighter under his chin. He knew all too well what they were dealing with and it wasn't a comfortable feeling out here in the frozen and isolated forest. He put his field glasses away and followed the sheriff, closely riding through the trees. The north face of the sheer cliff wall loomed larger in the distance. The gray sky offered little help with visibility at ground level.

Zeus suddenly bolted from the sled barking and running full bore ahead and covering ground more quickly than the snowmobiles could.

"Zeus, come! Zeus, come back!" Troy shouted to no avail. The big dog heard or sensed something that Troy and the sheriff were oblivious to. Troy had never seen the dog not obey a command.

"We gotta catch him!" Nick shouted back at Troy, who was already on the throttle. "He must've caught wind of the Squatch!"

The two men raced along the frozen ground chasing

267

after the dog that was already out of sight. They could hear Zeus barking occasionally, but the wind made pin-pointing a direction too difficult. The tracks the dog left behind were the only way they would be able to find him.

Nick hit a small rise unexpectedly, and the snowmobile leaped into the air throwing frozen snow in a giant arc. He leaned into the jump and landed the sled expertly.

Troy, following too closely behind the sheriff, wasn't so lucky. The sled seemed to drift in slow motion as he hung in the air for what seemed like an eternity. He lost his seat when the snowmobile pitched forward and in turn lost his grip. All he could do was watch as the machine slipped away underneath. He did his best to balance himself in midair to land with a tuck and roll. The sled landed and shot forward into a small pine. The right-side rudder caught on the tree and snapped the sled around in a semi-circle before coming to rest. Troy hadn't reattached the kill-switch cable to his wrist, and the engine was still running, though the machine lay on its side. Troy's landing didn't fare much better. He attempted to land on his feet with his knees bent slightly ready to tuck and roll, but his right foot caught on the top of his left boot top, and he landed at an awkward angle before splaying in the snow.

Nick hit the brakes and slid around in a half-donut and hit the throttle hard to circle back around to Troy.

"Are you okay?" he asked, jumping off the sled to check on his friend.

Troy was lying on his back with his head lower than his feet. He was struggling to sit up.

"Yeah, I think so," he said, finally able to get an elbow underneath him and push up to a sitting position. He no longer had his goggles on. They were lost somewhere in the snow.

Nick helped him to his feet then ran over to the sled and shut the engine off.

"Sled's busted, it's done for. We'll have to double up for now. We need to find Zeus. I know he spotted that son of a bitch or heard it or something." Nick said. "Are you good? Nothing broken or sprained?"

"Nah, I'm good, just dazed a bit." Troy slugged through the snow to the sled and pulled his rifle free from the scabbard. The binoculars had been tossed out of the case, and he stooped to pick them up. "Busted," he said, holding them up. One of the glass objective lenses was shattered, and the focus wheel was broken. "Just great - sleds busted, bino's busted, but at least I'm not. Let's get going."

Troy climbed on behind the sheriff with the rifle slung over his shoulder. Troy had opted for his Marlin 1895 Modern Hunter in the .45-70 Gov't. It packed six rounds in the magazine of four-hundred and five-grain Core-Lokt projectiles capable of knocking down the biggest of north-american game at over 1,330fps. He was more than confident the weapon would have little trouble taking down even the biggest adversary. He carried an extra ten rounds on his belt.

Nick had to swerve around a large patch of rocks and veered to the left side. The wind had created a snowdrift on the opposite side more than four feet high.

"It's going to get more like this the closer we get to the canyon wall," Nick said. "Do you see any tracks?"

Troy looked all around as Nick slowly maneuvered around the rocks. "I'm not seeing anything. Tell you the truth; it's getting too dark," Troy said, wiping away the tears from his eyes before they froze to his skin.

"I know," Nick said. He hit the brake and stopped suddenly. "Hey! Do you hear that?"

It was faint but distinct. It was a dog barking. Zeus was close.

"There!" Troy pointed. He caught a flash of movement not more than fifty yards ahead of them.

"Hold on!" Nick shouted, hitting the throttle. "Be ready to shoot. If Zeus has that damned thing cornered, we're in for a fight!"

Troy ducked behind the sheriffs back and covered his eyes with a gloved hand.

Nick slalomed around small pine trees and scrub brush growing in the rocky terrain, bouncing over the trail at break-neck speed. They could see Zeus running ahead of them, zig-zagging around trees and over rocks. He was hot on the trail of something, though they could not see where the creature was.

Troy was concentrated on watching the trail for the beast as best he could given the circumstances, but his mind also had time to contemplate the ordeal he and his friends went through so long ago when the Sasquatch attacked them at his cabin. The ragtag group of law enforcement officers, mountain folk and himself, held the clan of Sasquatch at bay for an entire night of terror. He saw first-hand how intelligent and clever the creatures were. They weren't simply animals; they were on a much higher plane of intellect. They fought together in unison. They made plans and carried out feints while others attacked on a different front. The Sasquatch were huge and powerful, but also sleek and cunning.

Nick followed Zeus as fast as he could maneuver through the natural obstacle course, but could not seem to close the gap.

"Look there," Nick shouted, pointing with his left hand to the ground. A huge set of tracks left by the creature along with much smaller tracks left by the dog. There were tinges of blood on the snow near the creature's prints.

"Zeus has it on the run!" Troy shouted back.

"Yeah, and they're headed straight for the canyon wall," Nick said. "We'll either stop it there, or it knows a way up!"

The men followed the trail, which was now mostly snow and easy to spot even in the dimming light. Zeus was out of sight, but his tracks were visible. As they neared the steep wall of the canyon rim, the graying light of the winter sky was nearly gone. The headlight from the snowmobile was brighter. They entered a small stand of scraggly pines and rode through as quietly as possible while keeping a close eye out for any indication the creature may have doubled back. When they emerged on the other side, the cliff face loomed over them, its jagged granite walls an imposing fortress rising nearly straight up almost two-hundred feet.

Zeus was twenty feet up on a small ledge that overlooked the gentle slope that cascaded down into the canyon below, but his attention was focused much higher up on the rock face. He barked feverishly at something beyond the trail but found himself unable to advance further.

Troy climbed off the sled followed by the sheriff.

"Look, there!" Troy shouted.

The giant tracks of the Sasquatch led straight up the wall where a bloody handprint the size of a basketball was imprinted on the granite.

"Zeus, come," Troy called, but the dog paid him no attention.

The frigid north wind came whistling down the cliff face with force enough to bend the evergreens that lay scattered below. Bringing with it an ensuing darkness that seemed to engulf the entire canyon as the men stood at the base looking up, desperately trying to see their quarry. They knew all too well the danger they faced. It was one thing to go up against a wounded animal such as a brown bear that fought only to defend itself and its territory. It was an entirely different scenario to face a predator that had no known natural enemies, including man.

Troy had his rifle out and ready, but could now barely see Zeus. He called several more times for the big dog to return to his side. Finally, faced with a reality that he could go no further, Zeus turned and trotted back down.

"Good boy, Zeus, good boy," Troy said, patting the dog on the head. "Do we have any flashlights?" he asked.

"Yeah," Nick said, reaching into his pack on the sled and handing one to Troy.

They shined the lights all over the cliff face but could see nothing.

"Hey, look over there where my light's shining," Nick said. "That may be a way up. It's wounded, maybe fatally. I'm gonna see just how far up I can go. I want to end this thing."

"I'm right behind you," Troy said. "Damn it!" he suddenly exclaimed. "My Ruger, it's missing. It must've fallen out when I wrecked my sled. I never noticed."

"How many rounds do you have for the rifle?" Nick asked.

"Six, one and ten more," Troy said, feeling his belt. "At least I haven't lost any of those."

He was a crack shot with the custom shop rifle. It held six rounds in the magazine that was as long as the eighteen and half inch barrel. It was a heavy big-bore rifle, but with the ammo he carried, it was also a formidable weapon against even the biggest game.

Nick pulled his Benelli M4 loose from the scabbard and

jacked a ten-millimeter shell into the chamber and replaced the one back in the magazine.

"The good news is, it's alone. The bad news is, we're on his grounds."

Troy swallowed hard, gripping the rifle in both hands. His gloves were thick, but he could still feel the contours of the laminated stock. The heft gave him comfort.

"Zeus, heel," he commanded.

The big dog was still agitated but had calmed down enough to listen to Troy's commands. He was ready to continue his pursuit. Troy had never seen him act this way but understood the behavior. It wasn't anything normal they were pursuing.

The path the sheriff found wasn't much better than the one Zeus was on earlier. The granite provided few natural walkways and what was provided was narrow, steep, and treacherous. The howling wind blowing across the cliff face wasn't helping with their precarious climb.

Nick led them up the narrow path, moving slow and cautiously. He stopped several times to shine the flashlight beams over the cliffs, ever cognizant of an attack from above.

About thirty feet up, the path widened enough that the two could walk side by side on the ledge. Nick stopped them suddenly when Zeus started growling.

"Zeus, quiet, quiet boy," Troy said softly.

"That looks like a cave up there. He sensed something. If it's in there and we have it cornered, it'll put up one hell of a fight." Nick said.

"What do you want to do?" Troy asked

"I want to go home and have a beer sitting in front of the TV, but since that's not happening…"

"Yeah, well," Troy said, clearing his throat and

swallowing hard. "I guess we're going in then."

"Yeah, guess so."

The two men slowed their approach, cautiously walking toward the cave entrance. All the way, Troy whispered to Zeus to heel and stay quiet. He hoped the dog would obey and silently prayed he wouldn't give them away. Somewhere in the back of his mind, however, he knew that if the creature were inside the cave, it already knew they were coming for it and they had to expect it to defend itself.

"Look, more blood," Nick pointed out when Zeus sniffed it and grizzled at it on the rocky terrace. It took Troy's constant reassuring of the commands to quiet and stay to keep the dog in check.

"I don't think I can keep him back much longer," Troy whispered.

Nick glanced over at Troy, but offered no suggestions, just shrugged. They were all nervous.

The entry to the cave wasn't much more than a standard door width, but it was well over ten feet tall. The opening was protected by a large rock outcrop on the opposite side of the men. The cave could not be seen easily from the ground. Their flashlights only showed a small sliver of darkness within the crevice of the wall. The rock terrace they stood on extended to the edge only ten feet, but it continued along the face of the cliff as far as their lights could shine.

Nick reached the cave first and shined his light inside. He could see that the cave widened just inside the mouth, but squeezed together the further back it went, which seemed to go on for hundreds of feet. He saw no signs of the Sasquatch, so he waved Troy in. When they stepped inside, they shined their lights all around, ready with their guns. The wind swirled snow at the entrance, but only a few steps in, there was a physical change in the ambient temperature. It was still cold, but without the brutal north wind, it was more bearable. They noticed a scattering of animal bones against the opposite side from where they stood, several loose rocks and a few large ones in various locations throughout.

Troy started pulling his balaclava down, but the cave reeked of a terrible bad odor, however, causing the men to leave their face masks pulled over their noses. The smell of rotten, decayed flesh was brutal on the senses.

"Dear Lord, the stench is awful," Troy said.

"Yeah, and you know what that means."

The statement wasn't something that needed to be said. They both knew what made the horrible smell. This was the lair of Sasquatch. It extended as far back as the lights could shine and on a gradual descent on smooth stone. The group moved steadily along the wall as quietly as possible, Troy whispering to Zeus the entire time to keep him calm.

"Hey, look at this," Nick whispered.

"Cheyenne?"

He shined his light against the wall of the cave. Dark red drawings depicted animals, people, and hunting scenes.

"Could be, but probably Ute Mountain tribe," Nick said. "Just another one of the many atrocities perpetrated by the federal government in the name of assimilation. Just a disguised land-grab really."

"Yeah, well. I appreciate the history lesson, but we have more pressing matters," Troy said.

Suddenly, Zeus barked. The deep throaty '*woof*' startled the men. When they turned toward the darkness of the cave Zeus bolted, heading straight back into the cave, growling and snarling.

"He must've heard something. Be ready!" Troy said.

"Let's follow him, but spread out. If he flushes that damned thing out, we'll have it in a crossfire."

Troy moved across to the other side of the cave, and together they advanced with their weapons readied. They could hear Zeus barking and the echoes ringing back through the cavernous fissure. He took his gloves off, removed the extra cartridges from his belt and dropped them in his pocket for quicker access. He moved across the cave floor and together, they advanced deeper into the cave, stepping over rocks and animal bones along the way.

"I don't hear Zeus anymore," Troy said.

"Yeah, me either," Nick said, shining his light to the ceiling of the cave and all along the walls. "Looks like it's getting narrower; only about ten feet wide here."

"I hope he's okay. It's not like him to disregard commands. He's trained a lot better than that, but this isn't something he's ever seen before."

The sheriff nodded silently in the darkness. Troy could barely make out his outline from the flashlight he carried. The men were more than two-hundred feet beyond the entrance of the cave when hy heard it.

"What is that?" Troy asked.

"What are you talking about?"

Troy pulled the face mask down from his ears and listened more carefully. It wasn't a steady sound; it came and went. It was a low-pitched thrum resembling a wide-throated steam horn way off in the distance.

The men shined their lights over the entire cave but could see nothing but the solid granite walls.

"I have no idea what that is. Let's keep going. Looks like it's turning back."

Nick was right. The cave did turn back and then began a

series of twists and turns never more than ten feet wide. The thrumming sound continued, not steadily, but coming and going.

"I think I hear Zeus," Troy said.

Nick heard it too. Shuffling ahead, he saw a split in the cave wall. He approached slowly. It was another passageway. The entrance was only a few feet wide and went up to the top of the ceiling. The main passageway continued into the distance. The flashlights revealed nothing more than jagged granite cave walls inside, but the new passage did widen out further back.

"I can't tell which direction Zeus's barking is coming from," Troy said.

"Me either, and this new one looks just as big as this main channel," Nick whispered.

"Hey, check this out. Is that blood?" Troy asked. He was shining his light on the floor just inside the new passage. He bent down and touched it with his bare fingers.

"Is it?" Nick asked.

"Yeah, looks like it went this way. I don't have to tell you how freakin' scary this is. My neck hurts so bad from being so bound up that I can barely turn my head."

"Me too, But we can't turn back now. There's only one of 'em, and it's already injured. He'll fight like hell, but we know they're flesh and blood and can be killed. We have enough firepower. Just don't shoot unless you have a good clear shot. Conserve the ammo."

Troy didn't have to be told. He knew all too well that if they ran out of ammo and the beast was still alive, the men wouldn't be for long.

They turned down the new passageway and were able to move a little faster as the floor was smooth and mostly level. The walls were damp, but also smooth.

The thrumming intensified and Troy had to work his jaw into a yawn several times for his ears to adjust.

"It doesn't seem like it just looking at it in the dark, but I know we're on a steady incline," Troy said.

"Been thinking the same thing. I can't make my ears pop."

"That sound is definitely louder now," Troy said.

The passage made a slow turn around a lazy bend then opened wide. The men made the turn and froze.

29

The limestone cave was cold, damp, and pitch-black inside. Their flashlights only illuminated exactly what they were pointed at with very little peripheral areas visible. The bright white conical beams punched a hole through the darkness like a light-saber when a Jedi first flicks it on. The erratic light danced all about the cave walls, bouncing with each step the men took, never shining in one place more than a few seconds.

It was quiet. So quiet, in fact, the men could hear their own footsteps even though they stepped as softly as they could. Even Zeus' barking had stopped, only the low thrumming came and went. The silence was unsettling. Troy was the first to speak.

"What the hell?"

The tunnel had turned directly into one of the largest caverns they had ever seen. Stalactites of various colors hung from the ceiling dozens of feet above them while tall spikes of stalagmites grew from the floor in a desperate attempt to reach the ceiling. They had no idea how far back the cavern went as their flashlights only penetrated the immediate darkness.

"I don't like this one bit. We're sitting ducks out there," Nick said.

Troy shined his light all around the cavern. An uncontrollable shiver came over his entire body. Something in the back of his mind was telling him, *Go back*, but all he could do was stand and stare at the massive cathedral-like cave.

"I'm with you," Troy finally said. "I don't like it either."

"A path that leads right through the middle of it. Looks well-worn too."

The sheriff's flashlight revealed a path about four feet wide that ran through the middle of the cavern. The floor was worn smooth and was clear of rocks. The cave itself smelled earthy, almost like wet dirt, damp and cold, but light, clean and easy to breathe.

Troy shifted the weight of his rifle from his shoulder to the crook of his left arm and moved his flashlight to his right hand.

"Well, let's see how far it goes."

The path led the men around huge rocks, and up and down undulations in the cave floor. They walked for several minutes without hearing anything other than the thrumming sound off and on, which they finally guessed were air currents throughout the cave system.

Troy had the uneasy feeling the entire time that they were being watched, but there was little he could do about it. They weren't turning back at this point. They were all in. He wasn't leaving without Zeus.

The slow, quiet shuffle along the twisting and winding path was somewhat mesmerizing to the two impromptu spelunkers, lulling them into complacency. At one point, Troy aimed his light above them and pointed out a bluish colored stalactite that dropped, what appeared to be, about twenty feet down and resembled an ice-cream cone turned upside down.

Suddenly a rock the size of a softball came hurtling through the air at the two men. If Nick hadn't seen the projectile move through the beam of his flashlight, the rock may have smashed into him which could've seriously injured or even killed him. When he saw it, he instinctively dodged thinking it was a bat. It was only when it smashed into a nearby stalagmite that he realized it was a rock.

"Take cover!" Nick yelled, as he ducked behind a large boulder.

Troy joined him, his rifle aimed in the general direction the stone came from, but he had no target to shoot at.

"There!" Nick shouted.

The flashlight picked up movement off to the right of their location. Something large loomed above a huge boulder fifty feet away. A flash of red eye shine gave its position away, but the Sasquatch moved too fast for the men to draw a bead on it.

Suddenly, another stone projectile came crashing toward them but was deflected by the large outcropping of rock the men hid behind. Nick moved his light quickly in the direction it came from again. This time he was ready with his handgun and squeezed a round off.

The blast of the Benelli M4 going off in the cave was so loud that the report caused both men to wince in pain and clutch at their ears.

Troy dropped his flashlight, and the rifle nearly fell as well, but luckily it when he fell back away from the sheriff's blast, the rifle dropped into his lap. His ears hurt from the sharp, loud explosion, but his survival instincts and adrenaline helped him push past the pain and scramble for the flashlight.

The Sasquatch roared in anger when the sheriff's 12-

gauge slug screamed past its head.

Troy grabbed his light and shined it toward the monster. He held the light under the forearm of the rifle with his left hand and tried to take aim, but the gunsights were too dark. He could only guess at his aim, and he waited until the creature showed itself.

The beast moved incredibly fast for how dark the cave was. *How could it see so well in the dark?* Troy thought. *Maybe it simply knew the cave so well that it didn't need much light.*

"The damned thing has us pinned down," Nick shouted, "with rocks!"

"What?" Troy said, still clasping his hands over his ears. He knew Nick was shouting something, but his ears rang with such intensity he was unable to understand the words.

Nick didn't hear him either but the Sasquatch had circled around them and cut off any escape from the direction the men had come. It seemed to be working its way closer, and with the darkness of the cave as cover, it could be on them within seconds.

"We need to move. Now!" Nick shouted, looking at Troy to make sure he understood, but he couldn't see the man's face in the darkness. He moved closer and clasped his shoulder.

"We've got to move. We're sitting ducks out here in the open. Let's head that direction," Nick shouted. He made a gesture with his hand in the ambient light of the flashlights.

Troy understood and was on his feet, instantly moving with the sheriff.

The flashlights bobbed and weaved through the maze of limestone as the two men moved quickly to find a better-protected position.

When the men ran through the maze, zig-zagging like a slalom skier. The creature threw more of the huge rocks at them, pushing them to change their course several times.

The men ran as fast as they could, but they were at a disadvantage in the labyrinth of mineral deposits. Every turn they made, they were forced to turn again as if they were the steel balls of a pinball machine. Several times they found themselves running in opposite directions, forcing them to stop and turn again and again.

"Where is it?" Troy hissed when they stopped for a breather.

"I don't know," Nick said.

Both scanned the area with their lights but saw nothing.

"Maybe it stopped chasing us?" Nick said, just as a rock the size of a baseball came whistling in, hitting Troy square in the left shoulder instantly knocking him down.

The flashlight fell from Troy's grasp, but he held onto the rifle, keeping it from hitting the rocks. Writhing in pain, he scrambled up to his knees, breathing hard.

Nick spun the direction the rock had come from. He waited until he saw the creature and squeezed off a well-aimed shot. The Ithaca barked its ten-gauge blast with authority. It was powerful enough to stop anything in its path with a direct hit.

The creature screamed in pain. It had been hit, but only a grazing shot on the arm. It felt all the weight and the sting of the giant slug ripping through its flesh.

The roars and screams were ear piercing, but being so close, it gave its position away. Nick seized the opportunity and ran forward. When he was only ten feet away from the beast, he raised his gun to fire, but when he went to pump another round in the chamber, he dropped the flashlight. He pulled the trigger then jacked another round in the chamber before reaching down for the light. Dropping to his left knee, he kept his right hand on the shotgun with the buttstock tucked under his arm. Not looking at the light, he reached for it in the darkness. At first, he missed it but didn't want to look away from where he thought the creature was. His hand trembled from the adrenaline and he still could not get a hold on the cold metal cylinder. He chanced a look down and saw his reach was too short. He had to lean forward more. Finally, his hand wrapped around the light, and he raised it alongside the barrel of the gun.

It was too late. The Sasquatch was already on him. Screaming in rage and fury, the beast reached down, grabbed the sheriff by the shoulders and slammed Nick to the ground.

Nick rolled onto his back when he hit the floor. He lost his breath in the blow, and he felt the sharp pang of a cracked rib when he tried to scramble back up. He felt the body heat of the creature standing over him. He smelled its awful, foul odor, but he couldn't move. He was pinned up against a rock. He could see the flashlight rolling back and forth on the rocky ground illuminating the giant creatures' feet. Nick was completely powerless to do anything about what was about to happen to him now.

A huge foot with a black scaly sole resembling pure leather, covered by long coarse black hair all the way down to the ankle slowly lifted above him ready to deliver the death blow, crushing the tiny human's head. There was nothing he could do to stop. A thousand things ran through Nick's mind as he prepared for his fate.

Lisa, his beautiful and only daughter. She had finally moved back to Hawthorn. He had missed her since she had gone off to college so many years ago. Sure, she came to visit during Christmas and always called on his birthday, but there was nothing like having her around.

Her mother passed away when she was young, and Nick never remarried. He always said he just didn't have time. The real reason was, he missed his wife too much. They were high school sweethearts. He had never known any other love than the one he had for her. He stayed busy though. He had been sheriff of Hawthorn for many years. Fact of the matter was, he never had to campaign. No one ever ran against him.

Darkness overtook him.

30

Michelle spotted the trail left by the snowmobiles. At first, she was confused by the directions until she saw the tracks of the Sasquatch. They were chasing it. She found where they had veered toward the north wall of the ridge and followed it up and over the hill. She wasn't far behind them but would have to go slow and careful so as not to get caught by surprise by the beast who had already injured two of their team members.

It would be dark soon. She wasn't afraid to be alone, but she knew the creature was better suited for nocturnal hunting than she was. She was already at a disadvantage.

The trail slalomed through the trees and sliced around giant boulders of solid granite. The wind was getting up and blowing crossways when she rode through tree cleared areas. An eerie feeling, she couldn't shake gnawed at the back of her neck. When she arrived at the canyon wall and spotted the snowmobiles parked at the bottom, it was dark.

Michelle pulled her sled in between the other two and shut the engine off and turned on her flashlight. She was leery of calling out for them in case the creature was nearby. She drew her Benelli out of the side scabbard, jacked a shell into the chamber as quietly as she could and slid another round into the magazine tube. Laying the shotgun across her arm that held the flashlight. She used her right hand to grab the two extra boxes of slugs, tossed them in her coat pocket, and set out to scout the area.

It didn't take her long to figure where the men had gone. Their trail was more than evident in the virgin snow, even in the dark. Her flashlight illuminated the path the two men had blazed not a half-hour earlier. Michelle was wary of the trail and the entire area. If the men had already become a victim of the creature, she could very well be next. The face of the ridge was nothing short of a wall of pure granite and limestone rising more than a few hundred feet. There were several places for an animal to hide, ready to ambush prey below, even for something as big as the Sasquatch. She was cautious, but not afraid. Resilient, headstrong, and determined. She would see this through to the end. She would find the creature, possibly the very one that killed her best friend so long ago, and she would kill it. She would show her parents, her therapist, the world even, that she wasn't crazy, that the story she told all those years ago was the truth. If she killed the beast and introduced it to the world, they would have to believe then. These creatures are real, not just fantasy. They're evil, dangerous and should be eradicated. Nobody should have to go through what she went through seven years earlier. Tonight, her nightmares would end.

The cold north wind blew over the top of the ridge winding its way through the trees, over the rocks and sweeping over the snow-covered slopes of the undulating hillside falling into the canyon below. Michelle felt the frigid bite even through her parka. She left her goggles on and pulled up her face mask tighter against the wind. She had scouted the area and felt comfortable in the fact that the creature and the men were inside the mountain. She had followed the tracks to the point where the men had ascended, and she spotted the cave entrance.

She went back to her snowmobile and grabbed a few more supplies. A few minutes later, she ascended the rock wall ledge and made her way along it until she got to the cave entrance. Ducking inside and scanning the area with her light, she felt safe enough to lean her shotgun against the rock wall and retrieve a pair of hands-free Nav7 night vision goggles and slipped it down on her head. Switching it on, she tested it, making sure it was at the right settings and firmly mounted for quick action. Next, she attached the flashlight to the M4 but switched it to infrared. She clicked it off for now. It may be needed later. She strapped two hunting knives with wicked nine-inch blades to each of her legs. After she checked her sidearm and made sure she had extra mags, she pulled the goggles down and followed the path into the belly of the mountain.

***

"Nick! Nick! Come on; we gotta get out of here!"

Troy tugged at the sheriff's coat to get to his feet. Nick was coming too slowly, not fast enough for Troy's sake.

Troy saw the creature pick the sheriff up and slam him to the floor of the cave. He had little time to react. He clicked the rifle's safety off and aiming the flashlight along the barrel, he fired.

The Sasquatch roared in pain and fury when the forty-five-caliber slug slammed into its shoulder, exploding into the solid mass of muscle.

Troy jacked another round into the chamber of the gun and ran forward. The creature turned just as he squeezed off another shot from the hip. The big-bore rifle bellowed, echoed through the cave, like a cannon blast on a cold, quiet morning battlefield of the civil war. The bullet slammed into a rock next to the Sasquatch, splintering shards of granite, lead and copper in a cascade of fiery sparks.

The beast roared in defiance then, disappeared in the cold dark gloom of the cavernous mausoleum.

Troy rushed to the sheriff's side.

"Come on, Nick. We gotta move."

Troy grabbed the sheriff's hand and forced the flashlight into it.

"You have to on hold this," He said, wrapping the sheriff's other arm over his shoulders.

Troy grabbed Nick's arm in a tight grip. He slung his other arm around the sheriff's upper body carrying his rifle in the same hand. He held Nick's left forearm in a tight grip, keeping the man on his feet they stumbled forward.

"There!" Troy shouted.

He stopped and grabbed the flashlight away from the still groggy sheriff. It was a ledge with what looked to be another passageway behind it. It was at least ten or twelve feet high.

"Wait, my gun. I must've dropped it."

"No time. We'd never find it anyway."

"How do we get up there?" Nick asked.

"Right there," Troy said, shining his light over a narrow ledge leading up to the rocky terrace.

"Looks like we can make it up there along that ledge. You up for it?"

"I'm good; let's go."

They heard the creature scream again. Its rage was followed by another large rock that crashed down near the men as they raced to the ledge. They scrambled up the narrow footpath and made their way up.

At any other time, the perch that overlooked the cavern below would have given them an incredible view. Under the circumstances, they didn't care about the location other than it gave them the high ground and a better position to fight back.

Troy's ears still hurt and rang, but at least he was able to hear again when the sheriff pointed his flashlight into the passageway behind the ledge.

"I'm not sure this is much better. Who knows where it leads?"

"At least we have the elevation for now," Troy said.

A low, drawn-out wail sounded in the distance. The creature howled. It sounded somewhat mournful, but angry at the same time. The men shined their lights toward the sound.

"Hard to tell exactly where it's coming from," Nick said.

Troy lay prone on the ledge overlooking the cavernous floor below them with his rifle aimed in the general direction of the Sasquatch. Try as he might, he wasn't able to position the flashlight well enough to allow him to see his gunsights.

"Nick, stand behind me with the flashlight so that I can see the sights too."

The sheriff understood his meaning and quickly moved behind him.

"Maybe, we'll get lucky if the damned thing shows itself."

They waited patiently, hearts beating rapidly positioned like a sniper and spotter on the battlefield when they finally heard it.

"There it is!" Nick said.

The creature moved quickly and was out of sight before Troy could get a bead on it. He followed it the best he could, but the Bigfoot disappeared as soon as it had appeared.

"It's too fast," Troy said. "I hate to waste a bullet unless I have a good chance to hit the damned thing."

Another huge rock crashed into the front edge of the ledge just in front of the men.

"Damn thing must be left-handed; I know I hit it in the right shoulder."

"So, what happened back there?" Nick asked.

"No time to explain really. Just dumb luck."

Troy backed away from the edge and rubbed his eyes from the debris of the crashing rocks as more came flying towards them.

"Let's duck inside this passage," Nick said. "Who knows, maybe we can get it to follow us and we can get it out in the open."

The men jumped up and turned into the dark corridor. The path went straight back about twenty feet then took a sharp turn to their left. They ran as fast as they could under the circumstances. Rocks crashed at their feet the size of a football weighing several pounds. If one of them found their mark, it could prove fatal.

As soon as they turned the corner of the narrow passageway, the solid rock under their feet suddenly disappeared. Neither men were able to stop in time. They slid, tumbled and crashed down the rocky incline falling nearly straight down for several feet. Their arms and legs were flailing in the air, banging on the rocks and finally they came to rest in a heap at the bottom of a twenty-foot fall.

Nick hit the bottom of the cave floor with a resounding

thud. He lay motionless and gasped for air. Air that seemed to have left him mid-flight to the ground. As he lay like that trying to remember exactly what had happened and where he was, a curious site came into view as he stared up. At first, it was merely a lighter shade of darkness, *if there was such a thing*, he thought. He let his eyes adjust and looked to the side of the apparition without looking directly at it. A deep thrumming sound surrounded him, ebbing and flowing. Finally, it dawned on him what the noise was and what he was now seeing.

Troy moaned somewhere off to the left.

"Troy, you okay?" Nick said.

A soft groan came from out of the darkness, "I think so. I dunno, really"

Nick struggled to sit up. He raised on one elbow, then pushed up with his hand against the hard floor. He rubbed his head with his other hand. When it came back wet, he knew it was blood.

"Banged up a little, but I think I'm okay. Nothing feels broken anyway," Nick said, rubbing the back of his neck.

Troy rolled onto his side and drew his left leg up gingerly. He felt a sharp pain shoot through his knee and winced. He tried straightening the leg out, slowly lifting and then bending it again. After a few times, he determined it wasn't broken, but it sure hurt.

"Guess we rolled more than fell. Still hurts like hell though." He sat up and started feeling around on the ground for his rifle and flashlight.

"I can't find anything, too damned dark," Nick said.

"Yeah, I can't even see my hand in front of my face. Need to find that flashlight."

A few minutes searching resulted in the rifle but no flashlight yet.

"Damnit! Just our luck. Feels like it took a beating. Can't tell with no light though."

Troy felt along the wall and made his way around the bottom edge of the passage where they fell. He moved to the other side and kicked something. He reached down and picked up the flashlight.

"Found it," he said and flicked it on.

The bright beam shined directly into Nick's eyes. He winced and pulled a hand up.

"Sorry, didn't know you were standing there," Troy said.

The lever of the rifle had opened, and the front site had been knocked off when it fell. There was a huge gouge in the forearm stock next to the sling mount. Nick saw the unspent cartridge and handed it to Troy who closed the breach and then slid the undamaged round back into the magazine.

"It's like me, a little beat up but ready to go. You, on the other hand, look like crap."

Nick touched a hand to his head, "Yeah, I can feel blood. It probably looks worse than it is. I don't feel light-headed or anything. My ribs are killing me."

Troy turned the flashlight to the top of the ledge they fell from. It wasn't exactly straight up, but there was no way they would be able to climb back up the smooth surface. The opposite direction split into two passageways.

"No way to get back up there," Troy said.

"No, and to be honest, we've already taken several turns in here. I'm afraid if we keep going, we may get stuck in this damn mountain for good," Nick spat.

As the men stood talking over their next move, the decision was made for them. A scream pierced the quiet solitude of the dark cave. It was too close for comfort.

"Choose one," Troy said.

293

"Let's go down the right. Any time we have a choice from here out, we go right. If we have to come back, it'll be easier to remember to go left."

"Sounds like a plan, unless we're forced back and have to take the left one," Troy said, striking out first with the flashlight.

"Cross that bridge when we get there. By the way, I think I know where that sound is coming from. That low-pitched wale, it's the wind blowing over crevices in the rock above us. There are openings up there, but they're too high to get to."

"Good to know."

The passageway started out wide and open, and the two men could walk side by side, but after a few hundred feet, it pinched down so small that both men had to duck down to get through single file.

"I have to tell you, I'm about ready to turn back and take our chances that Sasquatch will help us up that damn ledge," Troy mumbled. "I'm starting to feel more than just a little claustrophobic."

"I agree. If this gets any worse, we should turn back and try that other passage."

"Wait, what's that sound?" Troy said.

Nick stopped walking and listened carefully. "Sounds like running water."

"It's not far from here. Let's push forward."

Troy had to bend way down to duck under a rocky overhang but punched through to a large open area on the other side of the pinch-point. He stood up straight and stretched, reaching as high as he could.

"That feels better."

It was physically cooler, and the air felt cleaner.

Nick stepped out of the narrow passage and stretched to

his full height again.

"Tell me about it. Can you shine the light over there?"

Troy did as Nick asked of him and was astonished to see a small pool with water dumping into it from several feet above.

"Underground river. We must be deep. Everything outside has been frozen over solid for a month or better," Nick said, walking toward the pool.

Troy followed him to the edge.

"Question is, what now?"

Nick knelt and scooped a bit of the crystal-clear water and drank.

"Freezing cold, but tastes good."

After they both got their fill, they stood and looked around the landing. The river was too wide for the light to show the far side, but the water was flowing. Stalactites, suspended from the cave ceiling reached down toward the water's surface as if to dip a toe in to check the water. Some were submerged, but most held back in silent reserve.

"Good news is, there's no way that the Squatch can follow us through here. The bad news is, I have no idea where *here* is."

"Yeah, me either. I'm so turned around, and there's no telling which direction is which. Not that a compass would do us much good at getting out of here."

"There's a ledge along the edge of the stream. Shine the light over there."

Troy saw it too.

"Looks wide enough and I don't see any other way to go."

The intrepid hunters followed the winding path of the

stream for the better part of an hour. Nick struggled with the cracked rib. Troy could tell it was hard on his friend to keep pushing forward. Nick was breathing heavy and laboring, much too intensely.

"Why don't we sit down and rest for a few minutes," Troy suggested.

Nick kept moving forward, "Nah, I'm good. If I sit, I may not be able to get back up and get moving again."

"Okay, but if you need to stop and rest, just say so."

Nick just grunted and nodded his head. Not that Troy could see him, but he got the idea.

Troy's thoughts were not focused on resting. He was preoccupied with the fact the pair had between them all of one flashlight, one rifle and a hunting knife. These were the only weapons the two had to defend themselves with. By his count, he had fourteen rounds remaining for the rifle.

There was a slight breeze. It came from the deep recesses of the cave that followed along with the rolling stream. Troy aimed the flashlight across the water several times, but there was never a place where they could see all the way across.

The air was cold, and as the adrenaline wore off, he became more aware of it. His coat and pants were well insulated, but that didn't stop the chill on his face. He pulled his balaclava back up and tucked it just under his eyes and made sure most of his skin was covered. His knee throbbed from falling down the rocks, and he struggled to straighten it with each step. He could feel it getting tighter as they walked, but was thankful that his friend didn't want to stop. Troy didn't think he would've been able to go on either. He heard Nick stifle a cough several times, but the sheriff wasn't one to complain. The thought of being lost in the cave was unnerving, so he concentrated his efforts on moving. Troy held the flashlight in his left hand, the rifle in his right and plodded along in silence.

Troy didn't notice right away, but when he did, he gently tapped Nick on the shoulder with the back of his hand and stopped.

"Listen. Do you hear that?"

"Yeah, the water's flowing faster. Another falls, maybe?" Nick replied.

Troy moved forward, being careful not to leave Nick walking in the dark. They were only steps away from the edge before they realized where they stood.

"Bloody hell!" Troy exclaimed. "What now?"

The precipice leaned lazily out over the darkness below. The flashlight, as bright as it was, was unable to locate the bottom. The prognosis seemed grim.

Troy's chest tightened as he shined the light over the water falling over the edge of the underground canal then over the cave walls. *Panic is not an option*, he thought. *There must be a way out.* He handed the rifle to the sheriff and lowered himself to his hands and knees, crawling to the edge with the light.

"Hey, there may be a way down," Troy said. His thoughts turning to the banged-up knee and the sheriff's cracked rib. "If you think you're up for it? Doesn't look easy, and to be honest, if we go down and it turns out there's no way out…"

He let the sentence hang. The sheriff knew that if they took the chance of climbing down and discovered no way out once they reached the bottom, the chances of climbing back up and back-tracking the way they came in would be nearly impossible. Both men knew their predicament, but neither had to say it out loud. They were scared. They started out as the hunters, now they'd become the hunted, running for their lives.

"I don't see an alternative," Nick panted.

"I'll go first," Troy said. He unwrapped the Paracord from his hunting knife and secured the flashlight around his neck. "It'll be pretty dark going down. We'll have to take our chances."

Next, Troy took the rifle from the sheriff, extended the sling, and pulled it over his head with the rifle hanging between his shoulder blades. He swung a leg over the edge and stretched down for the next foothold. Once he was safely down to the next foot and handhold, he shined the light up for Nick to follow.

Half an hour later, the two men stood together at the bottom of a fifty-foot drop. The stream was much narrower at the bottom, and they could see the twenty feet or so to the other side. The landing had a low ceiling of only about eight feet, but the main feature was several water eroded tunnels along the side. Some passageway openings were large while others were so small that only small kids or animals could possibly crawl through.

"We said we stick to the right every time we could," Troy said.

"Yeah, but it's a bit small. I hate to say it, but I'm starting to feel claustrophobic. Not to mention the fact that I'm freakin' starving," Nick replied.

"You're telling me. I've been thinking the same thing. Why don't we check the tunnel out and see how far we can get? If it's not promising after a while, we come back and try the next one?"

"Sounds like a plan."

The passage walls were smoothed from millions of years

of water rushing through. The walls threatened to close in a few times but remained easily passable. Though they felt it more than saw it by the air pressure and sound, they emerged into a large limestone cavern an hour later. It was the feeling of being alone in a small room and another person enters. One may not have seen the person enter, but the ambient change in sound and air is perceptible, like a sixth sense woven deep in man's DNA.

"I'm not sure where the hell we are, but I already feel better that we're no longer trapped inside that small tunnel. I have no idea how my uncle survived Viet Nam as a tunnel rat," Troy stated.

"Tell me about it," Nick wheezed. He too felt the change. "I feel like I can breathe now. I know it's all in my head, but I sure feel better."

Troy shined the flashlight all around their new area and landed on one stalactite in particular - a large bluish spike in the shape of an upside-down ice cream cone. "Don't speak too fast. I have good news and then not so good news."

"What's that?" Nick asked.

"The good news is, I think I know where we are, which means I know the way out. The not so good news is that we're right back in the same cavern where the Sasquatch almost killed us."

31

"I'd say let's stay and fight, but neither of us is in good enough shape. I can barely move, and you're staggering like a ninety-year-old man right now. We need to get the hell out of here."

"I'm afraid you're right," Troy said. "I'm in no shape to put up much of a fight."

"We know it's worse off than we are now. If you hit it like you think you did, anyway."

"I know I hit once, maybe twice."

Nick eased down to a sitting position on a nearby rock. "I doubt it will cause much more problems on the mountain for skiers or campers. Not right now, anyway. We should have time to heal up and get the team back out here. We can prep better and come back another time, now that we know where it lives."

Troy followed suit and found a nearby rock and settled down with the rifle carefully laid across his lap. He switched the light off, and they sat in the darkness catching their breath.

Troy's mind wondered. He thought about Zeus, worried about where he might be. He had confidence the dog could take care of himself out in the open, but here in these caves was another story. It was a labyrinth with corridors and pathways that led every which direction. Troy had no idea if the dog would be able to track his way back out or not. As damp as the cave air was, it could prove challenging even for a bloodhound. He and Zeus had been together since the big rottweiler was just a pup.

Five minutes later, Nick held his ribs tightly and stood gingerly. Wincing in pain, he tried stretching as erect as possible. It was difficult, but necessary. He was aware of the danger of complacency.

Troy took a deep breath and pushed up off the rock. "Yeah, guess it's time to move." He flipped the flashlight on to look for a path. When he did, he saw the danger just in the nick of time. The Sasquatch stood ten feet away!

Troy threw the rifle to his shoulder and squeezed the trigger only to find the safety was still on. By the time he flicked it off, the beast was on them screaming in a frenzied rage.

Lunging forward the huge Sasquatch covered the distance easily with one leap. A giant hand with dark skin reached out and with one glancing blow knocked Troy off his feet and into a large boulder. It felt like being hit by a club covered in a coarse rough-out leather. The flashlight flew against the hard granite cave floor, flickered a couple of times then faded out. It plunged the weary warriors into pitch black.

Nick pulled his hunting knife from the sheath and stabbed at the spot where he saw the beast last, thrusting straight in and back out, but found nothing but air. The creature was too fast in its strike and move fight sequence. The sheriff knew the general direction Troy was thrown, so he hurried carefully toward him. He could hear his friend groaning in the darkness, but could not hear the Sasquatch.

"Troy, you okay?" he whispered, trying to listen for both

Troy and the beast.

Troy groaned but could say nothing. The wind had been knocked out of him when he hit the hard surface.

Nick flicked the knife handle around in his hand so that the blade ran along the outside of his forearm facing away from his skin. Clambering down on hands and knees, he found his friend.

"I can't see a damned thing. No idea where that sonofabitch is. Are you okay?"

He felt Troy roll onto his side.

"Yeah, I think so. Everything inside hurts from my teeth to my feet," he said groggily.

"We lost the light, not sure where the rifle is, but I have a general idea. Gonna try for it," Nick said, sliding the knife back into the sheath on his hip.

"Shh, it's close."

Nick crawled as quickly as he could to find the gun. Using his arms, he felt around the cold, damp surface of the cave floor like a desperate person who had dropped their glasses and couldn't see anything without them. His fingers touched something cold and round. He latched onto the barrel of the rifle just as he heard the beast's heavy footsteps thudding on the floor near him. He knew which direction Troy was. He wasn't in the line of fire. Nick rolled onto his back, clicked the safety off, and fired.

The muzzle blast illuminated the Sasquatch. It towered nearly nine feet above him, only steps away. The creature used a huge, hairy arm to shield its eyes from the gunfire which forced it to pause for a split second. Nick jacked another round into the chamber and shot again and again. Each blast echoed throughout the cavern, reverberating off the solid stone and crashing into one another until it sounded like one massive explosion.

Click!

The firing pin hammered down on empty space. The rifle was empty, but the Bigfoot was still standing. Nick had risen to a knee but now stood and grabbed his knife from the sheath expecting the beast to take advantage.

After a tense moment, Nick let a breath out that he didn't know he had been holding. His body shook from the adrenaline that coursed through his veins like electricity. He heard Troy stir again and turned to him.

"Where is it?"

"I don't know. I think it's gone. I...I don't hear it."

Nick stepped closer.

"I'm out. I need more rounds."

Troy reached in his pocket and quickly handed over more of the heavy .45-70 rounds to Nick who wasted no time reloading the weapon.

"We need to find the flashlight!" Nick hissed. "It's gotta be around close."

Both men scrambled to find the light, but with so many rocks, stalagmites, and pure darkness, their task was nearly impossible.

Suddenly they heard the creature's feet thudding on the cave floor, running straight at them. Nick jacked a round into the chamber and blasted the direction it seemed to be coming from. It missed but made it duck and cover from the loud noise and the projectile that flew screaming by its head. Nick fired again, but this time the creature was ready and ducked behind a huge boulder.

"Move back!" Nick shouted.

The men tried to move back, but the darkness, along with the unfamiliar cave, made the going difficult. They shuffled and felt their way around a large rock and hunkered down.

Troy kicked something on the ground. It didn't feel or sound like a rock. He reached down and found the flashlight. He clicked the switch on, but nothing happened. He tried shaking it a few times then banged it against his palm. The light flickered just as a large rock smashed into Nick's left hip knocking the man to the ground.

Nick screamed in agony.

Troy saw the beast had moved around to flank them and kept the light aimed straight at the large boulder it hid behind.

"Are you okay?" he shouted.

He heard Nick moan again.

"It's my leg," Nick hissed, clearly hurting.

Troy grabbed the rifle that Nick had the fortitude to hold on to and protect as he fell. He felt in his pocket and found two more rounds and reloaded the gun. He had no idea how many were left in it, but that was all they had.

"Do you have your knife?" he asked Nick.

"Yeah. Yeah, I think so."

The blade had fallen at his feet, but he heard it clank on the floor and scooped it up. Nick tried to get to his feet. The leg was too bad and wouldn't allow him to put weight on it. He could feel blood oozing down the leg.

Another rock came crashing in and shattered against the boulder where he lay. Troy turned and aimed the light along the barrel of the gun just as another rock came flying in and hit him on the shoulder. He staggered backward, tripped over the sheriff and collapsed in a heap trapped against the large rock. He dropped the flashlight again, plunging them back into darkness. Troy lay sprawled on the cold hard ground, unable to move.

Nick crawled over to him and found the rifle and the flashlight that he saw fall to the ground at his feet. The light was a tough, tactical light, but it had seen its final use. It was done. Nick tossed it aside with a curse and scrambled to a knee. The pain in his leg was almost unbearable, but the adrenaline helped him overcome it. He dragged himself up to lean on the nearest rock and listened for the Sasquatch. Finally, he heard it breathing hard and laboring toward him. He took a careful aim at the sound and pulled the trigger.

The creature roared in rage as the bullet found its mark in its gut.

Nick jacked another round in the chamber and squeezed the trigger. The blast missed. The creature had somehow moved out of the path just in time. Nick levered in another round and squeezed, but the trigger only clicked. He was out.

"That's it," he yelled, but Troy couldn't answer. He was out cold.

Nick shrunk behind the rock, and when he felt the beast draw near, he swung the rifle as hard as he could, catching the creature in the bicep.

The Sasquatch screamed down at the tiny man and swatted him against the rocks with a backhanded blow.

Nick banged against the rocks and crumpled like a rag doll onto the floor. He was still conscious, but he was unable to move. He lay still, gasping for breath.

Just as the huge beast was about to crush the men, Zeus leaped at the creature's throat, driving it backward. The dog was quick, and its teeth found flesh with its powerful jaws set. The Sasquatch screamed and tried desperately to shake the dog off, but the dog's teeth sank even deeper.

***

Michelle heard the shots echo down the passageway. She ran as fast as she dared through the corridor. She emerged into the vast cathedral-like cavern just in time to see the creature lumber over the men laying on the ground. The beast halfway roared and screamed in a primal rage. Was she too late to save them?

The Bigfoot was huge, easily twice her height. She found a pathway through the middle of the cavern and zig-zagged her way through. There was a possibility there would be more than one of the creatures, especially in this huge cave complex, but that was of little consequence now.

Suddenly Zeus was there, driving the beast back away from the men.

Michelle found the advantage she needed to get closer. She leaped on to a large rock then jumped to a bigger one where she had a better view. The goggles were great with just a little light, but the cave was pitch black. She reached into her bag and pulled out several chem-sticks. Breaking them, she threw them all around the area. It was more than adequate lighting for the goggles. From her vantage point she could see the men lying on the ground. She could also see the creature shake the dog off and fling the small animal somewhere into the darkness. She thought she heard a welp, but then silence.

Her actions with the chem-sticks drew the attention of the beast. Drawing her sidearm, she squeezed the handle to turn on the laser sight, and she aimed. The .454 Casull round belched its heavy metal bullet in a powerful blast and screamed straight at the creature's head.

The Sasquatch moved slightly at the new threat just as the bullet slammed into its thick muscled shoulder. It staggered backward but still stood.

Michelle aimed the laser at the creature again, but the

beast ducked behind the boulder. Much too close to the men for her comfort. If she were to miss, the bullet could ricochet and hit one of them. She leaped from the rock, running along the pathway at full speed. The glow sticks gave her all the light she needed to maneuver through the maze of rocks. She moved quickly, leaped on one rock and effortlessly jumped from it to the next.

The creature ducked down behind the nearest boulder and veered around to try to flank this new menace.

Michelle expected the move. She was doing the same thing. Each combatant was circling the other, looking for a weakness to exploit. She leaped onto a rock, then another and another until she saw the creature again only twenty feet away. She aimed the laser once more and took careful aim, but before she could squeeze the trigger, a well-placed rock flew directly at her. She didn't see it until the last second. She ducked just in the nick of time but lost her perch on the round boulder. She fell off the rock to the hard surface five feet down. She tumbled in a side roll and came up on her feet as quick as a cat. She ran forward and bobbed down behind a boulder just as the creature lobbed another rock at her, shattering the mineral deposit directly in front of her.

Screaming in fury, the Sasquatch moved quickly to counter her and cut her off from the downed men. It was angry that she had hurt it.

Michelle saw the beast tuck in behind a huge boulder and peak out on both sides. They were at a standoff. She glanced around the vast cavern. An idea sprouted when she looked above the creature's position. A large stalactite hung down several feet straight above it. She took careful aim and fired into the limestone and mineral deposit. The bullet slammed home, but the mineral deposit clung to the ceiling. She could see the creature peak out and lob another rock. She aimed and squeezed the trigger.

The cone-shaped rock shook loose from the cave ceiling, rocked a couple of times, then plunged straight down.

The Sasquatch looked up just in time to see the falling limestone and tried to catch it and sidestep it at the same time.

The spike ended rock was about five feet tall and at least a foot around weighing more than a couple of hundred pounds. The creature was able to miss a direct blow, but the rock was more than even it could bear, and the beast fell to the ground.

Michelle reloaded and moved from giant boulder to boulder with moves a gymnast would admire. This is what she had trained so hard for. She was fast and determined.

Before she could get in point-blank range of the Sasquatch, it got to its feet and leaped over some strewn boulders before ducking behind another tall mineral deposit screaming at the assailant.

Michelle reached in her bag and found the few remaining chem-sticks she had left, cracked them open, and tossed them all around the area, lighting the cavern to a greater extent.

She parkoured from rock to rock until she stood on one that was about fifteen feet high. She could see the two men, still down and several yards away, but what she couldn't see was the Bigfoot. Michelle crouched on the giant rock and hurriedly scanned the cave, but saw no sign of the creature.

A giant hand reached out and grabbed at her foot, attempting to pull her from the boulder. The creature had somehow gotten around to her backside. Michelle spun and kicked desperately to free her foot from the grasp. The sidearm she carried fell from her hand as she desperately clung to the rock. The monster was stretched as high as it could and had a loose hold on her pant leg to pull her down. Michelle's backpack had caught a snag on the boulder, which aided her in staying up. She kicked with her free leg at the giant hand when a desperate thought occurred to her. She slid out of the backpack, reached in, and grabbed a flare. Just as she pulled it out of the bag, the creature yanked, jerking her to the ground where she hit with a solid thud.

The vision goggles clattered off her head, but she didn't need them now. But the breath she lost when she hit the ground was desperately needed. A chem-stick lay near her face, and she could see the beast step over to her. Her brain screamed, *move, move, move.* She saw her weapon had fallen just a few feet away, and she scrambled on her knees to reach for it. Just as she tried for it, the creature was on her lifting her off the ground.

The Sasquatch hoisted her directly in front of its face to get a closer look at the tiny enemy. One arm hung limp at its side, useless. Blood was matting over most of its body. It was littered with slugs, but still, the beast was stronger than anything she had ever seen. It pulled her closer to its grotesque face to study the woman.

The giant monster screamed at Michelle as it held her in front of it. Drool dripped from its huge teeth, and its breath was scorching hot to her face. The stench of the beast was that of a dead carcass. When the creature stopped, Michelle screamed back at the beast, not out of fear, but defiance.

The creature was startled at first, but then a snarl came to its lips accompanied by a low guttural growl. Michelle read the look. The Bigfoot had decided that it was done with her. That's when she capped the flare and slammed it against the nearby rock.

"This is for Jenni, you son of a bitch!" She screamed.

Turning the flare around in her hand like a knife, she stabbed the beast in the eye, driving it in as far as she could. The Sasquatch roared madly, but it had to drop the woman from pure reflex to deal with the scorching flare. Michelle fell from its grasp. She was on her feet in an instant, leaped for her weapon and spun around to shoot. The sasquatch screamed in frenzied panic as the hair on its face caught fire from the near twenty-six-hundred-degree flare. The deputy squeezed the palm of the handgun, and the laser slowly climbed from the floor to the chest, then rested between its eyes. She slowly squeezed the trigger, releasing the hammer which slammed the firing pin into the primer of the brass casing of the .45 caliber slug. The bullet exploded from the barrel, and an instant later slammed home exactly where intended. The beast, like a skyscraper imploding, crumpled slowly to the ground, dead.

***

Troy was on his feet, helping the sheriff up when Zeus plodded over with a slight limp and lay at his feet with a whimper. The dog whined a few times, but once Troy gave him a reassuring pat on the head, the four-legged protector quieted and waited.

"Over here," Troy shouted. He didn't know who the person was that had saved them from an inevitable fate at the hands of the Sasquatch, but he had an idea.

32

Michelle dug into her pockets until she found what she was looking for a cell phone and a flashlight. Relieved it powered on, she began taking photos of the Sasquatch that lay dead at her feet. She had pulled the flare out and threw it on the ground nearby. The scorched hair on the beast had an almost unbearable stench.

The Sasquatch was at least nine feet tall, and she estimated weighed eight-hundred to a thousand pounds. The body was covered entirely in long, coarse reddish-black hair and was pure muscle. The head, cone-shaped with a low, massive brow ridge, rested on a thick short neck with massive deltoids that would keep the beast from turning its head beyond a few degrees from side to side. It was unlike anything imaginable. The only similarity to a gorilla was that it was covered in hair and the only thing in common with a man was it walked erect. The long arms ended with huge leathery hands that could easily crush a man's skull if so inclined. The legs were just as muscled, and Michelle could bear witness to the incredible speed and agility of the creature. The last few flashes of the cell phone camera were closeups of the creature's face. She started to turn away when something caught her eye.

She put the end of the flashlight in her teeth to free both

hands and pulled the creature's bottom lip down. She couldn't believe what she was seeing. On the inside of the lip was a tattoo of a bar code.

"What the hell?" she said in astonishment. "Someone is studying these things!" *If there's a bar code, there's probably a tracking chip on it somewhere,* she thought.

She tried the roll the creature's head around. Whoever was tracking it would have the forethought to place the tracker just under the skin somewhere that the Sasquatch wouldn't tear it out or where it could get damaged. Probably the back of the neck or somewhere in the back area.

"Who's there?" She heard a weak voice call out.

"It's me, Michelle," she responded.

"Is it gone?"

"Yeah, it's dead," she yelled back.

A long pause.

"Sheriff's hurt pretty bad."

"On my way."

Michelle took a few pictures of the bar code tattoo then used her knife and cut one of the creature's fingers off along with a tuft of the thick fur and dropped it into a sealable plastic bag. She was all too familiar with how these creatures mysteriously disappear. She wasn't about to let evidence go.

She and Troy carried the sheriff out of the cave with his arms draped over their shoulders. Zeus trailed along not leaving his master's side.

The ride back into town was slow going with the sheriff's busted leg, but he never complained. He rode on back of the sled with Michelle, and Zeus was sitting in front of Troy on his. Troy's arm helped the dog stay on the seat as the snowmobile sped along.

Michelle tried calling for the others when they reached a high point on the ridge, "This is Deputy Evers, need assistance, does anyone have a copy?

Static

"No, stop. Don't call for help. I'll be fine once we make it back," Nick said. "Just don't call anyone yet."

"What are you saying?" Michelle asked. "We need an extraction team."

Nick was weak and coughing. "Not yet. I'm fine," he said.

"We need an ambulance to meet us, not to mention that the whole damn world needs to know about these things. We've got to get that body out of there."

She tried again, "Anyone have a copy, over."

"Michelle, just think about it. Someone out there is listening and doesn't want the world knowing. We need to know what we're dealing with first," Nick said.

She turned around and stared at him, the look on her face resolute. She could see he was in pain and still weak from the climb down. "We need to get you out of here, but know this. Those things killed my best friend, this one almost killed you...*both*, of you! They're dangerous, and people need to know about 'em," she argued. "I'm not about to cover it up."

"I agree. I'm not asking for me, but for the town. At least, not yet. Let's just get to the hospital and then we'll talk about it, okay?" Nick said.

She didn't like it, but she knew it wasn't the time to argue. She needed to get these men to a doctor quickly. Troy wasn't in much better shape than the sheriff, and she had plenty of time to expose the creatures. She would call the university, the press, and anyone else she could think of. She wasn't going to allow another cover-up. Not like the last time when she went to the authorities, and they completely denied that the attack was anything but an angry grizzly. No one would listen to her. Months and months of therapy made her begin to doubt herself. It wasn't until two years later when she heard about an attack right here in Hawthorn that she pulled herself together and started training. Two years of nightmares, anger, and fear. Suddenly, she knew what she had to do, and tonight. She would take care of it.

***

Michelle left the men at the hospital after the sheriff's daughter arrived. Lisa had hurried in when she learned the news.

She dropped Zeus off at the local vet to get checked out. Her plan was to head home to take a shower. She was exhausted and had a lot of work left to do but it would have to wait until she cleaned up and got something to eat first.

She rode her sled over to the sheriff's office to drop it off and pick up her car before heading home. The parking lot gate was open when she arrived. She rode inside the entrance, parked the snowmobile, and grabbed her gear. She was too tired to notice two full-sized SUV's parked inside the lot.

Michelle entered through the back entrance, relieved that the door handle wasn't locked when she turned it. Dispatch was always turned over in the evenings to central, so being as late as it was, she didn't expect to run into anyone. Any deputies on patrol wouldn't be back at the office until their shift was over and that was a couple of hours away.

The ambient light from the street lamps was adequate to see inside the hallway when she entered so; there was no need to flip on the lights. Besides, her hands were full. She stowed her gear in the back room but was surprised when she saw the light coming from under the door of the sheriff's office.

I'll turn that off before I leave, she thought. That's when she heard the strange voices from inside. She froze.

"We've scoured the building, sir. We have it all, there's nothing more," a man's voice said from behind the closed door.

"Let's wrap it up," another man replied.

Michelle set her gear bag down in the hallway of the back room, took her cell phone out and laid it down on her desk. Her hand hit the 'On' button, and the screen came up with the last photograph she took, which was of the barcode tattoo on the sasquatch. Not taking any chances, she powered the phone down and slid it to the back of a drawer and eased it closed. She crept over to the sheriff's office door, drew her weapon, took a deep breath, and pushed the door open.

The three men were poised to walk out. Michelle stepped out with her gun drawn, "Let's say you fellas stop right there and identify yourselves."

The men were all wearing black fatigues, black face paint, and armed like a SWAT team. The first man, tall and lean with black hair, carried a black duffle over a shoulder. He stopped and slowly raised his hands, and a wolfish smile spread across his face.

"Woah there, missy, We're not bad guys. Easy with the bang-stick. Nice trigger discipline."

"Who are you and what the hell are you doing in the sheriff's office?" Michelle demanded.

"That's entirely none of your business, is it?" a voice behind her said.

She felt the muzzle of the gun on the back of her neck.

"Let's be reasonable here. Why don't you hand that peashooter over so that we can all be safe?"

Michelle knew she was outgunned. She was angry at herself for getting outmaneuvered so easily, but she was exhausted and going on no sleep more than twenty-four hours.

"Have a seat, Deputy," the man behind her said.

She didn't move.

"That was more of a demand than it was just being polite," he said with a nudge in her back.

Michelle ambled across the room, turned and sat down glaring at the man who had gotten the drop on her. She was somewhat shocked when she saw the jagged scar on his face. Even behind the black face paint, the scar was gruesome, starting at his temple down to the corner of his mouth.

"Who are you, and what are you guys doing?" she demanded again.

"Deputy Evers, you are in absolutely no position to be asking questions. The less you know, the better off you'll be."

One of the men pulled out zip-ties and secured her hands and feet to the chair.

Michelle watched the tall redheaded man cock his head off to one side. She thought it odd, but then she noticed the tiny ear-bud in his right ear. Someone was talking to him.

"Yes, ma'am…Roger that," the man said.

"That's it, men. Everyone get moving. I'll wrap up," the tall redhead said. He reached behind his back and came around with a silencer. He slowly screwed it on the handgun as the other three men cleared the room.

"Wait a minute, I know you," Michelle said as the came around and faced her. "Chris?"

***

The evening air was frigid, but the wind chill made it seem much colder. The grand opening at the Buckhorn Lodge was in full swing.

"Nick, so nice to see you. What's with the cane?" a tall gentleman in a black tuxedo asked with a jovial laugh. He clasped the sheriff on the shoulder and extending a hand.

"Mr. Mayor," Sheriff Blaine greeted the man. "Oh, just a little four-wheeler accident I'm afraid."

"Pardon me. I believe that's Mrs. Darrow just arriving. I really should say hello. One of the biggest donors to the Hawthorn Community Playhouse, you know," the mayor said as he scurried off.

Nick shrugged, used to the way the mayor acted during social events. He made time for everyone but never truly paid attention to anyone.

Troy saw the hurried exchange and sauntered over next to his friend.

"I'd shake your hand, but...well," Troy said while looking down at the sling his right arm rested in.

The sheriff laughed, "That's okay. I've done enough glad-handing tonight to last me the rest of my life."

"I hear ya."

Nick shifted nervously and pulled at his collar. "I hate this monkey suit."

"Don't you dare take that off," said Lisa Richards who had just walked over.

317

She greeted her father with a kiss on the cheek and a hug. "Don't you look handsome, old man? Minus the cane, of course."

Nick chuckled, "Yeah, well, that's what I get for riding reckless on snowmobiles."

Lisa laughed at her dad's attempt at humor before turning her attention to Troy.

"I'm really glad you came too, Troy. Was hoping to get a chance to visit," she said, smiling.

Troy returned the smile, "Someone has to keep this guy in line, and I figured you would have your hands full tonight as it is with the party. We've been here for almost an hour and just now saw you slow down long enough to not be a blur."

Lisa laughed and took a quick sip of her drink, "Sorry, I guess I have been scurrying around like barn rat. And, you're right. This guy," she put her hand on her dad's arm, "Does seem to find trouble a lot more these days. I think he's getting older." She leaned closer and put her hand up to hid her mouth before whispering, *"but don't tell him that."*

"I'm standing right here, you two, I can hear you," Nick said with a chuckle. "But, if you'll excuse me, I need a drink."

The sheriff walked away to give the two what little privacy they could find in a room chock full of dignitaries.

"So, what really happened out there?" Lisa asked.

"What are you talking about? I'm sure your dad filled you in. Just got tangled up on the sleds, that's all."

Lisa gave Troy a hard look, pursed her lips, biting back her thoughts. Instead, she changed the subject.

"How's Zeus?"

"He's good. No worse for wear. Don't tell the hotel manager, but he's hiding out in my room upstairs, enjoying the many amenities this fine establishment offers," Troy said, smiling. "Just hope he hasn't gotten into the mini-bar. Not yet, anyway."

"Seriously? How did you get him in without anyone seeing?"

Troy took a sip of his bourbon before answering. "It was easy, really. Zeus just flashed his badge. He's law enforcement, you know."

Lisa laughed, "I guess I'll have to go up and say hello at some point."

"You definitely should. It's a very nice room." He reached out and touched her arm, his gaze drifting from her eyes to the necklace she wore. His smile disappeared. His eyes shifted as if to find the words he wanted to say next, but simply came up with, "The necklace I gave you for your birthday?"

"Yes, it is. I wear it all the time," she said. She caught his eyes and held the gaze.

"Look, about…" he started to say.

"No, stop. Let me go first, please? I was an idiot. I really was. I got scared, and when I realized that I had made a mistake, my stupid pride got in the way of admitting it. I'm sorry. I wished I could take it all back and pretend that it never happened. I miss you."

"That's easy enough. I'm willing to forget how badly you broke my heart, how you ripped it out of my chest and smashed it on the rocks just before using it as a hockey puck. It's really not a problem."

Her throat tightened. She couldn't say anything. She didn't know if he was being honest or simply teasing her.

"Breathe," he said, a smile spreading across his face.

She didn't realize that she had been holding her breath. She slowly released it and drew another.

"Can we start over?"

"I would love to," Troy said.

Just then a lady from across the room spotted the couple and waved for Lisa's attention.

"Oh, no. Looks like I'm needed right now," she said.

"Before you go," Troy said, reaching into his pocket, he drew his room key-card out and slipped it into her hand. "337."

"See you there," Lisa said, smiling. "Now, if you'll excuse me, I have to get back to my other guests."

"Sure, I need a refill anyway," Troy said, giving her a quick kiss on the cheek.

When Lisa walked away, Nick came back over and handed Troy a fresh drink.

Troy took it, handed his empty glass to a server passing by, and took a sip. "Still going with the four-wheeler accident story?"

Nick took a deep breath and let it out before answering.

"I think it's best. With Evers disappearing with nothing more than a two-sentence resignation letter on my desk, which said absolutely nothing as to why or even where she's going or what she's doing, and the collapsed entrance to that cave? Nah, it's best that we leave it alone," Nick said. "Besides, there are too many things working against us here. It's like someone, or something in the universe just doesn't want us to expose the truth about those damn things."

"Yeah, I know. First, the guy that videos the thing, then the missing couple?"

Nick cut in, "And the missing car and all the evidence."

"I don't know what the hell's going on, and I heard or read a hundred stories where people swear there's a government conspiracy. I'm beginning to think there's something to it. Anyway, I hope that's the last we'll see of, *Bigfoot*."

"I dunno," Nick said, slowly shaking his head. "Maybe that was the last one of their clan. Hope so anyway. I think if we want any more answers, we're going to have to dig deeper and do it off the grid so to speak."

"Do you think we should? I mean, those guys that picked up Billy on his way back in, they gotta have something to do with all this. They couldn't have just shown up out of the blue clear sky right where they were out on that trail. That's not fortuitous, that was planned. It's like they had been following them, or at least knew where they were."

"I agree. They showed forestry division credentials, but a few calls and no one ever heard of 'em. Reeks of the feds. Don't forget that blacked-out SUV at the site of that car wreck on the mountain had government plates."

"Could explain a lot."

"Yeah, and leave a lot of questions too," Nick said, taking a long pull on the tumbler full of bourbon.

"No evidence that the damn thing even exists. That's the worst part of it all."

The sheriff stared into the bottom of his glass and shook the two ice cubes around. "Yeah, well, about that," he began. "Remember when we collected evidence at the car crash?"

"Sure," Troy said intrigued.

Nick continued sloshing the ice cubes around. "Well, I had collected some tissue, blood, and fur samples in an evidence bag, but then forgot to put it in the collection that mysteriously vanished. Instead, I put it in my lunch bag in the filing cabinet. They must've missed it, but I found it this afternoon."

33

The winding, deserted road twisted slowly down out of the mountains in a gray, misty early morning gloom. The dim yellow headlights of the late model sedan did little to illuminate the road in front of it, but the driver wasn't in a big hurry. She may have been a few hours ago, but the further away from Hawthorn she got, the more relaxed she became.

Leaving in the middle of the night with nothing more than a hurriedly packed suitcase, a laptop and what little cash she could get her hands on was not an ideal situation, but the alternative of staying behind with a bullet in her skull was a far worse condition. She had to disappear. That was made clear. She had little choice in the matter. Leave and live, or stay and die. Didn't take a genius to figure that one out. Running was not something she was accustomed to. She had trained hard to never be afraid again, but this was different. This was something bigger than she ever imagined. By all rights, she should be dead right now, but what stopped the gunman's finger from pulling the trigger?

It was a one-time event, a rare occurrence like two passing ships in the night, but much more significant. When the man looked her in the eye, she stared back defiantly. He hesitated, a split second later she knew why.

Those eyes, that hair, the voice, were all familiar, but the scar that ran down his face from his right temple down to his mouth was like a fingerprint. She knew him.

Two days later, she turned off the highway and parked in front of the run-down motel. The kind that didn't care who stayed there if you had cash.

"That'll be forty bucks, sign here," the portly man in the greasy wife-beater said, spinning the registration book around for the woman to sign.

The lady wore jeans, a dark green jacket, and a ball cap pulled down low. She handed the man the cash and signed the register as *Jennifer Tsul Ka Lu.*

"Indian, huh?"

"Native American," she corrected.

"That's what I meant. Room 16 Miss Soo…Sull…" the man stammered.

"It's pronounced, Jooth Kaw Lu," she said tersely. "It's Cherokee."

"Yeah, right," he said, handing her the key. "Whatever."

She took the key without another word, strode out of the office to her car and drove to the end of the dilapidated motel to park in front of the room. She stared at the place for a moment then with a resolute sigh then got out. She grabbed her bags, unlocked the room, and ducked inside.

Tossing one bag onto the bed with an obviously well-worn concave mattress, she pulled her laptop out, set it on the small desk and turned it on. A few minutes later, she pulled up a photo from the cloud and opened the editor program to clean up the image. Once she was satisfied, she turned on the cell phone and opened a QR reader app.

In a dark room filled with dozens of monitors a single computer stirred alive. The office building a thousand miles away, hidden in the middle of nowhere in the Pacific Northwest was staffed continuously. A single beep alerted the user. The screen lit up with a large red banner. The man at the monitor console spun around in his chair to see what the issue was. When he read it, the coffee cup in his hand fell, shattering on the floor.

Classified
Subject 112-A Has Been Scanned

ABOUT THE AUTHOR

Paul G. Buckner is an Amazon Top 100 selling author, a Cherokee Nation citizen, musician, and an avid outdoorsman. He attended Northeastern State University and holds a bachelor's degree in Business Management and a Masters of Business Administration. He lives in Claremore, Oklahoma with his wife Jody and son Chase.

CPSIA information can be obtained
at www.ICGtesting.com
Printed in the USA
LVHW081119281020
670044LV00016B/894

9 781732 300781